04

ℓ

t

Mr
SOU
C4 6a

Published in 2012 by Marplesi

ISBN 978-0-9566983-9-1

A catalogue record for this book is available
from the British Library.

Soulseeker

by

Sinclair Macleod

Marplesi Books

Also available by Sinclair Macleod

The Reluctant Detective Series

The Reluctant Detective

The Good Girl

The Killer Performer

Dedication

To Margaret (my other Mum) and Paul.
For all your love and support through
both the good times and the bad.

As always, in memory of Calum,
my wonderful son and constant guiding light.

Acknowledgements

I've had a lot of help with this book from a wonderful group of people and it is an honour to thank them through these pages.

Willie Scott, the manager of Glasgow's new mortuary was kind enough to give me a guided tour of the fabulous facility. Cheers Willie.

Emma Purdon is passionate about her role as a Forensic Pathology Technician and her enthusiasm shone through as she guided me through the processes and procedures of her job. Thank you Emma.

Geoff Fisher supplied an amazing depth and breadth of knowledge on the workings of Strathclyde Police, garnered over years of notable service. Thanks Geoff for your time and all the information you supplied.

Any technical errors will be mine, although I have deliberately used some dramatic license in areas of the story.

The staff of my local coffee shop have been patient, friendly and interested as I used their store as my office. Thank you Tracey, Ruth and all the team, for my caffeine fix.

One man has been a constant throughout these four books. Andy Melvin is not only my editor but also my cousin and occasional drinking buddy. Thanks again, Andy and I hope you will continue on this journey for a good few books more.

As always my love and thanks also go to my wife of 25 years, Kim and my incredibly wise and gorgeous daughter, Kirsten. I could not write these books without their continued love, support and inspiration. xx

PROLOGUE

*M*y name is Soulseeker and here is my confession. I killed my mother. Please don't misunderstand, it wasn't out of cruelty or hatred, anger or greed; it was an expression of my love for her. It was a decision taken to eliminate her pain and allow her to move on to a better place. It was my duty as a son.

I had watched her slip away over the span of four years, drifting further from me with every passing week. That which was familiar became unfamiliar; my face became that of a stranger, the house she had lived in all her married life became alien and distressing. It became her prison filled with a new terror every day.

I took her to see a hospital worth of doctors who diagnosed early onset Alzheimer's - a disease they

9

couldn't treat - but they were wrong. I knew the truth. I knew the pain of losing my brother Joseph, had been too much for her; she had a delicate mind too fragile to cope with the overwhelming grief and hurt. It tried to protect her from those agonising memories by gently removing her from the cruel reality of this world; a reality filled with loss and anguish.

It started with two police officers at the door, an older, gruff male detective and his younger female colleague. The man was the messenger while his colleague was there to offer comfort as he destroyed our world with his words. The simple sentence that informed us of the death of her first son and my only brother was like an injection of toxin into our lives. They said a drunk had killed Joseph during a night on the town; a knife flashed in alcohol-fuelled rage, blood spilling like wine, and at seventeen years old his life was over. No amount of sympathy the female officer could offer would ever help to erase that memory or ease that anguish for my mother.

In time, she forgot the details of his death and his funeral. There was a massive turnout for him; the congregation comprised of friends of the family, Joseph's friends from college, neighbours and relations; all of them offered condolences but none of them understood what we were going through, not even Dad. My wonderful father, who was nothing but a selfish, useless bastard; the man who left us to our grief, totally unable to offer the support that we needed. He was just another man who failed to address his own feelings while being unable to cope with the emotions of his family. It was easier to run away than face up to our loss and his responsibilities as the so-called head of the household. I shouldn't have been surprised. The only emotion he was capable of showing was anger and self-loathing. He would go out on a Saturday night, drink himself into near oblivion and come home and beat us for our sins. He would force us to go to church the following morning to hear the priest tell us how those sins would see us burn in hell. He would sit in the church with his suit on, the very epitome of the respectable Christian. He was a despicable human being and in time I was pleased he had left.

Within a year of him leaving, the signs began to appear; she would forget the name of someone she had known for years, she would buy washing powder three shopping trips in a row or she would board the wrong bus and find it difficult to get home. A year later and the doctors' diagnosis confirmed that a life of sorrow lay ahead for both of us.

My life at university was cut short as I took

on the function of a full-time carer. A little worm of resentment began to burrow its way into my sensibilities as I left my old life behind.

I did what I could for her, but it became impossible. She became impossible. She asked me constantly why Joseph never visited; the memory of his passing was erased and with it any connection to time. She would sit and tell me how he was getting on at college and talked about his girlfriend, all as natural as if the clock of our lives had stopped the day before he was killed. The days I hated most were the days that she blamed me. She would fly into a rage when I told her he was dead; I despised the very sight of her when she threw boiling tea over me, the anger nearly overwhelmed me and I came close to finishing it there and then. I tried to empathise and understand what she had been through. After a couple of days, I forgave her but I also knew that I had to end our torment, for both our sakes.

In the end it wasn't difficult, the blessed release from that daily torment. I let the gas escape from the old fire in her bedroom, went for a walk and came back to see her just as I had left her, but now she was at peace. Aided by the diagnosis given by the doctors, the police put it down to a tragic accident caused by the confusion of the disease. I believed that I had *given her the escape she needed but as time passed the doubts began to appear. Sunday school and church tales of the immortal soul began to plague me.*

Ten years have gone and now I need answers to the questions that haunt both my sleeping and waking hours. Where does a soul go? Did the fact that I murdered her stop her soul from attaining heavenly peace? Did it trap her in purgatory forever? I need to ease my conscience and know for sure that she has moved on to glory. They say that the body loses a tiny amount of weight at the point of death; if it is measurable then there must be a way of detecting it.

I need to find a way of witnessing the soul begin its journey and know that it is ascending to a better place. I need to be sure that she is truly at rest with Joseph by her side. The only way to do that is to find others I can help. God's messenger will help me find them; the depressed, the confused and the anxious; those whose life is now too much for them to bear. I will give them a route out of their despondency; I will salve their wounds and allow them to travel far from their troubles. I know my soul is condemned to an eternity in damnation but at least I can help them and watch them begin the final journey to a place where all their suffering is removed for good. It is my calling.

Soulseeker

I am the Soulseeker and I search for the essence of humanity; the soul of man. I will not cease my quest until I find the truth.

CHAPTER 1

Alex Menzies opened her eyes slowly; sleep cling-
ing to her with a tenacity she was determined
to beat. She turned slowly to her left, hoping the clock
would tell her she had five more minutes before she had
to begin her day. Instead, the red LEDs flashed a warning;
there had been an electrical outage during the night and
the clock numbers indicated that it had resumed just two
hours previously.

"Crap," she shouted as she jumped from the bed.

Her fiancé, Andrew Black, mumbled a sleepy response,
"Eh, what is it?"

"There's been a power cut," she replied as she walked
briskly out of the bedroom. In the living room, she found
her phone and the display told her that it was seven-
thirty. It was half an hour later than she would have liked
but better than it might have been.

"Crap!" she exclaimed again.

She hurried through the hall towards their bathroom.
"It's half seven," she shouted to Andrew as she passed the

bedroom.

"OK," he mumbled from below the duvet.

In the bathroom, the shower was slow to warm up, unlike Alex's stress levels, which were raised by another couple of degrees very quickly. This was not how she wanted to start her first day in her new job.

The move to the Major Incident Team had come out of the blue. She had been quite happy investigating the seedy world of vice, even if moving in the same circles as the pimps and madams, the perverts and pond scum that inhabited that strata of society had drained her faith in humanity occasionally.

She had attracted the attention of Detective Superintendent Russell when she was involved with a multiple murder case a few months previously. Her former boyfriend, the insurance investigator turned private detective Craig Campbell, had dragged her into the investigation of the murders of members and friends of a Glaswegian rock band. Her work had impressed the Detective Superintendent and when one of his team retired, he suggested to Alex it would be a good idea to apply for the vacant Detective Inspector post. It was a significant promotion and she thought a job in the top investigative team in the city was too good an opportunity to miss.

She uttered another curse at the shower as chill water continued to fall rather than the pleasantly warm cascade she was expecting.

Riled, she shouted, "We need to get this crappy boiler fixed."

Andrew grunted an affirmative.

Naked, she stormed through to the cupboard that

held the boiler and pressed the reset button on the unreliable old water heater. By the time she returned to the bathroom the water had begun to feel a little less icy.

She washed herself with more haste than she would have liked; she normally took her time in the mornings, allowing the minutes under the water to prepare her for the day to come.

Washing complete, she dried herself rapidly with the towel. Her hair would have to do as it was; there was no time to dry it and style it as she would have liked.

She walked back into the bedroom and began to search for underwear. She pulled on a pair of functional white knickers but the drawer that held her bras had nothing comfortable to wear for a day at work. After another expletive, she retrieved one from the pile of ironing that was lying in the spare bedroom.

She dressed in a simple pale blue blouse, navy trousers and a pair of comfortable but formal dark blue shoes. She liked to feel smart when she was at work but never to the point that it felt restricting.

She brushed her light brown hair and applied a little eyeliner and eye shadow around her duck-egg blue eyes. She then pulled her hair into a band to hide the fact that she had had no time to dry and brush it properly.

Her normal breakfast was a leisurely bowl of cereal accompanied by a coffee but she would have to make do with just the muesli this morning. As she was pouring it into the bowl, her mobile phone rang.

"Hello, DS Menzies."

"Hi Alex, its Tom Russell. Don't you mean DI Menzies?"

"Yes sir, sorry, I'm not used to it yet."

"Don't bother going to the office this morning, we've got a body."

She felt a rush of adrenaline. She had joined MIT to investigate this kind of case but she hadn't expected to face a new murder before she had even been in the office.

"Where?"

"An old warehouse close to the canal in Port Dundas. I'll text you the address, but get here as soon as you can."

"Right, will do."

"See you when you get here," the detective superintendent from her new squad said before ringing off. The text with the address arrived soon after he had ended the call.

She poured milk over the oats, nuts and fruit before gulping the lot down as quickly as she could.

She found her handbag, checking that she had a notebook and pen before she placed her phone in beside them. The bag also contained her car keys, a lipstick, some perfume, a small make-up set and an eyeliner brush.

"Andrew, I have to go. There's a body."

"OK. I'll see you later." He stuck his head out of the bedroom as she walked past and gave her a brief kiss.

She lifted her coat from the hooks close to the front door and began her journey.

Their flat was at the top floor of a red sandstone tenement in the Scotstoun district of Glasgow. As she set off to find her beaten-up VW Golf, the rain began to fall in small drops. She admonished herself for forgetting to lift her umbrella and moved quickly through the puddles that were beginning to form on the cracked pavement. It was two minutes before she reached the car, which was parked three streets away from the flat. Due to the down-pour, her hair was as wet as when she had stepped out of the shower and she was glad that she had not spent time drying or styling it.

The car was originally dark green but due to the layers of dirt it lacked the tone and the shine that it should have had. She always chided herself at the state of it when she saw it but very rarely did her embarrassment result in the car getting the wash and valet it required.

She opened the door, threw her handbag into the passenger seat and adjusted the driver's seat and mirror. She reached into her bag and took out her mobile. She tapped the details of the address of the crime scene into the navigation app and requested a route. The car radio was tuned to a discussion programme on Radio Scotland but despite her best intentions to try to improve her mind and keep informed of the news, she always retuned it to a music station. That morning she found a station where Fleetwood Mac were advising her to go her own way and that's what she did - after one false start from the car that included a cloud of blue smoke and some more swearing from Alex.

She sang along with the tune as she drove towards the centre of the city. The voice on her phone drowned out the music to tell her to take the Clydeside expressway and then she joined the M8 for a short time before exiting at the junction for St George's Cross. She drove under the motorway up to Port Dundas and a small industrial estate that sat on the banks of the Forth and Clyde canal.

She didn't need the GPS system to tell her that she had reached her destination. The area was filled with fire engines, cars, an ambulance, fire officers in their protective clothing, and sullen uniformed police officers who all looked as if they were questioning their choice of career. Technicians and detectives were either already wearing or pulling on overalls that would help protect the evidence at the scene from being corrupted by their DNA, clothing fibres or the remnants of their breakfast.

Alex parked the car a little way from the hive of police activity before lifting her phone and bag from the seat. As she opened the door the distinctive smell of smoke filled her lungs and a little shiver of apprehension trembled through her. She lifted her notebook and pen before transferring the bag to the boot of the car then walked to join the organised chaos that surrounded the scene.

As she was ducking under the crime scene tape, Superintendent Russell stepped out from the melee around the warehouse and came towards her. He was a man in his late forties, tall, relatively fit but showing the first folds of middle age spread. Below a head of thick but well-trimmed greying black hair his face was still handsome. He was dressed in an immaculate dark grey suit with a white shirt and a red and black striped tie. He was protected from the elements by a huge golf umbrella that sported the logo of a bank.

"Hi, Alex. Sorry for the early start but we've got a strange one here. We'll get ourselves a set of overalls before heading in. We're just waiting for the photographer and we'll get the briefing started. We're having the meeting just inside the building." He gestured towards the old warehouse that was the centre of the activity.

At the crime scene technicians' van they were each given a set of overalls, blue plastic overshoes and a mask. The technician directed them to a tent with one open side that had been erected at the door to the warehouse. It protected both of them and their colleagues from the rain as they dressed in their crime scene attire. The drops had increased in size and frequency, and both officers were glad of the shelter. Alex slipped a small bottle of Bergamot oil from her bag and poured a little on to her finger before rubbing it between her top lip and her nose. When she became a detective her first DCI had taught her the trick to help cope with the aromas associated with crime scenes, many of which could be overpowering.

"You ready for this?" Superintendent Russell asked as they wrestled into the strange paper suits.

"I think so. Is the body badly burned?" she asked hesitantly.

"Bad enough. As I said before, the whole crime scene is more than a bit weird. I've never seen anything like it, anyway. You'll see what I mean."

When they were ready they stepped out of the tent and into the cavernous space of the brick-built structure.

Inside, a circle of sizeable floodlights lit up the middle of the space. Cables snaked from the lights towards a noisy diesel generator that had been set up just outside a large shuttered doorway at the other end of the warehouse. When the warehouse was in use it would have been where vans entered and exited. The floor was wet as a result of the fire crew's efforts to put out the blaze and the lights reflected in the puddles like multiple moons in the landscape of some distant world. The smell of burnt wood and flesh mingled with the fumes from the generator, making Alex feel a little nauseous despite the oil under her nose.

A small assembly of people stood to the left of the entrance; their faces looked strangely devoid of colour and their features were flattened by the intensity of the bright floodlights.

"Everyone, this is our new DI, Alex Menzies," Russell said to the group.

"Alex, this is Jacqui Kerr, the Procurator Fiscal who deals with homicides; Detective Sergeant Billy Hendry from Stewart Street, who is managing the scene; Richard Johnstone, one of his DC's; Dr Eilidh MacNeil is the new pathologist around these parts; Senior Fire Officer Willie Ferguson and the Senior Crime Technician, Sean O'Reilly.

Alex shook each of their hands in turn as they were introduced.

When the formalities were complete, an English voice shouted from the door, "Good morning, everyone. Sorry I'm a bit late."

Alex turned to see a gangling, black man with a cheery grin and a confident swagger. A camera was draped around his neck and he carried a large bag that looked heavy.

"Alex, this is our photographer, Noel Hawthorn. He comes from London but we don't hold that against him. Noel, DI Alex Menzies," Russell said.

"I'm more of a Scot than you'll ever be, mate; at least I can hold my drink," Hawthorn responded, his cockney accent belying his words. His eyes twinkled with mischief as he turned his attention to Alex. "Pleased to meet you, Alex. Tough on you if you've got to work with this grumpy old sod."

"Nice to meet you too, Noel." Alex couldn't help but warm to Hawthorn's self-assured, chirpy character.

Jacqui Kerr took control of proceedings. "Now that we're all finally here, we'll get started. Mr Ferguson, can you run through what you have so far?"

Ferguson was a burly man in his late forties. He was dressed in full fire protection uniform, although he had removed his helmet to reveal a crop of unruly grey hair. He spoke with a broad Glaswegian accent but what he said was formal in structure and it sounded like he was reading from a report.

"At approximately six-thirty this mornin' a security guard in the building opposite noticed a fire while he wis oot on his rounds. He reported it immediately and the brigade responded. Two engines were dispatched and when we arrived we discovered a small blaze in the middle o' the warehouse. The fire was brought under control very quickly as it hudnae been burnin' that long. At the centre we discovered a boady. Initial investigations from our arson team reckon the man had been laid out on top o' a pile o' wid, somethin' like a funeral pyre that had been doused in an accelerant, probably petrol or lighter fuel - but we'll get that confirmed - and the boady was then placed oan tap. We'll compile a full report but that's oor initial impressions. Ah'm sorry but the fire and oor hoses huv probably restricted whit you'll be able to get in terms o' forensics."

"Not your fault, Willie," Russell reassured the fire-man. Jacqui Kerr gave Russell a scornful look, irked by his contribution. Alex had come across her before during one or two investigations and had always found her aloof and too full of her own self-importance. Her primary responsibility was the investigation of any murders in the city but Russell thought she was in over her head and many of his colleagues agreed.

The Procurator Fiscal turned to the pathologist. "Doctor, your initial findings?"

Eilidh MacNeil hailed from Barra in the Outer Hebrides and had been part of the team of Glaswegian forensic pathologists for a couple of months. She was tall at over six feet and her broad frame gave her a manly appearance. She had left the island to become a doctor but found that she had a passion for forensic pathology and as a result her career path had gone in a direction she had not anticipated when she left behind the slower pace of island life.

"I've only had a brief look so there's not a lot I can tell you at this point but the victim is a young Caucasian male, around twenty-five to thirty-five years of age. There is a hole in the front of his skull that could be a bullet hole but I'll know more when we do the post-mortem. The burn injuries are extensive but as they aren't too deep, we should still be able to learn quite a bit from him." She spoke with the soft lilt of her native island and it seemed incongruous coming from such a sizable woman.

"Do you have an opinion on cause of death? Was the victim alive when the fire began?"

MacNeil shook her head. "I'm afraid that will require the full PM before I can say with any certainty."

"Thank you, Doctor. Mr Hawthorn, will you begin the photography? Make sure you get a few shots of that hole in the skull, the position of the body and the immediate environs."

"Will do." Noel cast aside his trademark smile and replaced it with a more serious expression as his professionalism took over. He began to unpack a flash unit for his camera from his bag while Kerr continued, "DC Johnstone, I would like you to take notes, please. If anyone spots anything, tell the constable." Kerr gestured in the direction of the crime scene.

The young detective was a reflective man with clever eyes that studied the world from behind wireframe glasses. His blonde hair was already showing signs of a bald patch appearing on his crown. He was slender, on the edge of skinny with sharp features. Alex thought that he moved with the simple economy of athlete or maybe a dancer. She watched him as he listened carefully to all that was said and he seemed to be absorbing all he could learn from the senior officers.

Alex was apprehensive as she walked with Johnstone and the rest of her colleagues towards the circle of intense light. Her natural fear of fire was increasing her anxiety and she could feel drops of sweat forming on her brow. She hoped the others would put it down to the protective suit she was wearing. She drew the mask over her nose and mouth, as the smell of scorched flesh grew stronger.

In the centre of the arc of light, the body had the appearance of barbecued meat. In parts, the skin and flesh were charred a deep black, in others the outer layer was browned and in some parts bright red muscle showed through cracked skin. The legs were drawn up due to the contraction of the thigh and calf muscles as the flames had dehydrated them. Alex thought about bacon in a pan and how much it shrinks; it drew a sudden wave of nausea that she fought off. The man's arms seemed to have been crossed, as if the body had been laid out for a viewing in an undertaker's parlour, although he had rolled slightly on to his right side. The skin and some of the flesh on his face had been burned away, making an easy identification almost impossible. The bones around his mouth were visible and combined with his teeth created a ghoulish grin.

The stillness of any murder scene often made it look like some artist's bizarre interpretation of a life frozen in time. This one seemed to magnify that impression as so much of what they were seeing had been staged. It all looked carefully positioned for maximum effect; the killer had taken their time to get everything set the way they wanted it.

"Impressions?" Russell asked.

"Whoever did this is one evil bastard," DS Hendry was the first to reply.

Alex considered the scene before she bent closer to the ground. She disagreed with her colleague's assessment. "No, there is something almost reverent about how the body was laid out. In some cultures this is how a body is disposed of; a pyre with the body covered only by a shroud. Look at the way the arms are crossed. This isn't the desecration of someone who has dehumanised the victim. Evil's not the right word, disturbed would be better."

DC Johnstone gave a derisory laugh, "You're kidding, right?"

"No, I think Alex is on to something. This isn't a

normal disposal of a body, whoever did it was very precise," Russell responded.

"Did you find any ID?" Alex asked Ferguson.

"No, but once the fire was out we didn't move anything, left it to the experts." Alex wasn't sure if there was a little inter-force sarcasm in his words.

Sean O'Reilly, who stood at the edge of the gathering, also reported a negative. The Irishman and his team had done a preliminary search of the locus and would only be able to complete their work when the body was removed.

Dr MacNeil bent over the corpse and looked intently at the victim's leg. "Looks like there might be a metal plate on his right leg. That might help with identification if there are no other means."

DC Johnstone took note of it although it would obviously form part of the post-mortem report.

"Is there anything else you need, Doctor?" Kerr asked.

"No, I think that's all we can learn here. I'll bag the hands; you never know, we might get something from the fingernails. Then we should get him to the mortuary."

"Superintendent Russell, would you complete the formalities please?"

"I'll get a couple of uniforms in to escort the body. Constable, can you go and get a couple of the unis, please?"

Johnstone walked away to attend to his errand while Doctor MacNeil completed her tasks. A body bag was brought in and a couple of forensic technicians stepped forward to help with the delicate task of transferring the remains into the bag. They gently lifted the corpse from the ashes - which were nearly all that remained of the

pile of wood - on to the black surface. It was zipped and
wouldn't be opened until Russell, as the senior investigating officer, gave his permission.

Alex watched the process with professional detachment but the sight and thought of how much human
flesh resembled the meat of other animals had disturbed
her.

"Doctor, when will the post-mortem be conducted? I
would like it done as soon as possible," said Kerr.

"We should be able to fit it in this afternoon."

"Superintendent Russell, please ensure your staff are
aware and attend as required."

Tom Russell bit his tongue before saying, "Yes ma'am.
I will attend along with DI Menzies." He felt that Kerr
spoke to everyone like they were rookies at a crime scene
or they were stupid. The fact that she had a poor reputation among the ranks of the police force either didn't
register or was an irrelevance to her.

"Right, I'll see you there." Kerr marched away.

Tom Russell turned to Alex. "Quite a first morning,
Alex."

"Yes, talk about jumping in at the deep end."

"Are you OK?"

"The smell was worse than I expected but I'm fine."

"We'll pop over and interview the security guard, see
what he's got to say for himself."

"Right."

The forensics techs were now working round the pile
of ashes and wood, sifting it carefully as they tried to
find some evidence that would help to catch a killer. The
doctor and the police officers walked back to the door of

the warehouse. They deposited the used overalls, shoes and masks in a waste bin in the little tent.

"It was nice to meet you, Alex. I'll see you later," Doctor MacNeil said before she headed in the direction of her car.

✝

Russell shouted to a uniformed officer, "Constable, is the security guard still about?"

"Yes, sir. He's in his office, I think he's looking forward to talking to you." A knowing smile spread across the constable's youthful face.

Alex and Tom Russell crossed the road to a more modern and obviously active warehouse. All along the length of the M8 there are places that store the goods that are the lifeblood of the nation. This one was a hub for the distribution network and as it was close to the city centre, it was particularly busy.

The two detectives walked through the gates into an enclosed area where a line of vans - each with the logo of a courier on the side - were waiting their turn to pick up the parcels they would deliver across the city and beyond. The yard was filled with the noise of voices and the rumble from the wheels of the various trolleys used to move the parcels to and from the vehicles. A trace of blue smog from the diesel fumes shrouded everything, giving the scene a cinematic quality.

Russell asked one of the drivers where the security guard's office was located, and he was directed to a small portable cabin close to the gates.

Russell knocked on the door and a rotund little man

in his early sixties opened it. Both detectives flashed their warrant cards as the senior officer introduced himself and his DI.

"Oh, come in, come in. Ah've been expecting ye. Wid ye like a cup o' tea? Ah like to huv a cup of tea before ah head hame. Stoaps me fawin' asleep oan the bus," he said hurriedly.

He was about five feet six; the considerable stomach that strained against the cheap material of his company shirt was the product of an appetite that was bigger than his height. It wouldn't take many more biscuits before buttons began to pop from it. Above the collar his ruddy face was topped with a shock of white hair that was attempting to cover a considerable bald spot on the top.

"No thank you, Mr…?" Russell prompted.

"Oh MacDonald, sir, ma'am. Norman MacDonald, ex of the King's Own Scottish Borderers, sir, ma'am." Alex thought he was about to salute but stopped himself. He had a small kettle on a table and he filled a cup with boiling water from it while they spoke.

"A fine regiment," she said in an effort to build some rapport with the little man.

"It is that, ma'am. Ah served ma twenty-wan years, man and boy. Ah've seen some things, ah kin tell ye." He lifted his cup and sat down on the only seat.

He looked as if he was about to launch into the story of his army career when Russell interrupted, "Mr MacDonald, can you tell us what happened this morning?"

"Yes, sir. Ah wis oan ma ootside patrol; ah patrol the inside o' the compound wance an 'oor an ootside wance every two 'oors. Ah take ma joab seriously, there's a lot o' valuable stuff comes in tae this warehoose every night. There's wee bastards oot there, pardon ma French, that wid nick the milk oot yir tea, so there is. That's why ah'm vigilant," he said proudly.

Russell had to cut into his monologue once again. "You were on your patrol and what did you see?"

"Ah wis jist comin' roon the final corner and ah saw a white van pullin' away fae the place across the road. It wis wan o' they Luton-style vans; ye know the wans wi' the big boxy bit at the back. Ah know because ma sister, Frances, hired wan a couple o' months back when she wis movin' hoose. Ah helped ma brother-in-law, Jimmy, wi' the move. He drove the big van and ah took the moator. They wur movin' tae sheltered hooses oot in Shettleston, cos they're a bit older than me; Frances has goat a bad hip, know?"

Alex could see the frustration begin to boil in her boss.

"Mr MacDonald, did you get the number plate of the van?" Alex asked before Russell could allow his exasperation to show.

"Ah didnae, ma'am, sorry. Ah didnae think anythin' o' it at first; there's vans aboot here aw the time. Ah wis just aboot tae come back in here when ah noticed the smoke. Then ah dialled 999 and that's aboot it. Ah heard there wis a boady, is that right?"

"We can't give you any details at the moment I'm afraid," Russell replied.

MacDonald seemed to have made up his own mind about the details of the crime, no matter what Russell had said. "Christ, whit's the world comin' tae, eh?"

"Thanks for your help, Mr MacDonald. We'll need

you to pop into the station at Stewart Street to make a statement," Russell told him.

"It'll be an honour, sir." This time he did salute as both officers exited and left him to think how terrible the world is.

"Quite a character," Alex said.

"He's a typical Glaswegian, loves to tell you his business whether you want to hear it or not," Russell said with an irritated sigh.

"I think he's probably just lonely. It can't be much fun being stuck in a place like that every night on your own."

"I suppose so. At least he gave us something we can use. We can check the CCTV coverage, we might get a plate for the van."

"Where to?" Alex asked.

"I think we'll work out of Stewart Street, it's close enough to use as an incident room. Do you mind if I come in your car? I left it mine in town" Russell asked.

"If you don't mind a rust bucket," Alex replied with a smile.

Russell laughed, "No problem."

There was little time for conversation on the two-minute journey to the station. Alex parked the car, took a deep breath and got set to begin a new phase in her career.

CHAPTER 2

Once they were parked, they walked towards the 'A' Division headquarters, home to one of the eight divisions that make up the Strathclyde Police force. The exterior is covered in two-tone blue plastic that makes it look like a kid's building block creation. The plastic is a façade that covers an older building and the windows are thin pieces of glass that offer little natural light into the interior. The badge of the force, a thistle topped with a crown, sits proudly above the main entrance.

Tom Russell escorted Alex past the reception, acknowledging the duty desk sergeant with a brief, "Hi Terry." Tom Russell's experience and roving role meant that he knew most of the station staff across the city. After being buzzed through by the sergeant, they took the stairs to the first floor.

"Follow me," Tom said to Alex.

They walked along a short corridor to a door marked Chief Superintendent Blair. The Superintendent knocked on the door, which was greeted by a gruff, "Come in."

Inside was a small office dominated by a large old-fashioned wooden desk; behind which was the boss of the station's CID, Chief Superintendent Fraser Blair. He rose from his seat and offered his hand. "Tom, good to see you again, and this is your new detective inspector, I believe."

"Aye, this is Alex Menzies."

"Good to meet you, Alex." Blair offered Alex a welcoming shake of his considerable hand.

"And you, sir," she replied.

"Have a seat," Blair said.

Alex sat in one of the chairs on the opposite side of the desk from Blair.

Russell and Blair had been colleagues for many years and they had a bit of catching up to do. While they talked of old times, she surveyed the office discreetly. There was a pair of filing cabinets, the huge desk and behind the head of the chief super a couple of shelves. In the centre of the top shelf was a picture of Elvis Presley, to the left a sign that read 'Keep Calm and Listen to Elvis' and on the right a group of young men dressed in the fifties style known as Teddy Boy. At the centre of that picture was a younger version of the chief super, recognisable despite the quiff of dark hair. The wall next to the door was covered in framed qualifications and commendations that he had earned over a distinguished career.

"Are you admiring my pictures?' he asked.

"Sorry, yes sir, I noticed them, it's a bit different from

my previous chief super."

"Some polis have pictures of the Queen, I prefer the King." He smiled at his little joke before he continued, "And yes, that's me with a few mates back in the seventies. We were part of the rock'n'roll revival back then. I'm afraid my quiff went a while ago." He indicated his head, which was now bald with a tightly cut rim of hair around the sides and back.

Alex studied him. She had seen him once before at the Strathclyde Police HQ but in this small room he seemed to be even more imposing. He was around six feet two in height, broad and muscular; he carried little in the way of excess weight and looked every inch the kind of traditional policeman that people liked to reminisce about. His penetrating blue eyes had a steely quality but there was no mistaking the intelligence in them. She had heard good things about him as both a copper and a leader.

"So, I hear you got quite a baptism this morning?"

"Yes sir, it was definitely a case of being dropped in at the deep end. I've never seen anything like it before," she replied pensively.

"Tom?"

Russell gave Blair a concise briefing that still managed to cover all of the pertinent facts of the crime scene.

"Any ID?"

"No, the victim did have a plate fitted on his right leg, from an accident we presume, so that should help narrow

Soulseeker

the field when we get have a look at the missing persons list."

"Good, well you've got the full use of the station and personnel as you see fit."

"We'll need it."

"Alex, if you need anything and hit any problems, don't be scared to shout."

"Yes, sir."

"You can drop the sir. Boss or gaffer'll do me. 'Sir' is for the old men who prefer the braid on their hat, a bundle of bureaucratic forms under their arm and going to management seminars rather than being a real polis."

"Yes, boss." She smiled at Blair's assertion.

"Now, my team's a bit of a mixed bag. DC Johnstone's still a bit wet behind the ears but I think he's got the potential to be a great detective. I would appreciate it if you can give him an opportunity to expand his skills when it's appropriate. DC Carrick is, unfortunately, a different proposition. He's a bit of a lazy bastard and at times his mouth runs well in front of his brain. The only good thing I can say about him is that he's good at the mundane stuff. He'll trawl through CCTV pictures or reams of reports and find something. He's pretty useless with witnesses, suspects and victims. In fact, he's pretty shite with people, full stop. Tom, I think you've dealt with him before but don't hesitate to report him if he gets really out of line. I would like to be shot of him but everybody knows what he's like and getting him out the door will be impossible when his uncle is an Assistant Chief Constable. Marsha

Collins is our civilian co-ordinator; she's invaluable, particularly when we're dealing with something like you caught this morning, she can keep things organised as long as she knows where everybody is. We're still a body down but I think we'll need to go with it, at least until the single force thing comes in. Any questions?"

"No that's fine, gaffer. We'll organise some extra bodies to get this moving."

"No problem. Good luck."

As the two detectives prepared to leave, Blair added, "There's a major incident room being set up on the second floor, directly above us. We've got some computers in there already and there are more on their way from IT."

"Cheers, we'll get settled in as soon as possible," Russell said.

The two detectives walked back along the corridor to where the Stewart Street CID were based.

Before they reached the door Alex decided to establish some parameters for her relationship with her new boss. "What is your expectation of me, sir?" she asked.

Russell turned to her with a slightly surprised look on his face. "That's the first time I've been asked that. All I need from you is to work hard and use your brain. You can bend the rules but don't break them. I'll not lose a case because somebody broke the rules; we lose enough to these bastard lawyers without us helping them. I want the real bad guys in prison but I'm not going to sweat the poor woman who steals a loaf to feed her weans. I don't give a shit about statistics, that's for folk with nothing else to do. That's the kind of cop I am, I think you're the same and that's why I wanted you on my team," he finished emphatically.

"Yes, sir." She smiled, as he had left little doubt about what was expected of her and she was delighted at what he had said.

"Right, we'll go in and say hello to the gang and then we'll have a briefing upstairs."

The main office had little natural light and everything looked to be in high contrast of light and shade thanks to the harsh overhead fluorescent lighting. It looked like a thoroughly depressing place to work. There were eight desks, four in one group for the detectives; another three in a line where uniformed officers stared at computer screens and a single desk close to the door.

There were three uniformed officers who introduced themselves as PCs Kenneth, MacIntosh and Bartram. They had already been called in to join the team for this inquiry, but there were bound to be more out canvassing the area around the scene looking for witnesses and doing the grunt work that was so important in any criminal investigation.

Alex was introduced to Marsha Collins, a woman she guessed to be about fifty years of age. She had an attractive face, sparkling green eyes and dyed-blonde hair. She was dressed in a bright pink blouse; a crucifix nestled in the upper regions of her considerable cleavage. She welcomed Alex with a warm smile and firm handshake.

Detective Constable William Carrick was a lot less effusive in his welcome. He was in his late thirties but looked older with a considerable gut that spilled over his belt. His thick black hair was greasy and lacked any particular style; it was beginning to fade to grey around the temples but this was not someone who was ageing gracefully. He wore designer spectacles on a round and unkind face. He wiped his hand on his suit, clearing the grease that had dripped from a bacon roll and then offered a weak, slimy handshake without getting out of his seat.

"Pleased to meet you," she said.

"Aye," he replied curtly.

As she turned from Carrick's desk, Russell gave her a look that spoke volumes about his attitude to her new colleague.

"Don't mind, Bill, he's a miserable bastard," Russell said cheerily.

"That's William, if you don't mind, sir," Carrick responded with heavy dose of sarcasm on the final word.

"Right, folks let's get organised. There'll be a briefing upstairs in the incident room in half an hour. There will be some other officers arriving from other stations soon but we'll start with what we've got. OK?"

There was a general mutter of positive responses before the two left the room.

The incident room was even more soul destroying than the main office. It was a bigger area that took up most of that floor of the building but the walls were bare and the majority of the desks were covered in a thin coating of dust.

"Home, sweet home until we put the bad guy away," Russell said with mock enthusiasm.

He indicated a desk to Alex. "Help yourself to the best seat in the house before the rest arrive. She chose one of the beige and brown plastic tables with a blue-covered chair that were both almost as old as she was. A corporate computer and flat screen monitor were the only things on the worn surface. Russell chose the desk directly opposite her.

Russell checked the phones that were already sitting on the desks. All had a connection and the numbers were clearly marked on the handsets. During the investigation mobiles would be the main method of communication but Russell liked to know that there was a landline available when required.

He used one of the phones to request a kettle, tea, coffee and mugs, which were promptly delivered by a member of the civilian staff.

They logged into the computers and began the process of compiling the information for the briefing. Noel Hawthorn had sent some preliminary photographs to Russell and he printed them on the colour printer in the incident room. He lifted them from the printer's tray and stuck them on to the incident board.

The various members of the team began to assemble on schedule. A few others from Maryhill and Baird Street stations joined the 'A' Division officers. The room was getting crowded but Alex knew that when the investigation was in full swing it would be like Hampden on cup final day.

Russell walked to the sparsely populated incident

board; the room fell silent and the whole team gathered round the detective superintendent. As he was about to start talking DS Billy Hendry and DC Rick Johnstone arrived from the crime scene.

"I'm just giving the team a quick run down on what we've got so far, gents."

Johnstone put a bag on a desk and along with Hendry joined the group.

Russell began the briefing. "A fire was reported at around six-thirty this morning by a security guard at the Fast Link depot in Port Dundas. A body was discovered at the heart of the fire. All we have so far is that it's a young man and that there is a hole in the centre of the skull, as you can see here." He pointed to a close-up shot that the photographer had taken of the victim's face.

"There was no identification available at the scene, there appeared to be no personal belongings and the victim had been re-dressed in some sort of shroud. The corpse was laid out as if for burial with arms crossed. Myself and DI Menzies will attend the post-mortem this afternoon as soon as Doctor MacNeil is ready for us."

"Did you get anything from the security guard, sir?" Johnstone asked.

"He saw a white Luton-style van leaving the scene shortly before he noticed the smoke. We'll need to check the CCTV on the approaches to the scene to see if it gives us anything. DC Carrick, that'll be your task."

He turned to three of the visiting detective constables. "You three need to check missing persons reports for the past few days, see if there's anything in that lot that might help. Rick, if you could check the HOLMES database to see if there's been anything similar anywhere in the country. I don't want to believe that this isn't an isolated case but the strange circumstances mean it's a possibility. Everyone happy with the tasks?"

There were nods of assent around the group.

The superintendent voiced his main concern, "Identifying the victim is the number one priority, people. We need to chase down any possibilities. Marsha, can you liaise with the constables to relay anything that needs to be checked out by either DI Menzies or myself? Everyone make sure that Marsha has your mobile number and when the list is compiled, Marsha, send everyone a copy. Communication is vital if we're going to catch the weirdo that did this." As he finished his speech, his phone rang. He retrieved it from his pocket and had a brief conversation.

"That was Doctor MacNeil, she'll be ready to do the post-mortem in an hour. We'll grab a coffee and then head over to the mortuary, let's get this case moving."

Alex nodded her agreement and the group parted to begin their separate threads of the investigation.

CHAPTER 3

Russell's Vauxhall Insignia was considerably newer and more comfortable than Alex's ageing Golf and Tom did not need to use any persuasive powers to convince her that they should use his car rather than hers. By the time they reached the motorway, the rain had increased to Hollywood volume, battering down on the car and bouncing about two feet in the air. The two detectives were on the westbound carriageway of the M8, heading towards the new Glasgow Mortuary. The sound of the rain was deafening, accompanied by the occasional thunder crack, which meant their conversation was restricted as the traffic around them slowed to a crawl.

The new building had only opened a couple of weeks previously and was sited in the grounds of the new South Glasgow Hospital complex in Govan. The main hospital was still under construction and the area was filled with heavy machinery rumbling, creaking and squeaking while the builders shouted, laughed and cursed as they erected the new building. Men and women dressed in high visibility clothing populated the grounds like an army of luminous insects.

As a nod to the shipbuilding history of Govan, the mortuary and forensics building had a distinctly nautical feel, with ship-inspired design cues like funnels on the roof.

It was Alex's first visit but her superintendent had been given a tour of the facility before the serious work began and he found his way to the car park with ease. The building was a triangular shape and in the centre there was a courtyard reserved for police cars and undertakers' vehicles. Before they got out of the car, Russell rang Doctor MacNeil and told her they had arrived. She told him that a technician would meet them at the police entrance.

As they walked to the door, the two detectives were sheltered from the worst of the elements by the height of the buildings surrounding them, but the torrent was still obvious in the wide puddles that were forming in the middle of the yard.

A young male technician called Brian led them down a flight of stairs and through a maze of security controlled doors to the police viewing area adjacent to the main homicide post-mortem suite. Alex was glad of the guide, as she felt sure she would have become confused rapidly in the labyrinthine corridors.

When they reached the viewing suite, Jacqui Kerr was already sitting at the large conference table that occupied the centre of the room. She was facing the television screen that relayed into the room details of the work of the pathologists. Broad windows overlooking the suite gave the visitors the option to have a more direct view of the proceedings if they preferred.

"Hi Jacqui," Tom said.

"Oh, you're here," she replied with a curtness that was matched by the sneer on her face.

Alex could feel Russell's antipathy to the woman but he chose to ignore the Fiscal's comment.

He led Alex to the window. "You can watch from here or use the TV screen, it's up to you," he told her.

She decided that the TV screen would give her enough distance from what was happening on the other side of the glass and chose to sit beside the Procurator Fiscal. It was a much better arrangement than being in the room with the pathologist and the body, and all the associated odours. As she turned from the window she noticed another area of glass that allowed her to see through to another suite and viewing area.

Superintendent Russell gave Brian the technician the permission to open the sealed bag and begin the autopsy. He left the viewing room and a few seconds later appeared with the two pathologists who would be performing the inspection of the body. Eilidh MacNeil dwarfed her male colleague; Doctor Rajesh Gupta was diminutive in stature, with the innocent, smooth face of a teenager despite his thirty-two years.

The doctors acknowledged the observers, Eilidh with the soft vowels of a Hebridean islander, Rajesh with the gruff consonants that were characteristic of a man born and bred in Glasgow.

Behind the doctors was Noel Hawthorn, who was there to record the pertinent details with his camera.

"Will there be anyone else joining us?" the leading

pathologist asked.

"No, that's it for today," Tom replied.

"OK, we'll make a start."

Dr MacNeil plugged a microphone she was wearing on her lapel into an electronic unit positioned above the table. It would allow her to dictate her findings to a machine in the floor above, and record the post-mortem on to a flash card that could then be passed to an assistant, who would type the report for all interested parties to read.

Before anything could begin in earnest it was necessary to complete a visual inspection of the corpse, which was still in the confines of the body bag. The doctor began by describing much of what had been recorded at the scene. She stated the sex, ethnicity and approximate age of the person whose life had been ended so abruptly. There were third-degree burns across around forty percent of the front of the man's body; another forty-five percent of the affected area was second-degree burns. There was a small area on his chest, abdomen and head that was relatively unharmed by the cruel lick of the flames. With the help of Dr Gupta and the technician, the body was gently turned over, and MacNeil stated for the record that she estimated that there were third degree burns across one hundred per cent of the surface of the skin on the back of the body, the area that had borne the brunt of the fire.

At certain points on her visual tour of the corpse she would ask Noel to take a photograph of something that would be relevant to the investigation. White screens were available on either side of the PM table that could be lowered from housings on the ceiling and the photographer could use them when he needed more light on the subject to capture the image properly.

When the visual tour and initial photographs were complete, Dr MacNeil scraped the victim's fingernails, commenting for the benefit of her report that it would be sent to the forensic labs that would test for traces of DNA. The samples were deposited in a small vial, which was then sealed in an evidence bag.

When she had finished with the fingernails, the doctor gently prised apart the fingers from the palms. In the right hand, the one that was resting above the heart of the victim, she found a small gold cross.

"Superintendent Russell," she called out as she showed the tiny cross to the camera.

"What is that, a necklace?"

"It looks more like a charm that you might place on a bracelet."

"Bag it and we'll have forensics take a look."

"I might be wrong but somehow I don't think it's something the victim would have owned. The killer may have placed it there."

"This gets weirder by the second," Russell said.

"I'll continue now if that's OK?"

"Of course, Doctor."

She turned her attention back to the body while Brian bagged and logged the cross. Under the victim's armpits, small traces of cloth were found where the flames failed to reach before the firemen had extinguished the blaze. Those remnants were placed into another evidence bag and labelled. There was so little hair on the head that there was no point combing it but the doctor did comb the pubic region and the little pieces of trace that were retrieved were also put in an evidence bag. She completed the examination by using tape to collect any fibres or other fragments on the places on the body that were unaffected by the fire.

When Dr MacNeil was happy with the initial assessment, she turned to the fiscal and detectives. "Is there anything else before we wash the body?"

Tom Russell looked to Jacqui Kerr, who shook her head.

"That's fine, doctor, please continue."

The body was moved gingerly out of the bag and placed on the cold, stainless steel surface of the table. The bag was checked for further trace evidence before the process of washing the cadaver began.

Once the legs had been straightened from their contorted position the body was weighed, measurements taken and recorded. The sound of the charred flesh crackling under the strain of the movement was amplified into the viewing room, causing Alex to shudder.

Brian ran water over the body as gently as he could but in certain areas pieces of burnt flesh and skin fell from the bones under the gentle pressure of the water. Alex turned away from looking at the screen as her stomach heaved in protest.

"You OK?" her senior officer asked.

"I think so," she replied with little conviction.

The post-mortem then began in earnest as the doctor created the Y-incision. She ran a scalpel from the tip of each shoulder to meet at the dagger point at the bottom of the sternum. She completed the procedure with another stroke of her scalpel from the bottom of the V-shape, across the stomach and down to the subject's pubic bone.

Alex averted her eyes as the technician, wearing a pair of goggles, began to cut the victim's ribs at either side with an electric saw. The vibrations of the instrument sliced through bone easily but had little effect on the soft tissue. When all the cuts were complete the ribs and sternum were removed, allowing access to the chest cavity.

The doctor reported that the victim's lungs showed no obvious sign of disease. They were then removed and weighed. A slice of the organ was taken that would be sent to the histology department for an analysis that would help to find toxins or disease. She inspected the trachea with a magnifying glass; a powerful spotlight that Doctor Gupta positioned for his colleague supplied the illumination.

"There is no sign of soot in the windpipe," she announced.

"So the victim was dead when the fire started?" Jacqui Kerr asked.

"That is correct, Ms Kerr."

"That's a blessing at least," Alex murmured.

The pathologist continued her assessment of the internal organs; everything was measured, weighed, recorded and sliced in exactly the same way as the lungs had been processed. The young man appeared to have been in perfect health prior to his death.

The contents of his stomach were retrieved and an analysis would be done to establish if there were any poisons or other harmful chemicals that had been administered through his food.

The digestion of the victim's last meal might help to establish a time of death, which had been difficult to establish at the scene. The heat of the fire had elevated the temperature of the liver and as a result ruined any possibility of a reasonable estimate of when the murder had taken place.

On the victim's extremities the blood was black; all the fluids had boiled away leaving a dry residue. However, around the heart there was enough liquid blood to allow the pathologist to draw some vials that would find their way to the forensic labs a few floors above the mortuary. The forensic technicians would look for anything that may give the detectives an insight into the man's death.

Dr MacNeil then turned her attention to the skull and in particular the circular cavity that had been created on his forehead. She made an incision behind the left ear and ran the blade across the crown of the head to a symmetrical point behind the other ear. With some difficulty, she peeled back the skin and the thin layer of the periosteum; the fire had made them brittle and inflexible.

When the skull was visible, she pulled the spotlight to focus on the circle in the centre of the forehead.

"There are circular tool marks on the inside of the opening, probably made by a drill of some sort."

"He wasn't shot?" Jacqui Kerr exclaimed.

"Someone drilled into his head? Was that what killed him?" Tom Russell's surprise was accompanied by an obvious revulsion at the thought of someone puncturing another person's skull in that way.

The doctor replied, "I can't be sure until I can examine the brain."

She inspected the surface of the skull before asking Brian to cut into it with a bone saw. He used the instrument to create a circle around the skull, taking care not to go all the way through to the brain. He completed the delicate operation by following the indentation with a small chisel and hammered through the last millimetre to separate the two pieces of bone. When he was finished his precise task, he removed the top of the skull.

The doctor manoeuvred the spotlight again and peered at the area behind where the hole had been created.

"There is no damage to the meningeal layer, it's not been punctured by the drill. It was done with surgical precision and I don't think it was done with the intention of killing the victim. That's obviously an opinion but from what I can observe it doesn't appear to be a fatal wound."

"I would have to agree with Doctor MacNeil's assessment, if it had been the murder weapon they would have continued into the brain," Dr Gupta added.

Alex voiced her thoughts. "We're back to ritual, aren't we? In some cultures it is believed that drilling a hole in the skull will release demons that are thought to be the cause of mental illness."

"That's right, it's called trepanning. Doctors still use it today from time to time to treat epidural and subdural haematomas on the brain," Dr Gupta said.

"Could the operation be the cause of death?" Tom Russell asked.

"I would say no but the shock of such a traumatic event on the body could be fatal. This injury, if it was created in a hospital operating theatre would not lead to a fatality, but outwith a controlled environment, without proper anaesthesia and nursing care, then it's entirely possible," Dr MacNeil replied.

"So are we looking at some ritual or someone practising medicine without a licence?" Jacqui Kerr asked rhetorically.

"Either way, it's not your usual murder," Russell responded.

"What are the other possibilities for the cause of death?" Kerr asked.

"I think that we will have to wait on the blood work results to be sure. Elevated levels of cortisol and other hormones may indicate that the physical shock was the cause of death but it's very difficult to be sure. Hopefully, his blood or organs will give us some definitive answers."

"So the fire might be an attempt to dispose of the body in a respectful manner after a botched operation. Could we be looking at an immigrant? There is a large population of asylum seekers at the Sighthill flats, which aren't too far away from the locus," Jacqui Kerr said.

"It's a possibility I suppose, but the victim is Caucasian. I think that would decrease the chances but it's worth bearing in mind," Russell replied.

The pathology team continued their examination and analysis but there was nothing that would move the investigation forward. They recorded the position, length and type of the metal plate that was screwed to the right leg of the victim, which the detectives hoped would be the key to identifying the victim.

"Is there anything else you would like to ask?" Dr MacNeil asked as she left the technician to finish returning the body to a condition that would allow it to be released and transferred to the undertaker when all investigations were complete.

"I've got nothing," the superintendent said.

"No, that's fine, doctor," Kerr added.

Both Russell and Kerr stood to watch through the window as two uniformed constables collected the evidence bags from the pathologists and transferred them to a designated room. The law in Scotland is very strict on the procedures used to preserve the chain of evidence and it was important that it was observed at all times.

The two detectives and the Procurator Fiscal then thanked the pathology team and walked to the evidence room. All the labels were checked and aligned with the case number, and each was also allocated a specific reference number. When the fiscal was satisfied that all the evidence had been processed correctly, it was time for the detectives to return to the office to see if the victim's identity had been established.

The entrance to the station was now occupied by a small group of people; two of them carried TV cameras while others were laden with SLRs, ready to capture the first images of the investigating team. They stood close together like Emperor penguins, trying to get some shelter from the chilling rain that continued to pour down from a cloud-heavy sky.

"Shit, the press," was Russell's concise assessment.

"Oh, great." Alex was equally lacking in enthusiasm for the members of the fourth estate.

As they walked to the entrance, Charlie Walker, a reporter from the local evening paper, spotted Russell. The detective had a lot of time for the eager young man who mistakenly believed that being a newspaper reporter was a long-term career. The superintendent had found him to be conscientious, a decent writer with the ability to compose a story succinctly, minus the sensationalism that many of his more senior colleagues in the industry favoured.

"Detective Superintendent Russell, any word on the body found in the warehouse this morning?" Walker held out his digital voice recorder as the television cameramen and photographers trained their lenses on the detectives.

"The investigation is at a very early stage and we will be releasing an official statement in the near future," Russell replied while continuing to walk towards the entrance. Both he and Alex were inside the door before a supplementary question could be asked.

When the two detectives walked into the incident room they could sense that there was an air of frustration. Everyone reported a lack of progress within the separate strands of the investigation, which was not what the senior investigating officer wanted to hear.

The fact that the PM had failed to offer a conclusive cause of death was just one of the barriers that the team were already facing. Missing persons had turned up two men who were in the right age group but a phone call to their respective families had established that neither man had medical metalwork done on his right leg. Everyone knew that the first twenty-four hours of an investigation were crucial but after nearly twelve, they didn't even have the name of the victim.

When the uniformed officers had completed the report of their findings, Russell turned to DC Carrick. "William, any luck with the CCTV?"

Carrick puffed himself up, mentally preening himself before delivering his report. "I managed to get a plate number from a camera in Milton Street."

"Brilliant. What did the DVLA say?" Russell asked. But his optimism was quickly extinguished.

"It belongs to a silver Citroen C4 that was sent for scrap two months ago."

"Do they know who scrapped it?"

Carrick checked his notes. "Kelvin Recycling in Mary-hill."

"Did you phone them?"

"No," Carrick said simply.

"You didn't think that it might be worth while?"

"What good would that do?"

"Are you being deliberately thick? Our killer might work there; he might have been a customer that showed a particular interest in that car, he might even have lifted the plate. Get on the fucking phone and organise a visit," Russell vented his ire on the hapless DC.

Alex could see what the chief superintendent had meant about Carrick not being the kind of detective a murder squad really needed.

Russell turned to Rick Johnstone. "Rick, anything on HOLMES?"

"No, sir. There was no record of anything similar to what we found at the scene," the junior constable replied.

"Try the word trepanning or check for reports of bones

being drilled. You never know, we might get lucky, fuck knows we need something - sorry Marsha." The superintendent had rarely had such a disappointing start to an investigation.

"I'll get right on it, sir."

"No, it'll do in the morning, it's a long shot anyway. Before you go, drop forensics a mail for me and ask them to make the cross that was found in the victim's palm a priority. When that's done get yourself off home."

"I'm fine, sir, I could do another hour." Alex sensed desperation from Johnstone.

"No, go home. That's an order," Russell insisted.

"Yes, sir," Johnstone responded unenthusiastically.

"There's no reply from the scrapyard," said a disgruntled Carrick, angry at the very public dressing down he had received from his temporary boss.

"Get on it, first thing. Let's finish up for the night, it's been a long and very shitty day."

Russell walked out of the office in the direction of the chief super's office to tell him the bad news. He regarded it as a courtesy to keep any senior officer of a station appraised of what was happening and as that officer was a friend and good copper, it was even more important.

Alex and the other officers packed up their belongings then said good night and began their journey home.

Rick Johnstone was the last to leave; the thought of going home was one that now filled him with dread.

His baby daughter, Emily, had been born three months previously and although he loved her more than he ever thought possible, her arrival had upset his home in a way that he had not expected. A woman on the edge of a psychological breakdown had replaced his once beautiful and cheerful wife. The community midwife who visited insisted that Georgia was suffering from post-natal depression but Rick felt that it was as if his loving wife had been transformed into someone he didn't recognise. She often railed at him, screamed at the baby and provoked his mother at every opportunity. Georgia's own mother was in Bournemouth and although she had come for a short holiday when Emily was born, she had been unable to stay very long to support her daughter. His own mum visited every day in an effort to help Georgia cope and Rick was surprised at the tolerance she showed for the extreme behaviour that Georgia had been exhibiting. It was breaking his heart that every conversation with the woman he loved was like walking on a floor made of crystal that could shatter with the slightest misstep.

He parked the car in the drive of their compact two-bedroomed semi-detached home in Baillieston. After he switched off the engine he paused and drew breath, trying to prepare himself mentally for what was to come.

The house was only three years old and they were the second owners. It had a small garden at the front with a more expansive area at the back, which they hoped would offer a safe place for Emily to play when she was a bit older. It wasn't much but it was all they could afford and it least it was in a child-friendly cul-de-sac. Every choice they had made when selecting the house was driven by what their new family would need but the arrival of that family had not been the happy event they had envisaged.

Johnstone opened the door to the sound of Emily crying. When he had hung up his coat and taken off his shoes, he drew a long breath before he walked into the living room. His mental armour was now in place to protect him from what he was about to face. His mother was walking in the middle of the floor, rocking Emily gently, and trying to get the unhappy baby to settle.

"Hi, Mum."

"Hello, how was your day?" she asked as Rick gave her a brief hug.

"We caught a pretty bad murder and didn't make a lot of progress, so it wasn't great. Where's Georgia?"

"In her bed." She shook her head; her concern for her son and daughter-in-law was obvious.

Her son drew another long breath that then turned into an equally long sigh. "Not again. When's this going to end?"

"I don't know, Richard, but you've got to do something. She isn't spending enough time with Emily to allow them to bond properly. It is so important when she is so young that her mother is there. Georgia needs help." It was a simple statement but an accurate summation of the problem that the family faced.

"I've suggested going to the doctor and the health visitor has told her the same thing, but she won't listen."

"Maybe you need to just do it. Book an appointment and take her yourself. I know drugs aren't a long-term fix but if the doctor can give her something that will make her feel better until she can see a psychologist, it would be better than what's happening now. You know I don't mind helping out but a baby needs her mother."

"I know, Mum. I just don't know what say to her or how to deal with her. It's like I'm living with a stranger."

Emily had fallen asleep in her grandmother's arms and the house was suddenly quiet.

"You better go and see her," Brenda Johnstone said.

"I suppose so."

He climbed the stairs to their bedroom as if it was a difficult ascent of a mountain; his stomach was churning as he approached the door. Georgia was lying on the bed facing away from the door. She turned at the sound of the door opening and her puffy eyes told Rick that she had been crying again. It was a look he had grown accustomed to over the previous three months.

"Hello, darling," Rick said kindly.

"Hello." Her response was dry and emotionless.

Rick bent to kiss her but she turned her lips away and he had to be satisfied with landing a peck on her cheek.

"How are you today?"

"How do you think? Do I look like I'm having a great day?" she responded with a venom that until recently had been alien to her.

"Sorry."

"Go attend to your daughter and leave me in peace."

"OK. We'll talk later. What do you want for dinner?"

"Pasta, whatever, it doesn't matter." It was a dismissal and Rick retreated with a feeling of hopelessness descending on him like an unwanted visitor.

He made the evening meal with mechanical movements, his mind on the parlous state of his marriage and his concerns that he would never get back the woman he fell in love with five years previously.

His mother went home when he had finished cooking the meal. She parted with further urging for him to call the doctor.

Georgia refused to come and eat with him, so he delivered the simple dish to her on a tray.

He sat in the living room, eating from a tray of his own while Emily slept in her cot. She awoke before he could finish and he spent the remaining hours before he went to bed attending to the many needs of his tiny daughter. As he talked to her, she suddenly smiled for the first time and Rick Johnstone sat with his daughter in his arms and let tears splash on her innocent face.

He rocked her to sleep and then placed her in her nursery where he hoped she would have a night of peaceful dreams. He gathered a sleeping bag from the cupboard under the stairs and laid it out on the sofa in the living room. His thoughts before he fell asleep were that it was a truly hellish day when the pursuit of a crazed killer was preferable to an evening with his wife.

JOURNAL

*I*t began at Sunday school, my terror of
what lay beyond this life. The teachers
would tell us every week how bad boys and girls went
to hell and only those who followed the doctrine of
the church would be allowed to enter heaven. The
descriptions were often graphic depictions of the
never-ending torment of the soul in the sulphurous
flames. When the teachers spoke of heaven it seemed
more diaphanous, more difficult to grasp; there was
nothing concrete about it. The descriptions sometimes spoke of mansions and a vague notion of float-
ing among the clouds. Hell, on the other hand, was
filled with horrors that were real and it was easier
for my imagination to construct a vision of it. As a
result my nightmares would often consist of my own
soul being consumed by the flames as the devil stood

and laughed. I came to hate Sunday mornings when father would drag me to a place where more terror would be piled on top of terror; where all I received was more fuel for my nightmares.

When I released my mother from her mortal pains, I felt only relief. As I took up my studies again I had nearly five years of light but the darkness began to reappear around the fifth anniversary of her death. It began with a single night when I dreamt that my agonies were transferred to my mother. She screamed and pleaded with me, asking my why I had condemned her to an eternity of anguish. She came again a couple of months later and then her haunting of my dreams increased in frequency. Now they happen every night and sometimes twice a night. The only way I can address it is to begin the journey for others. I must know that my nightmares are the product of my guilt rather than a message from beyond the grave. If I see ascension I will know that the destination is paradise not damnation.

However, my first attempt failed; there was no great revelation, no light or any other indication that the soul had taken flight to a new level of existence.

Releasing him from his earthly bonds was easier than I thought it might be; it felt - as it did with my mother - like an act of mercy. His life was filled with pain and sin, but now all of that is over. I believed that creating an opening in his head would provide his soul with a doorway from which it could escape, a way to ease the beginning of its journey to heaven. But I was wrong.

One big problem is that I don't know what it is that I am looking for but there must be something tangible that will signify that a human being is more than a collection of atoms and molecules; that we have something that lifts us beyond an accident of chemistry and evolution. Proof that we are true masters of God's creation.

They didn't tell you in Sunday school or church what a soul looked like. There were pictures of angels and the risen Christ but they are immortal and everlasting. What about normal mortals? You'd think that was something elemental, something that priests and ministers should know. Maybe they do and they keep it to themselves, a secret only for the initiated.

What if I have been going to the wrong church or worshipping the wrong god? Maybe the answers lie somewhere else, with another deity. But I can't believe that; my mother, my teachers and the priest all told me that ours is the one true path. I know I must go on, no matter the cost to my own soul; I have to do it to be sure that mother is truly at rest.

Maybe God's messenger chose the wrong person for me; maybe he didn't have the type of soul that would be given the keys to the kingdom. There are many within the Church who say that homosexuality is a sin. Maybe his soul was dragged to hell before I could see it or maybe the devil already had it from the moment he chose to have sex with a man. Would Jesus Christ condemn a person because of who they love? He always preached that we must love one another but the Church has a different interpretation. I don't know which is the correct one.

Did I kill that man for no reason? Was his death pointless? I've thought long and hard about it and have come to the conclusion that I have relieved him of the torture of stress, the agony of a broken heart and the guilt of the sins he committed. He will be in a better place. It's a shame I didn't see his voyage to glory begin but it is only one failure.

I must design a new plan, a new way to find what I seek. If the brain is not the source of the soul, where else could it be? The heart is the key. Mankind has long believed that the heart is where our emotions lie and it must be where the soul has its roots. I know what I must do with the next person I will save.

I know who she is; the messenger of the Lord has guided me to her. She is lonely and far from home, she feels the pressure of her job is too great and she takes pills to ease her burden. I will take that cumbersome weight from her and send her to a wondrous new life. I'll do it tonight and hopefully my quest will be complete.

I am the Soulseeker and I search for the essence of humanity; the soul of man. I will not cease my quest until I find the truth.

CHAPTER 4

The following morning, it was obvious that the mood of the team had changed. There seemed to be a buzz of discussion going on and everyone looked more enthusiastic - which was a considerable contrast to the despondent group Alex had left the previous night.

"What's up?" she asked Marsha Collins.

"We think we've got an ID. The boss is going to brief us when everyone's here."

"I better get a coffee before he gets started then," Alex replied with a smile.

While she was preparing the coffee, William Carrick walked into the office. "That's what I like to see a woman doing woman's work. Get us a coffee, would you?" he shouted as he walked to his desk.

"Sure and then I'll kick you in the nuts," Alex replied under her breath.

"What was that?" he replied with a surly tone as he packed his bulk in behind his desk.

"I just said that I'm sure that you're more than capable of getting it yourself." Alex restrained herself from reacting to Carrick but it was obvious that he was an arse and that at some point she would probably have a frank discussion with him, but not on her second day.

"Charming, is it your time of the month or something? That's aw we need, another moody cow." He looked at Marsha Collins as he spoke and the poor woman flushed a deep crimson. Alex was about to put Carrick in his place but Chief Superintendent Blair heard the exchange as he walked in with the Tom Russell close behind him.

Blair glared at his detective constable and said, "Carrick, for once in your life, please don't be a fuckin' arsehole - sorry Marsha. Alex, Marsha try to ignore him but if you feel like punching his lights out, I'll look the other way."

"Right folks, if you could gather at the incident board, we've got some news," Russell ordered.

The officers surrounded their boss and as he addressed them his face was tense and lacking its usual warmth.

"It looks like we might have an ID for our warehouse body and it is not good news for us. Crimestoppers took a call from Howard Marr's office last night. His political assistant was due to meet him at a constituency function but didn't show. The officer that took the call asked for more details and established that the assistant was in the correct age range and fitted the physical characteristics. He then asked if this guy had ever been in an accident and was told that his right leg was smashed in a car crash four years ago and he had a metal plate fitted. That will give us something to go on by checking his medical records. We'll need to get some DNA to be sure but it looks like we've got a starting point."

"Am I supposed to know who Howard Marr is?" Carrick asked between bites of a chocolate bar.

"He's the MSP for Clyde Valley East and member of the Justice Committee of the Scottish Parliament. This means that it's not just the sliver braid brigade that will be breathing down our necks. We'll have the press and our political masters all over us like a nest of fire ants. We need to get moving on this and find this bastard." Russell's gravitas emphasised the scrutiny they would be under.

Blair ran his hand over his balding pate in a gesture that further highlighted how high his stress levels had climbed as he was bound to get some of the same pressures applied to him.

Tom Russell said, "The suspected victim is this man." He placed on to the incident board a posed photograph of a handsome, well-groomed man in his late twenties.

"This is Graeme Mathieson, twenty-eight years of age. He is a graduate of St Andrews University, and he has been climbing the political ranks since he left school. He lives alone and Marr's office were either unable or reluctant to give us many details about his life away from work. We need to get as much information as we can about known associates, family, friends, the works."

"Alex and Rick, I want you to speak to his parents. I'll take a run out to Marr's office and see what I can find. DC Carrick will accompany me as my silent partner, won't you DC Carrick? " Carrick was about to object when Chief Superintendent Blair's scowl stopped him mid-breath.

Russell then turned to the uniformed trio. "You three check his background. School or uni pals, any relationships he had, anything at all. We'll also need a couple of uniforms to visit his house and they have my permission to break in if they get no reply. If he's not there, tell them to bag anything that might have his DNA and get it to the lab ASAP. Got it?"

All three replied positively.

Blair added, "No one but Superintendent Russell or the media team speaks to the press on this, not even a fuckin' 'no comment' - sorry Marsha. I don't want any stories getting out of control, do I make myself clear?" he asked forcefully.

"Yes, sir," was the unanimous response from the team.

"Let's get cracking."

Howard Marr's constituency office was in Lanark, one of Scotland's most historic towns and a place that has links to a national hero, William Wallace. It is close to a World Heritage Site in the shape of the small former mill town of New Lanark. The MSP worked out of a converted shop in a side street off the town's broad, traditionally Scottish High Street.

The smell of frying sausages and bacon permeated the air from the café next door as the two detectives entered the constituency premises. Russell's mouth watered and he could almost see Carrick drooling. The food was dismissed from his mind, as he knew that he had something more important than his stomach to consider.

He introduced both himself and his DC to a studious

young woman in the front room of the building. She welcomed them with practiced warmth and came from behind her desk to shake their hands. She turned and knocked on a door and then led them through to see the MSP.

Howard Marr was a burly man who seemed to dominate the room when he stood up to greet his visitors. He had broad shoulders, which were attached to meaty arms, and he offered a hand the size of a dinner plate for the officers to shake. Russell noticed his bright blue eyes that were flecked with traces of slate grey; perceptive eyes that were appraising his visitors and making a quick assessment. His hair was a reddish-blonde colour and his complexion looked like he didn't spend all his time in the offices of power. Russell thought he was the kind of man who would not have looked out of place on the deck of a Viking longboat, wielding an axe as he led a raid on an unsuspecting coastal village.

"Thank you for seeing us, Mr Marr," Russell said as he took a seat across from the politician; a modern glass-topped desk separated them. Carrick sat beside the detective superintendent and took out a notebook and pen. At least I don't always have to tell him how to do his job, Russell thought.

"Anything I can do to help, believe me I will, Superintendent Russell. Would you like a tea or coffee before we start?" He smiled at them with as much sincerity as any politician can muster; it was the smile of a man who was used to canvassing for votes.

Carrick was about to reply before Russell said, "No thank you. We had one before we left the station."

"Have you found Graeme?" Marr said, getting straight to the point.

"Not yet. We need you to tell us a little more about Mr Mathieson."

"I've known him for about ten years and he's been my assistant for the past five. He's my right-hand man, a great worker, I don't know what I would do without him."

"What kind of person is he?" Russell was careful to use the present tense.

Marr pondered the question before answering, "He's very ambitious, absolutely driven. He wants to go as far as he can in his career. I hope it's with me but if not he'll try to find a way to the top by whatever means he can and I wouldn't stand in his way because he is that talented." Russell thought that is was a strange thing for a politician to say; rivalries, even within political parties, were normally enough for everyone to be a little wary of ambitious colleagues. Was Marr trying to hide a rivalry?

"What about his private life? What can you tell me about him outside of his career?"

Once again Marr was thoughtful and careful with his answer. "Not a lot because I'm not sure he has much of a life outside of his career. He did have a partner up to a couple of months ago, but they split and I think it hit Graeme quite hard. He had to take some days off, which is very uncharacteristic for him. Jason, his partner, couldn't take being second best to the job. At least that's the impression I got."

"So he was gay?" Carrick asked with a hint of distaste in his voice. Russell glared at his subordinate.

"Was? Has something happened to him?" Marr's voice

cracked.

Russell raised his hands in a placating gesture but before he could say anything, Marr interrupted him.

"Superintendent Russell, I would like to know the details. If necessary, I'll call the chief constable - who is a good friend of mine I hasten to add - to get the information," Marr said haughtily. The dynamic of the interview had changed in a second; Marr had gone from cautious but helpful to concerned and forceful. The politician using the characteristics of a man seeking power was replaced with one willing to use it.

Russell was resigned to telling Marr what they knew; the last thing he need was the chief constable nagging him or anyone else. "A body was found yesterday that could match the physical description of Mr Mathieson."

"The fire in Port Dundas?"

"Yes. I'm afraid the body is not in a condition where we can rely on a physical identification, we will have to get the DNA confirmed before we can be sure, but it seems likely that it is Mr Mathieson."

Marr sat for a couple of minutes obviously distressed at the confirmation of the source of his original anxiety for his colleague's safety. Russell gave the MSP the time to compose himself while watching for the tell-tale signs of guilt. He also took the time to look around the office. One wall was covered in photographs of Marr with a selection of fellow politicians including the First Minister. There were other prints of him presenting awards to children or receiving cheques for charities. It was a portrait of a man obsessed by his own image; he was in every sense a very modern politician.

"Sorry, superintendent, it's come as a shock," Marr said sadly.

"Was the split between Mr Mathieson and his partner amicable?"

"No, there seems to have been some acrimony. I think there may have been another person involved but I really don't know all the details."

"What is the partner's name?"

"Jason Hunter, I think. Ask Fiona on the way out, I think he was Graeme's emergency contact when they were together."

"I will do, thank you. Can you tell me, when did you last see Mr Mathieson?"

"Monday. We worked until about eight on a case we are looking into for a constituent. I knew that we had the function to come the following night so I told him to take the day off and that I would meet him at the dinner. I thought something was wrong when he didn't appear at the meal and I tried phoning him but there was no reply. When the dinner was finished, I tried calling again and then I phoned your people about one o'clock this morning."

"How was he at the meeting? Did he seem worried about anything?"

"He was fine, in fact happier than I had seen him since the break-up. He was looking forward to the dinner but as I say he was tired. It had been a tough few days between constituency and parliamentary work."

"Were you both here on Monday?" Russell asked indicating the constituency rooms.

"No, we were in Glasgow all day. I took him for a

working dinner in a restaurant in the Merchant City while we finished going through the papers. He said he was going to walk home, his flat was in the converted whisky bond close to the Forth and Clyde canal."

"I know the one you mean, it's not far from where the body was found," Russell voiced his thoughts. "Can you think of anyone who would want to harm Mr Mathieson?"

"No, he had political enemies like everyone else in this line of work, but that's it. But we don't bump off our political rivals, Superintendent Russell. It's not ancient Rome, at least not yet."

"No, of course not. Had he ever received any hate mail or threats due to his sexuality?"

"Not to my knowledge but as I say he kept his private life very private." Russell thought he was telling the truth and wondered how much the politician knew about the lives of the people who worked for him.

"I'm sorry to have to ask this Mr Marr, but was your relationship with Mr Mathieson strictly professional?"

Russell was expecting some indignation but he replied calmly, "Yes, I'm a happily married man, superintendent." The detective could not hear any deception in the answer.

"Was he a religious person?"

"No, I don't think so, why?"

Russell did not want anyone outwith the team knowing anything about the religious aspects of the killing and in particular the cross. "We're just trying to establish a possible motive and in this part of the world, religion can be a motive for some of the local bampots. Did you notice anyone taking any special interest in the two of you at the restaurant or when you left?"

He paused before saying, "Not particularly, no."

Russell was frustrated that the MSP had so little to offer; he hoped his DI was having better luck with Graeme Mathieson's parents.

"Thank you, sir. We'll need you to come to Stewart Street to make a statement regarding your dinner on Monday. You will need to come in within the next twenty-four hours."

"Of course, no problem."

"If there's anything you can think of that might help before that, just give me a ring."

The huge hand was offered to both detectives, Marr assured Russell of his full co-operation and then said goodbye.

Russell got the details of Mathieson's partner from the young woman in the outer office before the visit was over.

When the detectives were clear of the building, Russell turned towards Carrick and said, "You may be the thickest prick to ever pass through Tulliallan. What did I say? Shut the fuck up. But no, you had to open your stupid fuckin' mouth."

Carrick shrugged it off. "What difference does it make? If he's dead, he's dead."

"That's the problem, you fanny. If he's dead! If he's not you've just created a situation that was unnecessary and with a guy who can make our life a fuckin' misery."

"It's not my problem. His type risk getting caught up with some lunatic, it's a choice they make."

Russell clenched a fist but decided against throwing it. "You can get the train back." He turned away and strode towards the car park.

"You're kidding, right?" Carrick asked as he trailed behind his superior.

"No, get the fuckin' train. I can't be in a confined space with you... for your own safety."

He slammed the car door and then drove away, leaving Carrick standing breathing heavily as the torrent of rain soaked him.

Russell called the station while he was driving and told them that Marr would be coming in to make a statement. He asked that if he wasn't there when Marr arrived that an experienced detective be present to try to find any cracks in the politician's story. The detective constable who took the call noted the instruction.

The journey helped to dilute the anger Russell felt towards Carrick. He thought that her would probably have to apologise to the man at some point but it wouldn't be today.

The initial attempts to contact Graeme Mathieson's parents had not been fruitful. Alex dialled their telephone number but it rang eight times before a brief message told her to leave her details. She ignored it and hung up; asking the relatives of a victim of crime to contact the police by leaving a voicemail message was never the best way of initiating a relationship.

Alex spent a couple of hours helping the uniformed officers and junior detectives as they tried to piece together some of the details of Graeme Mathieson's life.

Rick Johnstone took a quick run to the scrap merchants

but there was nothing of any interest. The owner said that there were frequent customers who came in search of spare parts but if someone had lifted the plates from the Citroen, he hadn't noticed. The owner was co-operative and was happy to give the details of his five staff to the constable but there was nothing about the situation that gave Rick any hope that it would lead anywhere.

A quick check of the criminal records database confirmed what he thought, the only member of staff with a record had been arrested for shoplifting twenty years previously and had lived a quiet life ever since.

By the time Carrick had been abandoned at the railway station in Lanark, Alex was back on the phone to Mathieson's parents. When she was told that the police wanted to speak to her about her son, Mathieson's mother gave her curt permission to allow a visit but there was no trace of concern in her voice.

Rick Johnstone was no keener to be in Alex's car than Tom Russell had been and it was his Focus they used to take the short trip to the Mathieson home.

The flat was in Belmont Street in the West End of the city. Johnstone was soon regretting his choice to drive. It took twice as long to find a space to park as it had to drive from the station, and the detectives still had a five-minute walk in the tumbling rain back to the correct address. The Mathiesons lived in the upper floor of a building that was once an elegant Victorian townhouse in a street filled with similar properties.

A press on the buzzer marked Mathieson and the officers were invited to come in by a refined female voice.

The flat was at the top of a grand staircase with an

extravagantly carved bannister and a stained glass window that illuminated the stairwell; a floral design in the style of the 'Arts and Crafts' movement, it threw light of different vibrant hues on the detectives as they ascended. At the top, there was a single dark door, gleaming with the glaze of multiple generations of varnish. It swung open and a woman in her late middle age stood awaiting their arrival; the expression on her face was filled with disdain for her unsolicited visitors.

She was slimly built and held herself with the rigidity of a board. The light from the window enhanced her green eyes and they watched passively as the detectives approached. Alex judged that Mrs Mathieson's clothes were expensive and in every way she projected an aura of moneyed superiority.

"Mrs Mathieson, I'm Detective Inspector Alex Menzies and this is my colleague Detective Constable Johnstone." She offered a hand and although the older woman took it, there was no real welcome in the gesture.

She led the police officers through a long narrow hallway that was decorated with original paintings; the majority of which were pastoral scenes, heavy with oil paint featuring farm animals and honest peasants going about their business. It was the kind of chocolate-box art that would have been popular with the first owners of the house. The doors in the hall were all of the period; substantial pieces of dark wood carved with consummate skill; they were both functional and beautiful.

She led them into spacious living area where a willowy man stood waiting beside a substantial fireplace. He was introduced as Basil Mathieson and in many ways he was the mirror of his wife. He was slightly taller but had the same straight back, fine features that had aged well and his blue eyes were clear and youthful. The contrast was a nervousness that indicated he was worried about what his unexpected guests were going to say.

"Please have a seat," he said, indicating an antique settee.

There was an absence of modernity in the room; Alex reckoned that none of the furnishings or ornamentation dated from the twentieth century, never mind the twenty-first. Large pieces of oak, teak and mahogany furniture dominated, while a beautifully woven, sumptuous Persian rug occupied the centre of the natural-wood floor. Above the fireplace, an oil painting of an idealised Scottish glen was the centrepiece and was sure to draw any visitor's eye.

Mr Mathieson continued to stand in nervous anticipation while his wife sat on the edge of an armchair, her back as straight as the Scots pine trees in the painting.

"We would like to talk to you about your son," Alex opened the conversation as Rick Johnstone sat poised with a notebook.

"We have little to say to anyone about that individual," Mrs Mathieson responded dispassionately.

Alex was surprised at the reaction; it was not one she had encountered before from a parent, but she did well to hide it. She looked to Mr Mathieson, who shook his head almost imperceptibly but did nothing to contradict or admonish his wife.

"I'm sorry but it's important that we have this discussion. Your son has been reported missing and there is the possibility that he has been the victim of a crime."

"We have nothing to do with him since he decided to follow the devil's path," Mrs Mathieson replied.

"Excuse me?"

"He decided to stray from God's love and guidance when he was a teenager, he has no place in our life."

"Mrs Mathieson, I'm not sure you understand how serious this is." Alex wondered if this was some sort of shock that was making the woman react so coldly.

Mrs Mathieson regarded Alex with a frosty stare. "To be honest, detective, he is not our concern any more."

Alex glanced again at Mathieson's father and it was obvious that her words were having a greater effect on him.

"Mr Mathieson?"

"I have to agree with my wife, Graeme made his choice many years ago." He put an emphasis on the early part of the sentence, as if he had no choice but to say he concurred with his spouse whether he did or not.

"And what choice was that?"

"He decided to lie with men, which is against the word of God and nature. He chose the path of wickedness that can only lead to an eternity in hell. That was not how he was raised." Mrs Mathieson's hand reached for a cross that hung on a chain from her neck and held it firmly in her right hand.

A buzz from Johnstone's pocket interrupted the discussion before Alex could respond.

"I need to take this, it's the office," the young constable said.

He stood and retreated to the hall. An awkward silence followed in the living room as they waited while one side of the telephone conversation could be heard indistinctly.

A short time later, Johnstone's head appeared at the door. "Inspector, can I have a word?"

Alex walked out to join her colleague, leaving the Mathiesons fixed in their unyielding tableau.

"What's up?"

Johnstone kept his voice low as he replied, "His medical records confirm that the victim is definitely Graeme Mathieson. They checked the metal plate and the X-ray of the break and according to Dr MacNeil, it is identical to the body in the mortuary."

"It's what we expected. We better get this over with."

Johnstone nodded and prepared for a duty that was always the worst that any police officer ever faced. When they returned to the room, Alex advised Mr Mathieson to take a seat.

"What's up? What's happened?" he asked.

"I'm afraid that I have some very bad news. That phone call was confirmation that the body that was found yesterday morning is your son."

Mr Mathieson's youthfulness seemed to be drawn from him by some unseen force. His starched appearance crumpled into a bent pose of grief but initially he cried no tears. In contrast his wife sat holding the cross like it was a lifebelt. She had her faith to cling to.

"What happened?" Mr Mathieson asked.

"It is of no consequence, he has reaped the harvest of his wicked deeds and he will pay with an eternity in hell," his wife interjected with a misguided anger.

Alex glanced at Johnstone, who looked puzzled at what he was witnessing. She felt both shocked and infuriated by the reaction of a mother to the death of her child.

"Mrs Mathieson, it is important that whoever did this is brought to justice. Your son was murdered, and his body mutilated before being set alight, isn't that also a sin that requires to be punished?"

"The person who sows for the benefit of his own flesh shall reap corruption and death from the flesh," Mrs Mathieson quoted.

A sudden urge passed through Alex to scream at the inhuman doctrine of the woman but the professional in her took control, preventing her from saying what she was really thinking. She turned to the victim's father in the hope that she could reach him. "Mr Mathieson?"

He looked up, tears were now brimming in his eyes, and his grief was palpable. He sighed and appeared to have come to a significant decision. "Graeme had been very upset since his split with Jason. They had been very close but it all became very bitter at the end."

His wife reacted as if he had slapped her. "And how would you know that?"

"Because those nights you thought I was playing whist, I was meeting Graeme. I have been doing it since you threw the boy out." His reply was so spiteful that it was almost as shocking to the two detectives as it was to his wife.

"You encouraged his wickedness and betrayed me?" she shouted at him.

"No, I visited our son. The son your precious God created. Everything he was, was created by your God but you put yourself in judgement over him and above your Lord."

"How dare you! You will rot in hell beside him." She was now close to hysteria.

"If heaven's full of people like you, people who have no love for their own flesh and blood, then I'll be better off in hell."

She suddenly sprang from her chair, screamed and reached for her husband's throat. DC Johnstone was the first to react, pulling her away, but not before she left a row of scratches on Mr Mathieson's neck.

"Mrs Mathieson, calm down now or I'll arrest you for assault," Alex commanded. Her tone seemed to snap the older woman out of her temporary mania.

"Now sit down. We've got a job to do."

As the rage dissipated, her body relaxed and Johnstone allowed her to return to her seat.

"I can't believe you betrayed me, Basil," she said with anger, but there was also a sense of resignation as she contemplated what the future would hold for them.

"I didn't betray you, Ellen. I did what any parent should do, I loved and cared for our son. Now you will have to live with what you've done but my conscience will be clear, I did right by our boy. Officers, I wonder if I could trouble you for a lift into town, I don't think I can stay here and pretend any longer."

Alex looked at Johnstone, who nodded.

"Yes, Mr Mathieson, we can do that, if you're sure."

"Oh, I'm positive," he asserted.

As he walked out of the room he looked like a broken man, diminished by the experience of the past few minutes. While the detectives waited, Mrs Mathieson returned to her inflexible pose in the chair. She appeared to be reciting a near silent prayer as she gripped her cross tightly in her hand.

Mr Mathieson returned wearing a trench coat and holding a small suitcase in his hand. "I'm ready to go, detectives. I've called Ellen's sister to come and look after her."

Alex and Johnstone stood and said goodbye to the lonely woman. Her husband said, "Goodbye Ellen."

His wife of thirty-five years didn't even turn her head. Alex noticed that she had gripped the cross so tightly a trickle of blood was seeping from her palm through the fingers of her right hand. She thought about pausing to offer help but knew that it would probably not be accepted. As she closed the door, Ellen Mathieson glanced up and Alex could see that there were tears falling from her face on to the bloodied cross. She would have to live with her own guilt and it may be a lonely road ahead for her.

On the journey into town, Mathieson's stoic control faded away and he wept copiously, his life had been turned upside down in the space of an hour.

The detectives took him to the station and asked him if he would make a statement. He agreed that he would do whatever it took to help to find his son's killer.

At one point during the interview, in between the sobs, he managed to tell the police officers, "I know you might find it hard to believe but she is a good woman but her church preaches only hell-fire and damnation, there is no love of God where they are concerned."

Alex wanted to learn more about the church behind the woman's beliefs. She asked Basil Mathieson and he gave her the details.

When he had completed the formalities Alex asked him, "What are you going to do?"

"I'll stay at a hotel tonight and contact my brother in Edinburgh. Hopefully, he'll be able to put me up until I sort this mess out."

"One question before you go, Mr Mathieson. Did Graeme still have religious beliefs?"

"No, not at all. He saw his mother's example of what faith does to someone and it drove any belief he might have had in God out of him."

"OK, thank you. If there is anything we can do, let us know."

He whispered, "When can I bury my boy?"

"I'm afraid it might be some time before we can release him to you." Alex knew how difficult that period would be for the poor man, it was a trying time for any family whose loved one had been the victim of a crime. For a man whose marital façade had just disintegrated, exposing the rot within, it would be even more difficult.

"I'll give you my brother's phone number, you can get hold of me through him."

Alex drove him to the Holiday Inn Express hotel, and he wrote out his brother's details before thanking the officers for their kindness.

When she returned to the office Johnstone said to Alex, "That was an interesting afternoon."

"I can't believe how emotionless that woman is. I almost think she's capable of killing him herself."

"The cross in his hand and the treatment of the body might fit but I can't see her drilling a hole in his head, can you?"

"No, not really, but it might be worth checking out members of her church, you never know. I think I'll pay them a visit."

"One thing we do know is that the cross didn't belong to Graeme."

"Small progress is better than none at all, I suppose."

They drove back to the station talking politely about their home lives, beginning the gentle probing of two colleagues getting to know one another.

✝

Before she went home, Alex decided to drop in on the church where Ellen Mathieson worshipped. It was on her way home and she wanted to get some idea of what kind of people could turn a woman against her own child.

The Church of God, The Alpha and Omega was based in a small building close to Kelvinbridge subway station. A low, square structure with a simple plaque on the door, it looked to have been built relatively recently. Alex had looked up the details on the Internet and discovered that it was a single building and the church had seceded from another evangelical organisation.

The lights were on as Alex pulled into the car park. There were another three cars occupying some of the ten spaces the area provided.

Alex walked to the door and into the church itself. It looked like a community hall rather than a place of worship. There was no altar or communion table, the chairs were arranged in a semi-circle and windows were simple pieces of undecorated glass. The only clue as to the purpose was a cross, shaped from rough pieces of metal that could have come from any scrapyard in the land.

Alex could hear voices drifting in from a door off to the right. She walked towards it and found herself in a small kitchen. Four people were seated around a table, mugs of tea or coffee in front of them with a plate of sandwiches in the centre.

A man in his early thirties rose to greet her. "Good evening, sister. How may we help you?"

Her warrant card already in her hand, she said, "I'm Detective Inspector Alex Menzies. I would like to speak to the minister, please."

"There are no minsters within our church, Alex. We are all teachers and students of the word of God. I am Brother Allan Duncanson, this is sister Barbara, brother Steven and sister Naomi," he said with a fixed smile. Alex was a little surprised at his familiarity in using her first name; a warrant card was normally the cue for some kind of formality.

"Would you be the person who would represent the church?" she asked, as he seemed to have volunteered leadership by taking control of the conversation.

"I was the founder of this church and dedicate my life to the service of the Lord. I am but one of his flock but I suppose I am as good a person as any to answer your questions." The smile never wavered and Alex was a little disconcerted.

"May I have a word with you in private?"

"If that is your desire." He indicated the door that Alex had walked through and ushered back through the church to a pair of seats in front of the distressed cross.

"What can I do for you, Alex?" he asked when they were seated.

"I believe that Mrs Ellen Mathieson is a member of your congregation."

"That's correct, sister Ellen is a contributor to our community of Christ."

"Her son was killed yesterday."

"I am sorry to hear that. That means he has died before he could be brought to the Lord, he will be condemned to an eternity in hell. That is truly tragic."

"Maybe you didn't understand me, he was murdered."

"The Lord will find always find a hand to do his work. Sinners must be punished if they cannot be brought to live their life as God intended."

"Funny, I thought that one of the Ten Commandments specifically mentioned murder," she replied sarcastically.

"That only applies to those who live in God's light. The servants of the darkness have no such protection."

"So you would advocate murder during your teaching sessions?"

"Alex…"

Alex interrupted him, "That's Detective Inspector Menzies."

His smiles slipped for a moment but it soon returned. "My apologies. I would not advocate murder, detective inspector, but I understand if someone feels the Lord move within to do His will."

Alex moved away from his lunatic philosophy and to the real purpose of her visit. "I would like a full list of your membership, Mr Duncanson."

"Why?"

"I would like to know if any of them have a history of violence. Mrs Mathieson's reaction was not that of a grieving mother and I am concerned that one of your flock may have taken the decision to help her remove her embarrassment. It can't be easy for a pious woman such as her to have raised a man who falls so far from her and her church's idea of grace."

"That is impossible. No member of our faith would do that. If you need our membership list, I'm afraid that will only be possible if you supply me with a warrant, detective inspector."

"If that's how you want it." She stood but before she left she said, "I wonder, Mr Duncanson, why you condemn yourself and members of your flock to hell?"

His smile wavered. "I'm not sure what you mean."

"I couldn't help notice that there were some prawn sandwiches on the table."

"So?" he was frowning.

"The same book in the Bible that proscribes homosex-uality also says that you shouldn't eat anything that crawls on the seabed. I believe that includes prawns. Or is that one of those rules that can be dismissed because it doesn't suit you?" She left the church before he had a chance to reply.

Alex would probably find it difficult to get a warrant based on what evidence there was but she would get someone to pester Jacqui Kerr in the morning.

Theresa Asher stepped off the train at Milngavie

railway station, physically and mentally worn out from another long day of disagreements and compromises. She was one of only five passengers that alighted and made their way from the brightly lit station. She searched in her bag to find a compact umbrella and raised it against the rain that continued to spill relentlessly from the clouds that had taken up residence in the Glaswegian sky. She wondered if it ever stopped raining in this grey city.

Theresa had come to Glasgow from her native city of Bristol via London. For the past four months she had been working for the organising committee of the 2014 Commonwealth Games. The tight budgets and political situation of the country had meant that the job had become a stressful balancing act. She had performed a similar role in London in the early stages of the planning for the Olympic Games but when the role in Glasgow had been advertised she thought that it would be the perfect antidote to the rigours and pace of the capital. She was wrong. The local council, Scottish Government and UK parliament were controlled by three different political parties and all of them wanted to claim responsibility for any successes and blame the other two for any problems. Sometimes she felt that it would have been easier being a diplomat in the Middle East.

Her thoughts began to drift to her house and the welcome she would get from her ginger cat, O'Malley, when she opened the front door. Like all cats, his love was conditional as he expected to be fed when he demanded it, but when his stomach was full, he was always happy to settle on her lap and purr away some of her troubles.

As she walked out of the car park into Gavin's Mill

Road, a pair of eyes watched her from the dark interior of a stationary car. He waited to make sure that there was no one else coming from the station that might be heading in the same direction as his target. When he thought it was safe, he moved the gear stick and rolled the vehicle up beside her.

Theresa thought nothing of the blue Vauxhall Corsa as it drew beside her. Her mind was on Jonathan, the attractive doctor she had met the previous week. There was a possibility of something special happening between them, they had made a connection and Theresa felt that it could be the first good thing that had happened to her since she arrived in this miserable part of the world. It could be a new start and maybe she would be able to stop taking the anti-depressants that the doctor had prescribed to help her with the stress and the isolation she had been feeling for months.

As she walked past the car a voice called to her, "Excuse me."

She backed up a little and bent down to see a serious-looking man in a formal suit.

"I was wondering if you could help me, I'm looking for Clochber Avenue, I've got an elderly patient I have to visit but I'm a only a locum doctor and I've never been in this area before. I'm afraid I've got myself a bit lost."

"Oh, you're in the right general area but there's still a bit of driving to do. Actually, it's just round from where I live."

"That's a coincidence. Maybe I could give you a lift and you could navigate for me. Mutual benefit; I could help you get home quicker and you could stop me wandering around using up petrol." He smiled with a reassuring confidence.

Theresa hesitated; she knew that getting into a car with a strange man wasn't a good idea. She looked at the doctor and all she could see were kind eyes and a guy obviously dedicated to his profession. A quick trip in the car would save her getting any wetter and she would be helping someone to look after an elderly person. She shook the worst of the rainwater from her umbrella before sliding the telescopic mechanism into its housing. She eased her way into the car and it was only as she settled in the seat that she noticed the light from the GPS system attached to the window on the driver's side. The door locks clunked loudly, the car pulled away from the kerb and she felt a needle pierce her arm. Her last thought before she fell asleep was, *'Who will look after my poor O'Malley?'*

CHAPTER 5

Detective Superintendent Tom Russell could hear a bell ringing faintly. In his dream he was on the deck of a ship. The sound was becoming clearer but it was omnidirectional; he couldn't pinpoint the source and it was annoying him. Then slowly his conscious mind began to take control and he realised that the source of the noise was his phone.

"Hello," he mumbled into the device without even looking at the display to see who was calling.

An English voice that Russell didn't recognise said, "Sir, I'm sorry to call you at this time of day but we've got another body that I think you'll want to see."

"Eh, who is this?" Russell asked from the depths of his confusion.

"DC Barnstead from Maryhill CID, sir." Russell glanced at his bedside clock, which told him it was four a.m.

"Well detective constable, why the hell are you calling me at this God awful hour in the morning if you work in

Maryhill?"

"Sorry sir, a body was found in a fire at the old Ruchill Hospital. My DCI told me to ring you because the circumstances are similar to the Port Dundas fire earlier in the week; a body laid out before being set alight," he said apologetically.

The fog of sleep was blown away and Russell was suddenly wide-awake. "Shit, when was this?"

"The fire was reported at two this morning. First uniforms on site reported the body about twenty minutes ago."

"What's your first name, Barnstead?"

"Martin, sir."

"OK, Martin, thanks for the heads up. Tell your DCI I'll be there as soon as I can."

"Will do, sir."

Russell hated living alone but early morning calls were one of the few times that he was glad there was no one lying beside him to be disturbed by the incessant demands of his job.

He felt he was like a policing cliché, divorced and living the life of a recluse, but it wasn't his career that had led to this situation. He had been the one who decided to initiate divorce proceedings when he came to the conclusion that his wife was completely and utterly mental. She had been possessive and jealous for years but when she became more irrational than any sane person should be, or any sane partner could tolerate, he decided enough was enough. He wasn't sure why it had taken eight years to see the light but it was better that he was out of the marriage before he ended up the focus of the professional interest of his colleagues. A cop who had murdered his wife would be the subject of some unwanted and probably violent attention in any prison.

The divorce had left him living in a tiny flat with very few material items. Russell's lawyer had been as incompetent as his wife was crazy. His mishandling of the divorce had basically allowed his opposing counsel to take Tom for nearly all he had. He tried to not feel bitter but it was difficult; his life was empty beyond the confines of his job. Even old friends had drifted away, choosing to believe the stories of infidelity his wife had told them.

He showered, shaved and dressed as quickly as he could; shirt and tie, pressed suit trousers and newly polished shoes. He took pride in his appearance and believed that a cop was more likely to get respect if he looked the part.

He called Alex and then Rick Johnstone to tell them to meet him at the crime scene. He gave them a brief sketch of what they were going to find and the chilling reality of what it could mean.

He pulled on his suit jacket and then a long raincoat to protect the suit against the elements. When he was ready, he lifted his mobile phone, car keys and house keys from the small shelf in his compact living room. He was on his way to the crime scene within twenty minutes of receiving the call.

✠

Dawn had broken over the Glasgow skyline, tinting the grey cloud with a hint of salmon pink as Alex joined her boss and the young DC at the second smoky scene they had attended in three days.

Originally, Ruchill Hospital was the city's treatment clinic for patients suffering from serious infectious diseases like tuberculosis. It opened in 1900, but the need for its services diminished in the sixties as vaccination programmes began to have a positive effect on the health of the population. It closed in 1998 after a brief renaissance as the primary centre for the treatment of AIDS and HIV during the eighties.

The Victorian majesty of the red sandstone buildings was now under attack from a triumvirate of destructive forces. Wind and rain had eaten away at the wood and eroded the stone. Plants had taken up residence between the stones, their roots tearing away the mortar and beginning to pull the fabric of the building apart. Human hands were also at work dismantling some of the oldest buildings around the imposing clock tower, salvaging what they could to reuse in some glamorous new construction.

A fence had been erected around each of the structurally unsafe buildings and it provided the police with a ready-made cordon. Russell added an outer ring, protected by police tape and a couple of constables that he hoped would prevent press or public intrusion. Outside a large block that once rang to the voices of nurses, doctors and patients, there was a group of anxious faces clustered together in animated discussion. The building had been unsafe before the fire weakened its fabric further and inside the fence the fire service personnel were in deep discussion with a group of people that Alex presumed to be engineers or builders.

"What's happening?" she asked Russell, having negotiated the first ring.

"The fire teams have extinguished the flames from outside the building, they're trying to work out if it's safe to retrieve the body without some sort of support being put in place. We can't put the forensic team in at the moment it's too dangerous. We'll not get much from the scene anyway, the fire was burning too long."

As he finished speaking, Dr McNeil walked up to join them. She was already dressed for the scene with white wellingtons and the unflattering coveralls that did nothing for anyone who wore them, but looked particularly unkind to someone of her stature.

Russell greeted her, "Good morning, Doc. Another bright and breezy start to a morning."

"There's nothing like the smell of burnt flesh to set you up for another miserable day," she replied morosely.

"It might be a while before we need you."

"I wasn't doing anything else, just sleeping." She smiled faintly, resigned to her fate as a forensic pathologist in Glasgow; a full night's sleep was never guaranteed.

"Doctor McNeil, Alex, this is DCI Jones from Maryhill. I think he's about to hand this little mess over to us gleefully. Am I right, Ian?"

"Looks like you've got this covered, no point in duplicating work." Despite the grin there was a trace of sympathy in his words.

"We might need some of your guys to do the door to door. See if anybody noticed anything, particularly a white Luton-style box van."

"You'll be lucky round here," Jones replied.

"I know, but as this is unlikely to be local, you might

get something from some public-spirited citizen."

"In Ruchill? Mair chance of finding Angelina Jolie riding a unicorn bare-arsed naked."

The others laughed at the joke before Jones departed, obviously relieved that he could leave the Major Incident Team to their investigation.

As the sun cast a watery light between the slate-coloured shower clouds, the team of engineers and firefighters continued to discuss their options. Johnstone had suggested to his boss that maybe the police should be involved but Russell thought that it would be better to allow them to continue and that neither he nor his colleagues would be able to contribute a great deal anyway.

The police and the doctor stood in a tight huddle, conversing about trivialities for about twenty minutes; the sense of exasperation at being unable to get started was preying on their nerves.

"Oh shite, here she comes," DC Johnstone said as he watched Jacqui Kerr park her car a short way down the hill from where they were standing.

"Constable!" Alex said.

"Sorry," the embarrassed young man replied.

"Probably sucking some lemons before she came out. Make sure she had the correct demeanour to start the day," Russell said.

The others struggled to keep a smile from their faces as the Fiscal approached. She was dressed immaculately in a business suit, her hair and make-up perfect. Alex wondered how long it had taken her to look that pristine at this time in the morning.

"Right, what's the story?" she asked abruptly.

Alex could tell that the camaraderie of the group had been disrupted with a single sentence from the uptight woman. Russell gave her a briefing about what they knew, which wasn't much.

"So you haven't seen the body?"

"No, we can't get close until the fire officer says it's safe."

"Then how do you know it's related to the Port Dundas murder?"

He wondered if she was being deliberately difficult or she was as obtuse as she appeared.

"The firefighters reported that from what they could see from the exterior of the building, the body was laid out in a similar way to the first body. Carefully arranged on top of the combustible material."

"It doesn't mean it's the same killer," Kerr stated.

"No, but it would be one hell of a coincidence," Russell replied caustically.

"Quite. When will you get access?"

"I have no idea."

"Well maybe we should find out." She walked in the direction of the other gathering of people.

"Willie Ferguson is going to be delighted to see her," Russell muttered.

Kerr was on her way back within two minutes. "They are progressing it and apparently I'm not needed."

Rick Johnstone had to turn away to hide the extremely broad grin he was sporting.

Five minutes later, Willie Ferguson joined them with news. "The engineers are gonnae get some equipment they use in search and rescue efter an earthquake. It'll prop up the building and then we can get the boady oot. It might take a while to get it organised, sorry."

"Cheers, Willie."

That left the group no further forward and it looked like they were in for a long wait before they could begin the investigation in earnest.

Russell turned to the DC. "Rick, you head back to the station, get the details about Mathieson's ex, then go and interview him when he's available. It'll probably be more profitable than hanging about here twiddling your thumbs. Tell the techs that we're probably not going to need a full team, so if they've got somewhere better to be, they might as well go."

"OK, boss. Anything else?"

"No that'll do for now. Let me know what you can, when you can."

Johnstone trudged towards the van that was used by the scene of crime officers and passed on the message from Russell. He then waded to the car park through the mud and rivers of dirty water that were sloshing down the pathway. Jacqui Kerr took the opportunity to return to her car, leaving with a warning to Russell that she wanted a full briefing later in the day.

"Some day I'll swing for that useless cow. I wish she was as domineering in a courtroom, then we might get a few more convictions," Russell muttered when she was out of earshot. Doctor MacNeil looked at him, not sure how to react.

"Sorry Doc, but once you get to know her you'll understand why we feel the way we do."

"I think I'm getting a pretty good impression," she

replied.

"Do they know how he got in?" Alex asked.

"He burst the lock on the gates at the bottom of the hill according to the demolition guys. Once he was inside, the majority of the buildings are easy to access," Russell replied.

"He took some chance in doing this. It must be important to him for some reason."

"Do you think he used to work here maybe?"

"Possibly, but it's the second time that the body has been found where there is a view across the city. Maybe he needs the elevation for some reason."

"Could be. Who knows when you're dealing with a psycho who is wired differently from everyone else."

As they were talking, Noel Hawthorn arrived, looking uncharacteristically grim. He acknowledged the police officers and the doctor before joining Sean O'Reilly at the van.

It was another hour before a small convoy of vans drew up just short of the crime scene. A team of men and women appeared and began to unload a piece of heavy hydraulic equipment, numerous scaffolding bars and substantial pieces of wood that looked like old railway sleepers.

Another meeting was convened with the engineers; Russell led his team to the edge of the circle to hear what was said.

The leader of the newly arrived squad took centre stage. "I'm Ed Peters, I'll be leading the retrieval operation. We are going to use this equipment to create a tunnel that should allow us to extricate the body. This work is pretty delicate and we will have to proceed with a deal of caution, so it may take a while."

Alex heard her boss groan.

"I understand the need for the police to establish what happened and quickly, but I'm afraid I can't say for sure how long this will take," Peters added.

"I'm Detective Superintendent Tom Russell. We wouldn't wish to put anyone at risk; we want the body intact but not at the expense of putting any of your team in any danger."

"Thank you, superintendent, we'll work as quickly as we can. Shall we get started?"

Although the sun was now well above the horizon, the thick grey cumulus meant the light was still insufficient to work on the building without the addition of more artificial lighting. Two substantial floodlights already illuminated the scene but Peters' team erected another three and the rattle of another diesel generator kicking into life added to the noise.

Alex was fascinated to watch from a safe distance as the hydraulic machine was used to lift some of the beams that had collapsed as a result of the fire. They were then supported by a complicated construction that used the wooden props and metal poles to create a safe area that would protect the people below it. It was painstaking work and the tunnel slowly evolved inch by inch; the skill of the workforce was obvious and their diligence, teamwork and mutual understanding impressed Alex.

Around ten thirty, after a couple of rounds of coffee for the spectators, the work was nearing completion. There was a feeling of optimism that the body could soon be brought out and everyone could move to the next stage of the extraction.

The ward that was the focus of the drama was at the top of the hill and on a clear day offered a view across a large swathe of the city. Rain showers had swept regularly over the observers during the time they waited for the construction of the tunnel. Now, Alex could see a much darker cloud approaching, the kind that seems to suck light from around it like a spectre in a children's story. A flash of lightning was followed a few seconds later by the ominous boom and roll of thunder.

"I think that's heading our way," Alex said to Russell.

"You might be right. That's all we need, another deluge."

She continued to watch the storm approach and within a few minutes another jagged fork of lightning raced down to touch the earth in several places. Its accompanying thunderclap reached them a second later.

"Let's get back to the car until this passes over," Russell shouted through raindrops that had intensified to a cascade.

They had taken just a few steps when the ground was suddenly bathed in dazzling blue-white light as the lightning rod of the old clock tower attracted the next bolt and the concussion of the thunder nearly knocked Alex from her feet. The old ward creaked and groaned before the crash of falling masonry was heard like the earth's wrathful reply to the violence of the heavens. Screams and shouts were audible from within and then the world was silent. With her other senses overloaded, Alex's sense of smell took control as the tang of ozone and the stale bitterness of masonry dust filled her nostrils. In the ominous quiescence that followed the clamour, she was concerned that there may be more than one body to be retrieved from the rubble.

CHAPTER 6

When DC Johnstone returned to the station, the first thing he did was call the home number of Jason Hunter; the one that Carrick had been given during his visit to Marr's office. He quickly established that Mathieson's ex-partner was unavailable and he tried the mobile number. Jason Hunter answered, told him he was at work and gave him the address.

Carrick was still fuming due to the treatment he had received from Russell the previous day; he sat sulking behind his computer and was more abrupt than usual with anyone who spoke to him. Rick Johnstone had thought about asking his fellow DC to accompany him for the interview but when he considered Carrick's mood and his general lack of social skills, he realised that it would be better to leave him in the office. Anyway, it was only a witness statement. He could handle it.

Jason Hunter worked in The Black Dress Gallery in Glasgow's creative heart, the West End around Byres Road. When he discovered where the gallery was, Johnstone decided rather than face the parking nightmare once more, he would take the underground across the city.

The Black Dress Gallery was a short walk from the Hillhead subway station and Johnstone was opening the door only twenty-five minutes after leaving the office.

A bell announced his arrival and a tall man in his early twenties walked through a short hallway from the back of the gallery.

"Hello, can I help you?" He spoke with a soft voice and an accent that originated somewhere round Manchester.

"Yes, I'm Detective Constable Johnstone, we spoke on the phone," the detective said while completing the formality of showing him his warrant card.

"You've come about Graeme. Howard Marr called me last night." His sorrow transformed him as his retail smile slipped away.

"I'm sorry, sir, but I have to ask you a few questions about how your relationship ended."

"You can't think I had anything to do with this!" Hunter said with indignant surprise.

"I am simply following a line of enquiry, sir. I'm sure you want to help us find who committed this terrible act." Johnstone was firm and assured.

"Yes, sorry. How can I help?"

"We believe that you and Mr Mathieson parted on less than friendly terms. Can you tell me what happened?"

Hunter was about to answer when the bell on the door stopped him. An elderly couple, draped in the trappings of tourists everywhere, entered and began to look at the paintings on the wall. Dressed in rain coverings and bright clothes, they both had cameras and the woman carried a large handbag. They were out early to explore the city, trying to pack as much as possible into their holiday. Hunter introduced himself to them and they told him that they were looking for some 'Scotch' art to take home to Indiana. As Hunter pointed out the works by Scottish artists, Johnstone took the opportunity to study the pictures. They were all portraits and posed figures; he had to force himself to turn away from one particularly graphic representation of a nude woman that was anatomically correct in every detail. He didn't know too much about art but he thought that the work on show was generally of a very high quality and that if he had the money he might even have bought a couple, although probably not the representation of female genitalia.

Hunter returned to his side as he left his potential customers to make a choice.

"Why is the gallery called The Black Dress? It sounds more like a fashion boutique," Hunter said.

"It's the name of a painting by Modigliani, the owner's a big fan. As we specialise in figurative art, he thought it was appropriate."

Johnstone nodded sagely as if he knew what Hunter was talking about.

The American visitors made a choice after about ten minutes, during which time Johnstone was itching to continue the interview. Hunter completed the transaction by taking payment and the details of his customers' address in Crawfordsville, Indiana. The picture would be shipped across the Atlantic and arrive at their home shortly after they did.

"Can you close the shop while we talk, please?" the

detective asked, trying not to show how irked he had been by the interruption.

"Of course, I'm sorry about that." He flipped the sign on the door to 'Closed' and then turned the lock.

"Now, you were going to tell me about your break-up."

Hunter looked uncomfortable before admitting, "It was all my fault."

"Why was that?"

"I did something stupid, very stupid."

"I'm afraid I'll need the details, Mr Hunter," Johnstone pressed.

"I slept with a woman," he confessed as if it was the most shocking thing in the world.

"Are you bisexual?"

"No, at least I don't think so."

Johnstone was puzzled by the response but it looked as though he wasn't the only one.

"We were invited to the first night of a new exhibition through in Edinburgh. As usual, Graeme couldn't go, he was always too busy with work to allow us to do anything together. I was angry with him and I started drinking before I even left Glasgow. I met this young female artist and we got to talking and then to drinking Champagne, a lot of Champagne. We liked the same artists and had a lot in common. We both ended up very drunk and when she suggested I go back to her place I don't know what came over me, but I woke up the next morning naked in her bed with her at my side."

Johnstone thought that drink was a weak excuse for infidelity but the way his home life was at the moment he could almost understand it.

"And Mr Mathieson found out?"

"I decided to be honest and tell him. He went ballistic, screamed at me and told me he never wanted to see me again. Things got silly after that; I threw an accusation of his neglect at him, he called me a traitor and our relationship disintegrated."

"And the night you told him about the woman, that was the last time you saw him?"

"Saw, yes, but we had begun to talk again just last week. He called because he had found a book of mine and wanted to return it but we started chatting and it was good, like old times. Then I phoned him the following night, I thought we had a chance at reconciliation, but that's all gone now." The realisation of Mathieson's death and its implications appeared to suddenly overwhelm him and he began to weep quietly.

Johnstone offered a tissue from a box that was sitting on the small desk at the front of the gallery.

"During your time together did he receive any threats connected to your relationship or to his job?"

Hunter managed to reply through his tears. "He got some hassle from some right-wing organisation through one of his social media accounts and e-mail but they were just the usual neds with a litany of hate. I don't think they would have done something like this."

"Do you have the details of the organisation?"

"It'll be on his computer."

"Thank you, Mr Hunter. I know this has been difficult for you. We'll need you to come into the station to give a formal statement."

"Yes, I understand."

The policeman finished with the usual speech about getting in touch if Hunter could think of anything else and left his card.

Johnstone hoped the computer techs would come up with the name of the organisation to help move the case forward.

As the cloud of dust billowed away there were a few moments of confusion as more shouts were heard from inside the building; grime-covered watchers wiped the grit from their eyes and everyone tried to get their bearings. The collapse had happened on the far side of the structure, which meant fortunately no one had been seriously hurt. One member of the rescue team had her arm broken by a piece of stone that had managed to find its way through the props but the rest of the injuries were restricted to minor scrapes and bruises. The paramedics treated the broken arm and offered to take the woman to hospital but she said wanted to wait until the work was complete.

The operation was paused for ten minutes while everyone took shelter until the storm completed its rapid traverse of the site. There was another brief meeting then the work restarted and within twenty-five minutes calls were made for a stretcher to extract the body.

Russell walked over to Ed Peters. "Is there any chance we can get some photographs of the body in situ?"

"I could get one of my team to do it, I wouldn't suggest that you put any of your people in there."

"OK, thanks, I'll get the crime-scene photographer to give you a camera."

Noel Hawthorn was dozing in the cabin of the crime scene team's van while Sean O'Reilly sat beside him writing a report from a previous case. Russell knocked on the window and Hawthorn jumped, O'Reilly laughed.

"What's up, we ready to go?" Noel asked sleepily.

"I need one of your cameras; one of the rescue team are going to take some photographs of the body."

It was obvious from his expression that Hawthorn wasn't too keen to entrust some of his expensive equipment to inexperienced hands.

"Do you fancy going in there?" Russell asked with a smile.

"You've got a point, I suppose it's better to leave it to the experts," he conceded. He moved around the van to the side door where he had stowed his bag and picked one of the cameras.

The camera looked like a toy in Noel's hands as he spent a few minutes showing one of Peters' team how to get the best from the various settings. When he was confident that his pupil was capable of getting the shots that were needed, he gave his permission for the photography to begin.

The temporary scene of crime photographer took as many pictures as the confined space would allow. When the camera was returned to Hawthorn he checked the shots and declared himself happy. Russell breathed a sigh of relief as the long morning of difficult work drew to a close.

O'Reilly joined the briefing and gave the rescue team

some instructions on how he wanted the body and any evidence preserved. It was decided that a body bag would be the best way to remove the corpse from the scene without compromising it any more than it already had been. The team were attentive and O'Reilly was pleased to see that they understood the significance of what he was saying and why it was important in the pursuit of the killer.

The removal of a corpse from a crime scene was always a task fraught with difficulty but the location of this one and its condition made it an even more delicate task. O'Reilly and Dr MacNeil were at the edge of the building, hard hats protecting their heads while they relayed instructions to, and answered questions from, the people inside the building. The teamwork was effective and with fifteen minutes a zipped body bag was delivered to an area well away from the reach of any further collapse of the masonry.

Russell, Alex, Noel Hawthorn, O'Reilly and Doctor MacNeil joined the small party who had gathered around the body as if to pay their respects. They included Peters and his team, Willie Ferguson and some of the demolition team.

"Give the doctor some space, please," the Superintendent said.

Everyone took a pace back and watched as Doctor MacNeil crouched beside the bag and gently drew the zip down to expose its contents.

There was an audible gasp as the charred skeleton was exposed and it was followed by the sound of someone being sick. The damage done by the fire was more extensive than that on Graeme Mathieson's body. No part of the flesh remained untouched by the destructive contact with the flames, with the majority burnt to black cinder. In places along the length of all four limbs the skin and muscle had fallen from the bone like dead leaves from ancient tree.

Alex stared in muted shock at the scene; her fear of fire had been ingrained deep within her as a child. Her mother and father, always concerned that she would go too close to their coal fire in the living room, had disciplined her if she disobeyed their instruction. Their lectures had become the subject of her nightmares and now those terrors were now more vividly exposed by the poor soul whose body lay before her. The first body had been bad enough but this was almost too much for her.

Doctor MacNeil calmly took control and began to detail her initial findings for the benefit of the police officers. "It is the body of a woman, the burns are extensive and it will be difficult to determine the cause of death until the PM. Four ribs above the heart have been removed, possibly using a bone saw, but I will have to confirm that in the mortuary. There is no sign of a trepanning hole in the skull. Noel, can you please record the details?"

Hawthorn worked with his usual diligence, pointing the camera at every important detail while the conversation continued around him. When he was happy with the still photographs he repeated the process with the video camera.

"Same killer?" Russell asked, having recovered from his own shock at what he was witnessing.

"I can't be sure. Apart from where the bone was

removed, it's pretty much the same MO as the first body. I would say as there were no details released to the media of the removal of pieces of bone from the previous victim, it's unlikely to be a copycat."

"When will you be able to do the PM?" Russell asked.

"Later today, I'll give you a bell."

"OK Doc, but we need it as a high priority. We'll get the body transferred to the mortuary and take it from there. Thanks, everyone, for all your help today. I hope I don't need to remind you that no one says a thing about this to the press, understand?" Everyone acknowledged and agreed to the instruction. The body bag was sealed and Russell called Maryhill police station to request two uniformed officers to escort the body to the mortuary.

The little groups dispersed and handshakes were exchanged before everyone began the process of packing up.

Two constables arrived to perform their escort duties. They reported to Russell and he gave them their instructions. The private ambulance departed with the body and officers on board, leaving behind a sense of relief amongst the majority of the witnesses.

"What do you think?" Russell turned to his DI as they walked back to their cars.

Alex put aside her own internal terrors and focused her attention on a professional analysis of what she had seen. "I think there's too many similarities for it to be anything other than the same killer. The placement of the body, the ritualistic fire and the removal of bone all point to the same person."

"The removal of the bone is the weirdest part for me.

Is he collecting souvenirs?"

"It could be, but there is something about this that is almost occult."

"Devil worship you mean?"

"Possibly but not necessarily. I feel there's some kind of religious undertone, maybe paganism. I thought that the hole in the previous victim was about some form of healing that had gone wrong. With this one that's probably not the case but do you know what I mean?"

Russell stopped and turned to meet Alex's gaze. "I'm not sure but I'm worried this guy's getting a taste for it and it might not be the last."

Alex dismissed an inadvertent shudder but she had to agree that what her boss had said was a distinct possibility.

"I wonder where the primary crime scene is? The two we've had so far are obviously secondary," Alex mused.

"Inside the white van? It's big enough."

"Could be but how do we find it?"

"Luck, probably. I sometimes think that police work is eighty per cent effort and twenty per cent blind luck."

"Back to the office?" Alex asked as they reached the cars.

"You look beat, why not take a break and come in refreshed in the morning?"

"I'm fine."

"I don't think you are. I could see the effect that corpse had on you. I'll go back and see how Rick's been getting on, I'll see you tomorrow," he insisted.

"Thanks, sir." In truth she was relieved and was eager to have a shower to clean the smell of smoke and scorched flesh from her hair and skin. A glass of wine would help to send her off to sleep later.

As she was opening the car door, she heard a shout from outside the cordon the police had established at the bottom of the hill. Charlie Walker was trying to get the attention of the detective superintendent by waving his notepad in the air. He was at the front of a small group of reporters and photographers that had assembled in the hope of getting some details of the activity in the grounds.

"Is this the same murderer, Superintendent Russell? Does Glasgow have a serial killer?" He continued in the same vein of wild speculation while Russell ignored him pointedly. His fellow reporters took up the same theme but they had no more luck than Walker in eliciting a response from Russell. Officially a serial killer was defined as one with at least three victims but in Alex's mind it was the term that best summed up what they were dealing with. Across the roof of the cars she exchanged a look with her boss that indicated he believed Walker might well be correct.

Russell walked wearily into the incident room in Stewart Street station; exhausted by the length of his day and the emotional drain of what had been revealed when the body bag was opened. Carrick didn't acknowledge him at all but Marsha's smile cheered him a little. Rick Johnstone looked eager to tell him what he had discovered, but a cup of tea was his immediate imperative and he held up his hand to his eager DC.

"Give me a minute, Rick."

Tea made, he walked to his desk and sunk into the ancient chair that sat in front of the desk he had chosen. It had been shaped by a number of backsides over time into a vaguely comfortable place to rest his tired bones.

When he felt a little refreshed and ready to face the next part of the day he stood up and asked the team to assemble. There were around twelve detectives in the room and well as the uniformed staff. He briefed them about the gruesome realities of the Ruchill crime scene; telling them every detail that he could remember. There was a moment of quiet as the team absorbed what they had heard. He didn't look forward to repeating the tale to Blair, who was already feeling the burden from the first murder.

"Anyone got anything useful to tell me?" he asked hopefully.

Johnstone was the first to speak and was pleased that he could offer his superintendent some good news. "Mathieson may have been the subject of some threat from a right-wing organisation; the IT guys are checking his computer to see if they can work out who it was."

"Tell them I want it as top priority. William?' Russell turned to Carrick, who seemed eager to tell him something.

Carrick announced, "The toxicology reports are back on the first victim."

"And?" Russell knew what was wrong with the recalcitrant detective constable but decided it was better to ignore his attitude in the hope that he would come out of puberty soon.

Carrick consulted his notepad. "Mathieson was loaded with a cocktail of phenobarbital, morphine and something called ketamine. Ketamine is normally used in hospitals to sedate a patient before an operation; the other two are used as anaesthetics. The lab reckoned the ketamine was used to disable the victim and that the other two drugs were administered as a fatal dose."

"Thanks, William. Shit - sorry Marsha - what kind of psycho are we dealing with?" Russell said rhetorically. He turned to the desk-bound uniformed officers. "You guys got anything worthwhile?"

The mumbled negative responses strained his patience but he realised that the frustrations of this case had nothing to do with the overworked people who were standing in front of him. This wasn't a simple case by any stretch of the imagination.

"I better go and brief the chief super, wish me luck."

The walk along the corridor to Blair's office felt like the Green Mile for Russell. The thought of telling his friend that Glasgow may have its own serial killer was hanging like a death sentence on the seasoned officer. He knocked on the door and was invited in to the office.

"Tom, please tell me you've got good news." The chief superintendent's words were not accompanied by any real hope in his voice.

Russell rolled out the mountain of problems that were now piling up on the team from the first victim and the addition of a second body. The small chinks of light in the progress of the first case were of little consolation.

"Fuck, Tom. I had hoped I'd get to retirement before something like this happened in this city. Ah'll take a common or garden Glesgae nutjob any day over a psycho with some motive that exists only in his head. We need to find who the second victim is and link her to the first if we can. Shit, shit, shit. It's going be a fuckin' feedin' frenzy with those bastards of Her Majesty's press. I want everybody razor sharp on this, we can't afford any fuck ups." His spleen vented, he sat back in his chair and took a long breath.

"I know, sir," Russell replied. "The computer might give us a place to start. There might be something there to get our teeth into."

"I've got to go to one of the fuckin' single force planning meetings tomorrow. The chief constable won't be too pleased to see our stats getting blown out of the water by some fuckin' bam. To cheer me up I'm going to need Elvis '56 on my phone before I go in; it'll give me some protection against all the negativity that's going to be coming my way."

Russell smiled for the first time that day as he visualised his boss rocking his way into a strategic planning meeting.

"I don't suppose that the killer left a wallet or a bag to tell us who the second victim is?"

"I'm afraid not, sir."

"Make identifying the poor woman a priority, same routine as early in the week, until the techies give us something from the computer. I'll get a press conference organised and you can brief them about what's happening; it might give you some breathing space for a wee while. Keep me updated, Tom, I need to brief this upstairs and they'll already be under pressure, and when they're under pressure the shite just falls to the bottom."

"I know, sir. We might need some more resources."

"Anything you need, let me know, this crazy bastard needs to be caught before he does it again. I'll deal with the flak from whoever's throwing it. Get to it."

"Yes, sir," Russell replied crisply.

As he reached for the door, Blair said, "Oh and Tom just remember…"

"What's that, sir?"

"Keep calm and listen to Elvis. Thank you very much," he finished with his own little impression of the King.

Russell laughed as he walked back down the corridor, which earned him a strange look from Marsha as he entered the incident room.

✝

Alex drove home feeling exhausted after her childhood fears had been further awakened and drained her emotional reserves. She felt a little guilty at leaving the team to continue the investigation but in her heart knew that Russell had been right to send her home; she probably wouldn't have been very productive that afternoon.

Due to her early return, she found a parking space just two hundred yards from the front door of her tenement rather than the usual five streets away. When she reached the flat she was surprised to discover that there was no resistance to the mortise key as she tried to open it; she thought that Andrew must have forgotten to lock it when he went to work. She used the Yale key to open the other lock and walked into the hall.

She dumped her handbag on the bookcase and swung open the door to their bedroom. Andrew and a woman that Alex didn't recognise were scrambling from the bed, desperately trying to gather their clothes to cover their nudity.

Alex took a breath and then a fury she had never known before took hold of her. "Andrew, what the fuck?"

"Alex, I'm sorry I…"

"Shut the fuck up, you bastard. You bastard. In our bed, you shagged this tart in our bed?" She pointed at the woman who was trying to cover her pendulous breasts in a ridiculous attempt at modesty.

"Excuse me," the woman dared to reply as if offended by Alex's comments.

"You, shut the fuck up, get dressed and get out my fucking house. You have no rights to say anything, didn't you see the fucking ring on his finger, you bitch? Move!"

The command broke through the woman's inertia and she scrambled to get her clothes into a bundle before racing out of the bedroom into the hall. Alex heard the bathroom door open and then slam shut. As the naked woman had rushed past, Alex noticed that her new enemy had dyed-blonde hair and that she was a little overweight. That just stoked the fire of wrath Alex was feeling which she would later realise was irrational; what difference did it make to an already horrible situation?

She vented some further levels of her outrage at her now ex-fiancé, "Get a fucking bag, put some clothes in it and get out of my house, you dirty, cheating, lying scum-bag bastard."

Andrew was still trying to gain some measure of

control, slowing his breathing and trying to stop his heart from pounding. Still nude, he walked towards her and put his arms on Alex's shoulder, "Alex, I'm so sorry, it just kind of… ahh what are you doing?"

Before he could react, Alex had reached down and grabbed his genitals, digging her nails in to his scrotum while simultaneously squeezing and twisting his testicles. The power went from his legs and he collapsed, replacing her hands with his as he clutched the painful area protectively. "What's the matter with you, you crazy bitch?" he managed to say through the tears of pain that were streaming from his eyes.

"Crazy? That's not half of what I'll do to you if you don't get out, you fucking treacherous troll. Now fucking move!"

He got up still trying to cosset his aching balls and walked gingerly to the wardrobe. Alex watched as he pulled on a pair of underpants, which caused him to wince, giving her a small feeling of satisfaction. He dressed as quickly as his predicament would allow and gathered some clothes that he threw untidily into a sports bag as quickly as he could.

"Alex can't we talk about this?" he pleaded.

Before she answered, she heard the front door close; the bitch had left.

"What is there to talk about? You shagged some fucking fat, cheap tart in our bed. That was your fucking choice; you chose a quick shag over a life with me. Here's your fucking ring, you can stick it where the sun don't shine." She slid the diamond and ruby ring from her finger and fired at him at high velocity.

"Sell it, it's no good to me." He took off his own ring and left it on the dressing table. The ring had been her idea, she wanted to give him a token of her love but now it was just a symbol of betrayal.

"Organise a courier to pick your stuff up and let me know when they are coming, you can have whatever's left when I'm done with it."

"Alex, don't do anything stupid," he protested.

"Well, you fucking started it," she replied bitterly.

He tried one last time to placate her, "Please Alex, think of what we've been through together, give me another chance, I can change, and we can sort this."

She drew in a long breath to try to still her. It worked and she was able to tell him calmly, "No, Andrew there is no sorting this. You're just another one of those guys whose prick dominates his brain. Oh you'll be sorry for a while but before long you'll do it again with the first gullible little cow that gives you the eye. I'm not stupid enough to watch you dip your dick in whatever little honeypot takes your fancy. Get out of my flat, get out of this relationship, get out of my life and I mean for good." The anger was dissipating and all she wanted was for him to go and leave her to pick up the pieces of a life that he had destroyed in the pursuit of his own selfish needs.

"I'm sorry," were his parting words. He grabbed the bag and she listened for the sound of the outside door closing before she replied, "You should be."

She sat on the edge of the bed; the heavy smell of sex still filled the air. 'I'll need to throw that bedding out,' she thought. That provoked a brief almost hysterical laugh before the emotion overwhelmed her and she burst into a long series of racking sobs as she slipped from the bed on to the floor.

She stayed curled up in that position for around half an hour. The tears came and went in waves as the new truth of her life became more apparent. The life she thought that she would have with Andrew was gone and something new would have to replace it. When she finally stopped crying, she decided she could not spend the night on her own.

She dialled her mother and father's phone number.

"Hi, mum," she said in as neutral voice as she could manage.

"What's up?" her attempt at disguise couldn't fool her mother, who seemed to have a sixth sense for knowing when her children were hurting.

Alex paused and then cried into the phone, "I caught Andrew cheating with another woman."

"You what? That bastard!" Her mother's choice of language surprised Alex; she had very rarely ever heard her swear.

"Do you want us to come up?"

"I don't want to be here tonight, if it's OK with Dad, I'd like to come down."

"Of course, it'll be fine." Her mum sounded confident but Alex wasn't quite so sure. Her relationship with her father hadn't been great ever since she had joined the force. He was a young miner when the industrial strife and pit closures of the mid-eighties devastated the economy of many a mining community, including his Ayrshire hometown. Like many former miners, he couldn't forgive the role the police had played in putting down the strike.

Stories of policemen in Yorkshire waving extravagant pay packets at the starving men on the picket line who were trying to save their jobs still rankled with her dad. He felt she had betrayed him by joining up and the close connection they had once enjoyed had faded over time. It didn't matter that the police were now on the end of the same budget restrictions as the rest of the public sector, he still regarded them as the enemy.

"Come down, pet. Home and family are what you need at a time like this," her mother reassured her.

"OK, I'll see you soon."

She packed an overnight bag and half an hour she was on the road to Ayrshire and her family home within half an hour. Her parents now lived in Coylton, a small village not far from the former mining communities of Auchinleck and Cumnock. They were both retired and their small pensions were enough to allow them to live with little worries although there wasn't a lot left over after the bills were paid.

When she had parked the car and stepped out on their street, she was stunned to see her father walking down the path to meet her at the gate. He opened his arms and she fell into them, buried her face in his shoulder and released a flood of her emotional troubles into it.

"Here, lassie. Don't let that clown get tae ye. Ye're better than he'll ever be." The previous tensions between them seemed to dissolve as he held her tightly. The smell of his Old Spice aftershave and the faint, distinctive aroma of the smoke from a coal fire transported her back twenty-five years to nights when her father would read to her before she went to bed. They would sit in the living room, the hot living flames from the fireplace warming her against the chill on one side while she nestled against the warmth of her father on the other. Back then she always felt safe, protected from all that the world could throw at her. Snuggled against him again, she found it was having the same effect.

Her mother had already prepared a feast of food for her to enjoy and despite the gnawing at the pit of her stomach, she was soon persuaded to savour the benefits of mum's home cooking. The three of them sat round the dinner table and discussed the events of the day in a way that was so familiar to her.

"D'ye want me tae sort him out?" her father asked. Alex was touched that her dad thought he could take on a strong man thirty years his junior.

"I think I might have managed that already," she replied with a melancholic smile.

"How, whit happened?"

"I grabbed his balls, dug my nails in and twisted."

Her mum giggled and her father started to chuckle, after he had winced in the way any man would. "Aye, that wid dae it, lass. Well done."

Her parents' amusement was infectious and before long the three of them sat laughing hysterically and it only got louder when Alex told them that he was naked when she did it.

A little later they were each sitting with a glass of wine, watching the evening news. Her trials of the afternoon had temporarily removed Alex's concerns over her first murder case with her new team. They were brought to the forefront of her mind once again when the smooth face of

Detective Superintendent Russell appeared on the screen.

They sat in silence as Russell briefed the press about what little the police knew, while trying to sound positive that they would catch the perpetrator. He did his best to dissuade the line of questioning that mentioned a serial killer but the reporters had been tenacious in their belief that their generation had their very own 'Bible John' - a killer who had stalked the dance halls of Glasgow in the sixties but had never been caught. Russell had wrapped up the conference requesting any information about the whereabouts of Graeme Mathieson in the hours before he was killed and any sightings of the white van.

Alex knew that the station would be inundated with calls from the well-meaning as well as the lunatic fringe. It would be a tough exercise trying to sort the real information from the extraneous data but every call would need to be followed up.

"That's my boss," she informed her parents when the piece finished.

"You're investigating these murders?' her mother asked.

"I'm afraid so."

"Is it the same guy?"

"We don't know yet, Dad. We'll know more in the next couple of days."

"Well ah hope ye hang him up by the balls when ye catch him."

"That's only for cheating boyfriends," she replied with a weak smile.

The rest of evening was spent in comfortable nostalgia as they each remembered moments from the family's life together when Alex and her brother were young.

At ten o'clock Alex announced that she was going to bed. Her mother asked her how long she would be staying but Alex said she would have to go home the following day and that she had to get back to work.

"Are ye sure ye're ready?" her father asked.

"I need to Dad, we've got to catch the killer. The team's short-handed as it is. Anyway, I'll be better if I've got something to occupy my mind."

"If you're sure, pet."

"Thanks, Dad, but yes, I'm sure. A new life starts tomorrow." She kissed him and walked upstairs to the spare room.

That night, Alex settled down to sleep relatively content with the belief that she would be able to cope. She was sure there were more bad times to come but for the moment, the comforts of home had eased her pain.

CHAPTER 7

Alex spent a demanding night fighting terrifying visions of the twisted cinder of a corpse that she had watched being pulled from the broken building. She felt there were times when this job took too much out of her physically, emotionally and spiritually. Her soul was being eroded a little bit more with every ghastly act that she encountered; each an innovative way for human beings to show the depths to which they could sink. In this case, there seemed to be a contradiction between the terrible mutilations of the bodies and the almost reverential treatment of the remains. The laying out of the corpse, the cross and the apparent cremation ritual didn't tie with the removal of bones or the act of murder itself. The inconsistency was a theme that plagued her thoughts all night and not even the wine she had consumed had helped her to an undisturbed sleep. She finally gave up trying at around five-thirty; she showered, dressed and made a slice of toast. She left a note of thanks to her parents and was on her way to back up the M77 to the station by six-thirty.

She wasn't the first to arrive in the office, as Russell was already sitting at his desk. He acknowledged her arrival and seemed to sense that something wasn't right with her but he didn't ask and she didn't want to tell him of her personal problems.

The room then descended into silence as Russell was immersed in the reports that the detective team had submitted. Alex was glad of the time to compose her thoughts; there was none of the incessant chatter, no phones ringing and no bubbling kettle, although she decided she would have to change that.

A few minutes later she was sitting at her desk with a cup of peppermint tea at her side, reading her e-mail, when Rick Johnstone arrived.

"Good morning," he said to his superiors.

Alex greeted him and Russell said, "Let's hope it is, Rick. Were you another one unable to sleep?"

"I like an early start, it's when my brain's at its best," he replied.

"How are things at home?"

"Still struggling on. Georgia's still not great but we'll get there," he said with more optimism than he truly felt.

"I'm sorry, Rick, but it looks like we've got a few long days ahead of us."

"I understand that, sir. My mother's helping out and I'm hoping to get Georgia to a doctor. That should get us back on track. What do you want me to do first?" He was guarded and was another member of staff who didn't want Russell to know how much he was struggling away from the office. As far as he was concerned, work was work and home was home and they shouldn't ever affect each other.

"Grab yourself a cup of coffee, check your e-mails, and see if the geek squad came up with anything. We'll have a briefing when everyone arrives."

As Johnstone set about his tasks, Russell ploughed his way through the apparently never-ending list of e-mails. Before he had even read it, the latest stupid memo from HR disappeared with a press of the delete key. People who knew nothing about policing and thought they could tell him how to do his job weren't worthy of his attention; he had more important things to concern him.

He had left until last a group of e-mails from Noel Hawthorn that contained the crime scene photographs. Noel had processed the shots from the scene with his usual care and each was annotated according to the time they were taken. Russell printed them to make them available for the other members of the team when they arrived.

The chief superintendent stuck his head in to say good morning and the bulk of the detectives had gathered in the crowded office by nine o'clock.

A quick call through to Blair established that he wanted to be part of the briefing and by quarter past nine they were once again convened around the incident board.

Russell began by placing the crime scene photographs in sequence on the board. Marsha Collins turned away and Rick Johnstone's usual pallor was tinged with green. Russell highlighted the points of particular interest with special attention to the removal of the ribs.

Johnstone and Carrick had been delegated to go to the PM the previous evening. Russell asked Carrick to brief the room on what had been found.

Carrick stepped forward and consulted his notes as he spoke. "There is a great deal of similarities between the two victims. Doc MacNeil couldn't establish a cause of death, so there's a good chance that the tox report will produce similar results if he has followed the same pattern. She's convinced that a bone-saw was used to remove the ribs, which further ties in with the idea that the perpetrator had some kind of medical knowledge. There was also a gold cross pressed into the victim's hand. There were no other obvious injuries to the victim and the doc reckons the woman was Afro-Caribbean."

Russell turned to one of the uniformed officers, Jordan Kenneth, "Any black women on our missing persons list, Jordan?"

Kenneth consulted his computer. "Yes, sir. Ms Theresa Asher. She's originally from Bristol. She was reported missing yesterday by one of her colleagues at the Commonwealth Games offices."

"Jesus, that's all we need," Blair sighed as the political implications of the case deepened further.

"Any thoughts about the similarities and differences?" Russell hoped his colleagues would have some insight and it was always good to get their synapses firing early in the morning.

Carrick voiced what they were all thinking. "The similarities are too many for it to be anything other than a single killer."

There were nods of agreement from the whole team.

"Except if there was someone at the original scene who decided to get rid of this woman in a similar way to throw us off their trail." The uniformed officer Tina Bartram was the one who gave voice to this uncomfortable thought. PC Bartram had impressed Russell in the previous cases that he had come in contact with her and with each passing encounter she was showing her potential to be an excellent addition to the detective squad at some point in the future.

The discovery of a second cross meant that the fire crew could probably be ruled out, as they knew nothing about it. Inter-force rivalry aside, he didn't want to think of any of the fire officers being capable of such a callous act. However there was protocol to be followed and it was always better to ensure that every possible angle had been covered. The detective superintendent said, "Tina, can you do a discreet background check on the fire crew who were present, just in case?"

"Yes, sir."

"Any thoughts on the differences?" Russell prompted.

"There's the fact that the second body is a black woman. Typically serial killers - if that's what we're dealing with - will stay within their own racial group and follow a similar pattern in their choice of victim," Alex contributed.

"True. Anything else?"

"It could be that he's trying to perfect a method. The first attempt didn't give him what he was looking for from it, so he has changed where he removes the bone to give him greater satisfaction," Alex replied.

Rick Johnstone offered an alternative. "Or he's a collector."

"Oh, no." Marsha had seen more than she ever thought possible since she had had been assigned to CID but the idea that someone would collect the bones of their victims was almost too much.

"It is a possibility, serial killers have been known to take souvenirs from their victims. For some it may be seen as a trophy, a medal to remind them of the victory over their target. Some of them use it as a connection to the past. For example, our killer may have been beaten and had his bones broken often when he was a kid. There could be an emotional attachment that he is either trying to reconnect with or purge from his mind." Alex had studied psychology as one of her degree subjects and she had kept up the interest when she joined the police by studying some of the profiling techniques used by the FBI in the US.

"Christ, it's Clarice Starling. More likely he's just a deviant who gets his kicks out of hurting and killing people," Carrick stated dismissively.

Russell was about to tell him to shut his mouth when Alex said, "You're right, his behaviour is deviant, but there is normally a reason behind it. It's up to us to stop him regardless of what caused him to behave that way, the psychologists can argue over the reasons later."

Blair nodded as she made her comments.

Russell continued, "Before we can establish that it is a serial killer and not someone with a palpable motive, we've got to find out more about our second victim. DS Hendry, could you organise a team to interview Ms Asher's acquaintances and report back to me."

"Yes, sir," Hendry shouted from somewhere near the back of the group.

"Billy, did Marr appear to give a statement?"

"Yes, sir. There was nothing of substance, his alibi for the night of the murder checked out. A taxi driver verified that he had taken him home from the restaurant and the CCTV in his flats confirmed that he didn't leave until the following morning."

Blair, who had stood quietly up to that point said, "We've got an incident room set up in Ruchill and some of the Maryhill team are going to take statements and do some door-to-door. I've arranged for two of them to join us here to help us with the phone calls we received after last night's TV report. I know it's going to get even more crowded but we need the extra bodies to filter through the crap. Superintendent, I'd like you make more use of DS Stephanie Anderson for the duration of this investigation."

"Will do."

"I believe you know DS Anderson, Alex." Blair said.

"Yes, sir. She's a good detective."

She held back her opinion of Anderson as a person. She had stated the truth regarding her abilities but she had found her to be arrogant, aloof and all too willing to hog the limelight when there were plaudits being handed out - though she was more of a shrinking violet when things went wrong. She also had a tendency to be abrupt with her colleagues and even at times with witnesses.

"She'll be with us this afternoon, Tom."

"Good, this could get unmanageable very quickly, so we need to keep on top of it. Rick, anything from the geek squad?"

"Yes, sir. Mr Mathieson was being targeted by a group calling themselves 'The Council for the Defence of Scottish Family Life'."

"And who the hell are they?"

"A newly formed political party and pressure group, apparently. According to the IT guys, their website says they are protecting the way of life of white Scottish families from the influence of…" He looked to his notebook before continuing, "…Jews; Islamists; homosexuals and the elitist left-wing media."

"That's what I like to see, all-inclusive fuckwits - sorry Marsha - they hate everybody." Russell felt another little parcel of energy get carried away.

"Any names?"

"Their leader is a Hugh Evans, based here in Glasgow." Russell turned quickly towards Blair. "It couldn't be."

"Nothing would surprise me," was Blair's reply.

"Sir?" Alex asked as puzzled as the rest of the group.

"Shuggie Evans was a serial pain in the arse back in the late nineties. He ran a crew of football casuals that were allegedly Rangers fans. He started with the post-football fights on a Saturday and graduated up to serious assault of Catholics and members of the Asian community. He was put away for a ten stretch back in 2001 when he left a young girl in coma after a kicking and slashing he administered up in the Merchant City. He's your typical bully who uses bigotry and racism as an excuse to vent his spleen."

"You think this is the same guy?"

"Good chance, he always had delusions of grandeur."

"Tom, you better have a look and if it is that wee shite - sorry Marsha - grab him by the balls and don't let go." Blair commanded. Alex almost burst out laughing as she remembered her conversation with her parents.

"Do you like Evans for this?" Russell asked.

"I don't know but he'll be guilty of something; it's about time he got reacquainted with our interview room."

"OK folks, everyone knows what you've got to do."

When Superintendent Russell checked the website of the group Johnstone had mentioned, he discovered that it was indeed led by the criminal formerly known as Shuggie Evans. The same self-satisfied smirk Russell remembered was still on his repulsive fleshy face. Some might have called it a moon face but only if the moon had a long scar down one side courtesy of an industrial knife. His eyes were tiny compared to the size of his head; the extra layers of fat he had accumulated in the intervening years seemed to be swallowing them, so that before long they would disappear altogether.

"That's him, all right."

"Fine example of the master race, isn't he?" Alex observed.

"Funny, every one of these clowns looks like they fell out the ugly tree and hit every branch on the way down. I think it must be lack of nookie that drives them nuts, what d'ye think?"

"You might be right, sir," Alex said with a grin.

"Right, let's go and pay this obnoxious little creep a visit."

On the way out of the station, the Superintendent pulled a couple of uniformed PCs from their break and ordered them to follow him in a marked car.

The headquarters of The Council for the Defence of Scottish Family Life was in the Gorbals area of the city. The tough working-class area clung to the south bank of the Clyde, a last bastion of the old city centre, being slowly replaced with new buildings and new people thanks to renovation and renewal. Evans' organisation was obviously targeting the socially excluded, trying to convince them that anyone who was different was to blame for their plight.

The squat building sat in the shadow of some high-rise blocks and looked like it may have been built for a small business, but only hate was being peddled there now, neatly packaged in empty slogans and disinformation.

Russell swung the car into a space marked 'reserved'. Alex could tell that he was relishing the thought of an encounter with Evans.

They headed to the door, Russell taking the lead and walking like a man on a mission, Alex and the two PCs trailing in his wake like children scurrying after their parent. He pushed hard to open the door, swinging it back on his hinges with so much force it hit the wall with a bang. Inside, a shocked, skinny little man in a shell-suit stood up as if he was on guard duty, appointed to keep unwanted visitors out.

"Sit on yer arse shitface, it's the polis." Russell's slip into the vernacular was accompanied by a flourish of his warrant card.

"Where's the pond slime that leads this bunch o' wankers? Through here?" He indicated a door and was through it before the animated twig could react. Alex walked in the wake of her boss, interested to see a different side to him and how he had taken complete control of the situation within a few words.

"Lads, you two keep an eye on shell-suit Boab here," he shouted over his shoulder.

Beyond the door, Evans was sitting behind a desk, dressed in a shirt and tie while two burly men sat on the opposite side. All three stood as Russell and Alex completed their dramatic entrance. Russell shook his head and said, "Shuggie Evans, on the outside world like a normal, decent human being. It's a sad fuckin' day."

"That's Hugh Evans, Sergeant Russell."

"That's Detective Superintendent Russell tae you, Shuggie boy. Whit's wi' the suit, bawbag? Ye got a funeral tae go tae? It's a shame it's no' yir ain."

"Hey, you cannae say stuff like that, man," the muscle bound suit on the left of the two doormen said with the nasal tone that was a characteristic of the dialect of the species known as Glaswegian ned. Both of the men were broad and brawny with the look of people who would enjoy a good fight but might struggle in an intellectual debate. They had moved to place themselves between Evans and the door.

"Who the fuck ur you two, the hard men? Sit on yir arse or ah'll haul ye in for being ugly bastards." Russell's sheer force of personality and confidence seemed to have the desired effect as the two men flopped down in their seats like obedient mastiffs.

"Detective Superintendent, you do know there is such a thing as police harassment. I am going about my legal business and you burst in here, abuse my guests and me. You seem very keen to land yourself in trouble." Alex had only just met him but she already felt that she wanted to erase the arrogance from the little man's self-satisfied fat face.

Russell laughed, a genuine hearty chuckle from deep in his stomach. "Whit's wi' the accent? Did wan o' the cons' plums you were licking get stuck in yir gob at the Bar-L?"

"I spent my time in prison educating myself, Superintendent, you should try it some time."

"Reading the fuckin' Beano and Mein Kampf disnae count as an education, ya wee shite. Now yir gonnae come wi' me tae the station fur a wee chat, ah've saved yir favourite interview room, so you'll feel right at hame."

"I don't think so. I've not done anything wrong."

"Whit aboot threatening behaviour, producin' racist material, oh aye, and murder?"

Evans self-confident smile disappeared. "Murder? Are ye fuckin' mental Russell?"

"Oops, yir mask is slippin', Shuggie. The wee nyaff fae Drumchapel is makin' an appearance. Oan yir feet, and let's go fur a wee chat."

"I'm going nowhere," Evans said, struggling to regain a measure of composure.

"DS Menzies wid ye get the constables, please?"

Alex opened the door as the other two men stood to try to prevent her.

Evans decided that it might be better to comply with the detective's request. "It's fine, guys. I'll answer the policeman's questions, and then I'll finish his career. Just get Mr Pirelli," he said as he moved from behind the desk.

Russell led Evans out of the offices with a trail of

people directly behind him. Evans was placed in the back of the marked Ford Focus while 'Mr Shellsuit' and the two heavies looked on from the door of the office. Alex almost expected them to wave a tearful farewell, like a scene from some sentimental movie.

Within twenty minutes the cars pulled in to the back of the station to avoid the small press pack that had taken up residence at the front. Evans was shown into a cramped interview room where he was left with a uniformed constable as company.

Russell and Alex walked up to the office. "We'll let him sweat while we have a cuppa."

"Sir, I didn't expect that," Alex said when they were settled with their drinks.

"What, the accent?"

"Well, yes."

"I still like to play the part of the old school Glesgae copper, when I can. Wee pricks - sorry Marsha - like Evans think they have everything under control; I like to disabuse them of that particular idea. Let them think the days of the polis being scary haven't completely disappeared." He beamed and for the first time Alex could see that her boss really enjoyed this part of his job.

Chief Superintendent Blair walked into the office, "Evans downstairs?"

"Yes, sir. Sounding like he was raised in Giffnock and he's wearing a suit. We're letting him get used to the surroundings again."

"Christ, doesn't matter how you much you polish a turd, it's still a turd - sorry Marsha."

"I thought you were going to the strategic planning

bollocks - sorry Marsha."

Marsha had become so used to their language that it no longer bothered her and she was amused how they still apologised to her.

"The ACC was keen that I stay here and oversee what you lot were up to." He managed a smile that was more of relief than joy. Even a lurid murder was better than a strategic planning meeting.

"Every cloud…" Russell replied.

"What's you're feeling about Shuggie boy?"

"Probably not our man judging by his reaction but that doesn't mean that somebody connected to his little bunch of brown-shirts isn't involved."

"Right, get to it, see what you can find out."

Before they could leave the office, Rick Johnstone called for their attention. "It's about the cross on the first victim. Forensics has had a look. There's nothing specific about it that would help us. It's a cheap nine-carat gold charm that you can buy in any of the big jewellery chains. It's too small for prints and chances are it'll be the victim's DNA that will be found on it if they can find anything."

"OK, thanks." The physical evidence was creating more questions that it was answering.

Before going into the interview room, Alex delivered a message to the desk sergeant to delay a Mr Pirelli for as long as she could. She was very happy to oblige when she was told that he was a defence lawyer.

In the interview room, Russell settled into the chair opposite Evans with Alex beside him. The table in between them and the suspect was tiny, in proportion with the room it inhabited. The tiles on the ceiling were dirty and broken, the walls looked like they hadn't seen paint in about twenty years and the carpet was filthy. The heat was turned up as high as possible, an old trick to keep the suspect as uncomfortable as they could. It wasn't a particularly welcoming room but it was good enough for scum like Evans. In comparison, the purpose-built rooms in the MIT's base in Helen Street station were cavernous and luxurious.

"So Shug, how long huv ye been tormenting Graeme Mathieson?"

"It's Hugh and I don't know what you're talking about. Shouldn't there be a tape running? I don't want anyone to miss your harassment."

Russell hauled the plug of the tape recorder from the socket. "Oops, looks like it's broken."

"I am going to finish you, Russell," Evans threatened.

"Ah'm quakin' in ma fuckin' boots. Look Shuggie yir suit and posh voice might impress a young officer like DI Menzies here but tae an auld hand like me, it's aw bullshit. Your little gang of Nazi wannabes has been sending hate-filled e-mails and social media messages to one Graeme Mathieson, who just happened to turn up dead on Wednesday."

"The poof? What's that got to do with me?"

"Well there ye go, ye're really no' that bright ur ye. How did ye know that Mr Mathieson was homosexual if ye don't know whit ah'm talkin' aboot?"

"Deviants like him are threatening the fabric of white family life in this country," Evans replied as if quoting from a leaflet.

Russell, obviously delighting in the cut and thrust

of the battle, turned to Alex. "White family life! Wid ye listen tae this piece o' scum? His mother wis an alkie and his faither wis some soldiers. Family life, ye wouldnae know whit a decent family life wis if it came and booted ye in the baws."

"Fuckin' watch it, Russell," Evans made an effort to stand but stopped when he realised that Russell was deliberately trying to goad him into losing control.

"Oh Shuggie, Shuggie, Shuggie. Ye were never cut oot fur this pillar o' the community crap ye're tryin' tae pull. Now did ye kill Mr Mathieson yirsel or did ye get wan o' yir stormtroopers tae dae it fur ye?"

"I've got no idea what you're talking about," Evans said, smoothing his suit as he spoke.

Russell began to consult the notes that the forensic IT team had compiled. "OK let's go go back tae the beginning. According tae Mr Mathieson's computer your organisation started tae send some threatening e-mails tae him about six weeks ago. He wrote an e-mail tae his service provider askin' them to block the mails and then he wis targeted through his social media accounts. On one you announced his home address and phone number. Dae ye deny any o' this?"

"We are waging a war against the people who would drag this country into the pit of cross-breeding and the promotion of queers at the expense of ordinary people. We are campaigning to get all the Jews, Muslims, niggers and queers out of the government so we can have a true white Scotland, free from their godless influence."

Alex realised her mouth had fallen open and closed it.

"Bloody hell, Shuggie. Ye don't half talk a lot o' shite.

So ye don't deny that yir pathetic little band are responsible for threatening Mr Mathieson?"

"I never said that."

"Well yir manifesto sure sounded like a call tae arms tae me. Ye could save yirsel' a heap o' trouble by tellin' me who did it."

"You're an idiot, Russell. I'm not sorry the queer's deid but it has nothing to do with my organisation or me. Some day ye'll thank the likes of me when we've driven out the Yids and the ragheids and put the queers in jail."

Russell jumped up from his seat, startling his DI and making Evans shrink back as if expecting a blow.

"Maybe ye should concentrate yir hate on the stupid cow that spawned ye. She's the wan that turned ye intae a fuckwit."

While Russell calmed down a little, Alex asked, "What about Theresa Asher?"

"Who's she?"

"She's the second victim in your little gang's killing spree," Russell said.

"Ur you smokin' crack or something?" Evans said, the smug smirk back on his face.

Before he could ask anything else there was a knock at the door.

"Come in," he shouted.

"Sir, there's a Mr Pirelli outside insisting that we let him see his client," Sergeant Dingwall announced as she put her head into the room.

"Shit. Bring it in," Russell said with resignation as he pushed the recorder's plug back into its socket.

A few seconds later a thin man in an expensive suit

walked into the room carrying a briefcase and a sense of self-importance.

"Detective Superintendent, I hope you weren't interviewing my client without his lawyer present. That's against his human rights, you know."

"Just waiting to get started, Mr… ?"

"Pirelli, as I think you know."

Russell pressed the record button and detailed the date, time and names of those present. Every attempt at extracting information from Evans was blocked by the persistence of his lawyer, who told the suspect not to answer any questions. Russell and Alex both knew instinctively that Evans had no involvement in the murders but his agenda of hate disturbed them enough that they wanted him off the streets.

The interview ended after ten minutes and as Pirelli and Evans were leaving Russell called back the lawyer. Russell knew him by reputation and he would normally be rolled out when some rich businessman had been caught with his hand in the till. The firm he worked for were very expensive and not the type to normally get involved with people like Evans.

"Can I ask you who is paying for your time?" the policeman asked as he held the lawyer's gaze.

"Mr Evans is entitled to the best representation possible."

"I can't help but wonder why someone like you is representing someone like him? Could it be that you or your partners have some sympathy for his political ambitions?'

"I have no idea what you're talking about. Mr Evans is

a client, nothing more."

"You're a bit more expensive than the briefs he used to have and that old cynic in me thinks that there is more to your relationship than meets the eye. I'll be monitoring your client's behaviour and if you're involved in any of his little crimes of hate; it's not just him that will need a lawyer. Do I make myself clear?"

"Is that a threat, Detective Superintendent Russell?"

"Call it a friendly piece of advice."

Pirelli walked away without another word.

"Prick," Russell muttered to the lawyer's back.

When Alex and Russell were back in the office he turned to her and said, "Maybe we should get special branch to keep an eye on this lot if they're not already on the radar."

"Can't do any harm, sir."

"I don't like the thought of a piece of scum like Evans having finance that could cause serious trouble further down the line."

"He seems to have got under your skin."

"Nae wonder. Not only did he put that girl in a coma, he carved a swastika into her face with a carpet fitter's knife. It was a hooked blade that left a ragged wound and the poor woman was facing years of plastic surgery to get rid of it. Can you imagine having to walk around with scars like that? The Fiscal made an arse of it and let him cop to serious injury and permanent disfigurement in court rather than the attempted murder we wanted. So you could say I'm very motivated to put him back where he belongs."

Alex nodded, "I know what you mean."

"I think I'm going to make life a little uncomfortable for Messrs Evans and Pirelli." Russell called the journalist, Walker, and told him that he might want to have a look at Evans, his organisation and Pirelli's law firm. He told him that this information was off the record and that he should treat it as such. The eager young man was happy to help as he could sniff the possibility of a story that would attract the interest of the nationals. Russell hoped that it might just scare off some of the financial backers of Evans' organisation.

"Evans is not involved in this, so we'll need to try something else," Alex stated.

"I know just the man."

CHAPTER 8

Alex followed her superintendent back to his car. He wouldn't say where they were going, so she didn't push it; accompanying him had been a little intimidating but she felt that she would be able to ask him a little more as their working relationship developed. His encounter with Evans appeared to have invigorated him and he seemed determined to make a break in the case; his enthusiasm was infectious.

They drove for about fifteen minutes to the Maryhill district of the city, close to where the second body had been discovered. The rain had eased to a steady drizzle with an occasional glimpse of blue sky visible through the clouds. Alex couldn't remember a worse summer and for Glasgow that was saying something.

The car pulled in to a rubble-strewn excuse for a car park outside what looked like a nuclear bunker. The building was a concrete block covered in a filthy grey render with tiny windows that were reminiscent of arrow-slits in a mediaeval castle. All around it for about a radius of two hundred yards was desolate ground as if this bunker was the only survivor of a major earthquake or a bombing raid. At the back of the building, the rusting shell of a burnt-out car lay abandoned like a piece of post-apocalyptic art.

When they walked to the front door, Alex finally realised that it was a bar. A sign above the door read 'As ral Pub ic Ba', which she presumed should have read Astral Public Bar. The Astral bar was legendary among police officers across the city for all the wrong reasons. It was an underground world where anything was bought and sold, from duty-free cigarettes to drugs, from guns to women. It was raided occasionally but generally it was thought to be worth keeping it open; the police would know where to look for at least some of the city's most hardened criminals.

The pub was well named as the door swung open on an alien planet, one with a dying sun where the inhabitants lived in near darkness. Within a pace, Alex could feel her shoes sticking to the remnants of a carpet where years of spills had congealed into a form of tacky glue. The arrow-slit windows did little to illuminate the dingy scene where people sat along the walls and around tables like a forgotten tribe. A ripple of speech ran around the room as the customers assessed the new arrivals. To the left, the bar had little to offer the patrons except a choice of two lagers, some cheap bottles of whisky or vodka on the gantry and a baseball bat if they should step out of line. Alex had never been in a more desperate or intimidating place.

Russell walked past the barman who attempted to stop

him by putting an arm out and saying, "We don't want your kind in here."

Russell stared him down, ignored him and continued walking to a small booth close to the rear of the building where he hauled a gaunt man in his fifties to his feet. Before the man could react, Russell had him in handcuffs and was marching him to the front door.

"Hey, whit the fuck ye daein'?" an elderly customer shouted.

"Nane o' your business, auld yin. Sit oan yir arse and drink yirsel' intae unconsciousness," Russell replied.

"Fuckin' polis bashtards," the worthy slurred in reply.

There were further mumbles of dissent but there was no one willing to stand up to the detective to protect their drinking buddy.

Alex had watched with amazement as her boss bundled the unsuspecting man out to the car. He put him in the back and Alex took up her position in the passenger seat.

When the car was on the move the man said, "Fuck sake, Mr Russell. Did ye need tae be so rough?"

"Sorry, Paddy, I didn't want you to get any hassle later. It's better this way."

"Could ye no' used the usual method o' contactin' me?"

"No time for that. I need your help. Give me five minutes and I'll let you know what I want you to tell me."

They drove a short distance and parked just off Great Western Road, a place where the pub's regulars were unlikely to see them together. Russell removed the handcuffs and the three of them strolled into the luscious green surroundings of the Botanic Gardens.

"So whit's up, Mr Russell?"

"Do you know about the recent murders?"

"The arson jobs?"

"Aye, what have you heard?"

The little man stopped and faced the two detectives. He was emaciated and the skin hung loosely from a face that had been well lived in. There was little of his face that wasn't covered in a network of craggy wrinkles. The changes in his pigment gave his face a patchwork quality and when he opened his mouth to speak his teeth looked like the remains of a circle of standing stones. His chin featured a collection of patchy hair pretending to be a beard of about four days' growth. His grey eyes looked tired as if life had worn him down but there was a still enough of a twinkle that indicated he wasn't quite beaten yet.

"Mr Russell, that's some crazy shit. No even the heid-bangers wid think o' laying out some poor bastard and setting them alight." He paused before adding, "Well, maybe wan or two wid."

"What headbangers are you thinking of?"

"Naw, don't get me wrang, ah didnae mean that. Majority o' folk are a bit freaked oot by this. We've no' hud a real psycho in Glesga since Bible John."

"So there's no one boasting about it or any suspicions that it might be one of the usual suspects?"

"Fuck naw, any stupid bastard boasting aboot it wid find his sel' oan tap a bonfire, ah think."

"OK, Paddy, but I want you to put the word out that if anybody hears anything they've to let us know and we'll deal with it."

"Nae problem, Mr Russell. Wis there anythin' else?"

"Shuggie Evans."

"That fuckin' wee shite! Ah heard he's oot again."

"Aye, and he's got himself a posh voice, a suit and some interesting pals, but he's still a hateful wee prick. Anything you get on him and his cronies, I want to know."

"You got it, Mr Russell. Ah can't stand that bigoted wee bastard."

Russell gave his informant a ten-pound note and dropped him outside a café with orders to eat a fish supper. As they drove away Alex watched from the car as Paddy found his way into the pub next door to where he was dropped, any thoughts of a decent meal abandoned in pursuit of his next pint.

"Who was that?" she asked.

"Paddy Niven, a one-time criminal and the world's worst burglar. I caught him three times when we were both a good bit younger. Eventually - after three visits to Barlinnie - he realised that a life of crime wasn't for him and ever since he's been the best snout I have."

"How do you usually get in contact with him?"

"I get one of the unis to phone the Astral and leave a message with the name of a horse and the time of a race at a specific course. The time of the race is when we meet; the course is the code for one of ten meeting places we've got. If he wants to talk to me it's the same routine."

"A bit elaborate, is it not?"

"Paddy insisted. He's a bit paranoid. He'll probably throw himself against a wall and tell the regulars in the Astral that I roughed him up a bit. In truth, he's a wee bit nuts, but people tell him things because he appears to be a harmless old man with a fondness for the bevvy. But he doesn't drink as much as it appears."

"You do know he didn't go into the café?"

"Of course, but I'll keep trying."

"So what next, boss? I feel like I'm just an accessory today."

"Sorry Alex. I'm not the best at realising people don't know what's in my head, I expect you just to know what I'm thinking." He smiled apologetically.

"I might work it out after a while but you'll definitely need to help me out a little until I'm used to the way you work."

"You're right. Let's see if we have a definite ID on our second victim."

A call to the station confirmed that Theresa's dental records had proved to be a match for the body in the mortuary. Russell asked for the young woman's address and turned to Alex. "It's confirmed, it's Theresa Asher. I thought we should go have a look at her house. See if there's anything there that might help us find a killer."

"Sounds good to me."

They arrived in front of the semi-detached house fifteen minutes later.

A uniformed officer stood outside the garden gate where the police tape across the path acted as the defined area of the potential crime scene. Despite his waterproof jacket he looked to be soaked to the skin and was thoroughly miserable.

"Constable, have the SOCOs been here yet?"

"No sir, they're on their way," he replied politely but with a touch of sullen attitude.

"We better suit up then."

They walked back to the car, Russell sporting a sympathetic smile as he remembered the days that he was the poor sod standing outside in all weathers protecting a scene; it was the most boring duty a police officer could have but it was an important one.

Theresa had been renting a house since she arrived in Glasgow and the police had contacted her landlord to get a key to the property. The PC at the gate was the temporary key holder as well as being responsible for the security of the scene until the crime scene team arrived.

When the two detectives were suited, booted and gloved they went toward the house once again. Russell opened the door, and a small bundle of orange fur wrapped itself around his legs.

"What the hell?" he exclaimed.

"Oh you poor thing," Alex said, reaching down to pick the cat from under the feet of her boss.

She read the nametag on its collar. "O'Malley, you must be starving. I'll feed him and then we'll get peace to check out the house," she told Russell.

"Fine, but be quick about it." Russell had a strong aversion to pets but he didn't want the cat to suffer. What happened to it after the police were finished would be a problem for the SSPCA.

Alex went to the kitchen and busied herself searching for a packet of food, cleaning the cat's bowls, and then spooning the food into one of them and filling the other with water. O'Malley was content to purr at her and rub himself against her legs until she had put down the food and then she was forgotten.

The two detectives began in a spacious living room to peer into a small window of Theresa Asher's life. It was sparsely furnished with a television and DVD player, a couch, a matching armchair and a small coffee table; everything was modern, simple and functional. There were no personal photographs and the only art on the wall was a black and white photograph of New York, the kind you can buy in most department stores.

Upstairs there were two bedrooms as well as the bathroom. Alex went into the main bedroom, which was decorated in a feminine and sophisticated way; Theresa's good taste was obvious in all the little touches that made it homely and welcoming. There was a single group photograph that looked like it was probably Theresa with her mother, father and three brothers. They were smiling and laughing, attending a family birthday or some other celebration, enjoying the moment, incapable of imagining the tragedy that lay ahead. Alex knew that feeling of joy was about to be crushed for all Theresa's family and friends; the time they would spend together in the future would be forever tinged with sadness as there would always be an empty chair.

The room contained nothing that indicated the killer had been there or even in correspondence with his victim prior to the act of murder.

Theresa had been using the other bedroom for storage and as a small office. Alex walked through to where Russell was sifting through a pile of papers on a small desk. He looked up as she entered, "Anything?"

"No, you?"

"Lots of bills and paperwork but nothing that might tell us who killed or why."

"There's no sign of a struggle and I don't think she was taken from here."

"I agree, same as Graeme Mathieson's flat. What are we dealing with here, Alex?"

"I don't know, sir. It's not following any pattern that would normally be associated with a serial killer. They normally stick to a single sex and within their own racial group. Maybe we are dealing with a real motive, something to do with contracts for the Commonwealth Games?"

"Could be, but I'm beginning to feel out of my depth. Twenty-two years on the force and I've seen nothing that has prepared me for something like this. Usually, I get a feeling for what the killer is about, some inkling to their motive or a clue from their method, but I can't get a handle on this guy. The mutilations don't tie with the respectful treatment of the body, that's the bit that's keeping me awake at night."

Alex pondered what he had said. "Me too. There is one explanation. That he feels guilty for what he's done and that something in his background tells him that he must atone. It might explain the cross and the cremation."

Russell's expression told Alex that this was a case that was getting under the skin of her boss. Every detective dreaded a murder that they couldn't solve, a victim who would never get the justice they deserved and a killer who would evade his punishment. This case was already in danger of becoming one that would haunt Russell into his retirement if they didn't get a major break soon.

"Check the bathroom, please, Alex," he said wearily.

"Will do."

She strode the length of a short hall into a pure white bathroom. A faint hint of scented candle hung in the air; a reminder of Theresa's last time of relaxation in this most private of rooms. The essence of what a person was seemed to linger for a short time after their death. Their little routines and moments of personal pleasure would outlast them until the crime scene team arrived and started to replace the sense of who the victim was with procedure, chemicals and their own professional characteristics.

The bathroom was as neat and tidy as the rest of the house. On a shelf, a line of perfume bottles, essential oils and skin products were arranged according to purpose and size. Alex opened a small medicine cabinet that contained some tampons and towels, shampoo, and conditioner. On the bottom shelf was a small pile of pharmaceutical boxes containing fluoxetine, commonly known as Prozac. There was also a bottle of herbal tablets designed to help achieve a night of natural sleep. Alex lifted a box of the anti-depressants and joined Russell once again.

"Sir, I was thinking about the medical angle to all this. Was Graeme Mathieson seeing a doctor for anything?" she asked as she held up the pills.

"I'm not sure."

"What if the two victims were in the same medical practice or had been to the same hospital department? It would give us a connection to each other and the fact we think the killer has medical skills."

"Not a bad idea, Alex. It's worth checking out. We'll

get the team to do some digging when we get back to the office."

They stood bent over the desk going through the rest of the correspondence together under a picture of Theresa with a group of people standing beneath the London 2012 Olympic logo. She was in the second row behind the recognisable faces of Lord Coe and David Beckham among many other famous people. The loss of such a beautiful young woman touched Alex's heart and strengthened her resolve to find whoever had brought Theresa Asher's life to an untimely end.

There was nothing that gave them any clues to either the killer or the motive for her murder but the scene of crime team would collect anything that might be worth further investigation. Something as simple as a credit card bill could point to somewhere that the two victims' paths had crossed and help to piece together a possible connection.

As Alex and Russell walked out of the front door, Sean O'Reilly and his team were walking towards them.

"Doing me job for me, Superintendent?" O'Reilly asked.

"Wouldn't dream of it, Sean. I know who the experts are."

"Glad to hear it," the Irishman replied with a smile.

Noel Hawthorn was close behind the technicians, as usual weighed down by his camera equipment. Like everybody involved with the case he looked exhausted but he still managed a smile when he saw the two police officers.

"Are you fed up with this grumpy ole bugger yet,

Alex?' he asked with a glint in his eye.

"He's not that bad," she replied loyally. There was something about Noel that Alex couldn't help but warm to.

"Give it time, you'll soon be needing a shrink or a drink. One of the two."

"Watch it, London," Russell said with mock outrage.

"Got much for me?" Hawthorn asked, gesturing his head towards the house.

"I don't think so, Noel. There's nothing to indicate that it's the primary."

"Well, I better get to work anyway. It's good to see you again Alex. Tom, I'll catch you later."

He walked up the path whistling a tune, leaving the two detectives to remove their protective clothing.

When they were back on the road again Russell said, "Alex, is everything OK with you? You seemed a bit distracted when you came in this morning."

"I had a bit of a shock yesterday."

"What happened?"

Alex explained the story of Andrew and his naked visitor. She masked her feelings but reciting the sordid tale suddenly brought the anger and sense of betrayal to mind again.

"That's shitty. We could make his life difficult if you want. Get traffic to stop his car, find some fault on it or fit him up for something serious. Anything you want." The way he said it made Alex think he wasn't joking.

"No, he's history now. I need to deal with it and move on. Anyway, I'm a single woman again, there's plenty more fish in the sea, as they say. Let's hope the next time

I don't land another slimy eel." She kept her voice light as there was no way that she wanted the pain she was feeling to be exposed to her colleague.

"Well, you know where I am and if you feel like a little revenge on your ex, I'm sure we could come up with something."

"Thanks." Alex retreated into her thoughts as they completed the journey.

✢

When they returned to the station they ran a small gauntlet of dedicated press hounds but as per orders they ignored them, much to the displeasure of the already disgruntled and drenched journalists.

The office was busy with frenetic activity but the feeling persisted that they were running to stand still and it hung in the air like a shroud.

"You must be DS Anderson, I'm Superintendent Russell," Russell said to a woman sitting at his desk.

She stood and offered a formal handshake. "Pleased to meet you, sir."

"I believe you know DI Menzies."

"Alex," she said.

"Stephanie," Alex acknowledged her but there was no smile or a sign of any close relationship between the two women. Russell noted that maybe pairing the two of them might not be as ideal as he had imagined.

He addressed the assembled officers. "What have we got, folks?"

William Carrick was the first to respond. "I've been in touch with Bristol CID and they're informing the girl's parents."

"Good, but I doubt it will move the investigation on any further," he said with a dismissive tone that Alex felt Carrick, for once, didn't deserve.

Rick Johnstone was the next to volunteer some information. "DS Hendry asked me to interview the people at Ms Asher's work. They say three of them had left work together around eight-thirty on Wednesday night. There had been no threat or intimidation from Evans' mob as far as her colleagues knew. She hadn't reported any concerns about anyone following her or anything that might have had her worried about someone wanting to harm her. They think she had been quite lonely as she worked so hard there was little time for socialising and as a result her only real friends up here were connected to her job. They did say that she had met a man at a party and they were due to go on a date this weekend."

"Did you get the details?"

"Just his name I'm afraid, sir. They didn't know any more about him."

"Stephanie, see if you can learn some more about him. It's probably a long shot that he'll be our man but check him out anyway, please."

"Yes, sir."

He turned back to Johnstone. "Do you know if she ever met Graeme Mathieson?"

"Mathieson attended one meeting regarding security at the Games back in March. Ms Asher was there but her colleagues didn't think there was any discussion between the two."

"Good, we need to know everyone that attended that

meeting, there were probably a few of our brass there."

He turned towards the part of the office that the uniformed officers occupied which was now populated with another two PCs. Elbow room was at a premium in the small area. "Tina, can you chase this up? It might be the best lead we've got. I want a full background check on anyone there. Pay particular attention to anyone with medical connections."

"It might take some time, sir," PC Bartram replied.

"I know, but pull in anyone you need to help you."

"Yes, sir."

"Alex and I were at the victim's house and it looks like she wasn't abducted or murdered there; the SOCOs will be able to say for sure. So we're looking at somewhere between her leaving her colleagues and arriving home. Rick, check how she normally travelled and allocate some of the uniformed team to speak to bus drivers or train conductors who might have seen her."

"Yes sir, but can it wait until tomorrow? I've managed to get an appointment at our doctor's surgery for Georgia."

"Of course, I'll check with the chief super but I imagine that the political interest will mean weekend working shouldn't be a problem. You get yourself home and look after your family."

"Thank you, sir."

"DC Carrick did you check the CCTV for the van on the approaches to Ruchill hospital?"

"No, sir."

"You do know it's OK to use your initiative, it's not against the fuckin' rules - sorry Marsha."

His apology fell on an empty desk as Marsha had gone home an hour earlier.

"I'll get on it," Carrick said, once again sliding back into a sulk with a large muffin for company.

"Alex, we need to do some digging into the victims' medical history and establish if there is a connection. That'll be your task."

"No problem, sir."

"I'll speak to the boss and find out what the score is for working this weekend and after that I'll be heading to the Station Bar if anyone wants to join me."

Chief Superintendent Blair looked distinctly unwell when Russell went in to see him. His skin was drained of colour and resembled old ivory forgotten in a tomb for three thousand years. He was also perspiring and his eyes looked a little glazed.

"You OK, chief?"

"I think I've got the flu coming on. That's aw I bloody need."

"You want me to get a doctor?"

"Naw, don't be daft. Now, are we any nearer catching this bastard?"

"Not really, but at least we've got a few things to follow up on."

"What have you learned, if anything?"

Russell told him about the meeting that both victims attended and Alex's thoughts on the possibility of a medical connection.

"Well a connection of any kind will be useful. It might take the psychos out of the equation."

"We're probably going to have to work this weekend,

is that OK?"

"Don't worry about that. I've had the Justice Minister on the phone telling me that money will be made available; he's taking a particular interest apparently. Amazing what can be done when politicians or their cronies are directly involved," he finished cynically.

"There's always money in the budget when it suits them. I'm glad we've got the go ahead, no matter the reason. We're going for a beer, do you want to join us?"

"No, I'll give it a miss."

He reached into his pocket and handed Russell a twenty-pound note. "Get a round on me. They're going to be under a lot of pressure in the next few days."

"Thanks, sir."

CHAPTER 9

Rick Johnstone arrived home at six o'clock, which gave him just enough time to pick up Georgia and get to the doctor's surgery for the final appointment of the week.

"Georgia, are you ready?" he shouted as he entered the house.

There was no reply from Georgia and no sign of her in either the living room or the small dining room adjacent to the kitchen. His mother was in the kitchen, heating a bottle of milk for Emily, who was lying in a bouncy chair playfully hitting the row of rattles that lay across it. He bent to give his a daughter a kiss before asking his mother, "Where is she?"

"In her bed. She says she's not going," his mother replied, obviously disappointed at her daughter-in-law's attitude.

"Christ." He stormed up the staircase and into their bedroom.

"Right, I've had enough. Get your shoes and coat on, you're going to the doctor."

"Oh, that would suit you, wouldn't it? Getting me declared mental, that would be just perfect for you," she spat her reply at him.

"What are you talking about? We can't go on like this. You can't keep treating our daughter like an unwanted pet. You need someone that can help you. Now get up!" He reached and then pulled her firmly but gently to her feet. He turned her head and made her look into the mirror on the wardrobe door.

"Look at that woman in that mirror. That's not the person I married and I don't want to believe for a second that she has gone forever. Look at her, you would have been ashamed to be this person a few short months ago."

Georgia stopped struggling against his grip and focused on the image in the mirror. Her hair hadn't been washed in three days, it was lank and a mess of tangles as it hadn't been brushed over the same period. Her skin was pale and greasy; dark grey circles surrounded her eyes, a result of the combination of her despair and the sleepless nights she had suffered. An old faded sweatshirt - good for nothing but the bin - hung from her in shapeless folds and ugly baggy jogging trousers that were equally distressed covered her legs. She realised that Rick was right; she was no longer the same woman. All the life had been sucked from her and she wondered if Emily had taken it with her when she was born like some kind of vampire. Until the moment he had walked into the bedroom, Rick had treated her with kid gloves but his actions had shocked her deeply and he had successfully broken through the barriers she had erected between her and the rest of her family.

"I'm sorry," she said before turning to hold her husband for the first time since Emily's birth.

"I know, let's go and see if we can get you some help," he managed to say as relief ran through him.

They arrived at the surgery just before six-thirty and parked in the near-empty car park. While they waited to be seen, Georgia clung tightly to her husband, trying to stop her hands from shaking.

When they were called they walked into a small, familiar consulting room. Doctor Young was their usual physician and he smiled warmly. Beside him was a man they didn't know who smiled reassuringly.

Doctor Young had been Rick's family doctor for as long as he could remember and he had welcomed Georgia to the practice when they got married. He had provided the primary care for her during her pregnancy and Georgia had grown to like him in the way Rick always had. The doctor had always been a formidable figure but his care for his patients seemed genuine and Rick trusted his judgement and advice. He was a big man with broad shoulders and a deep, resonating voice that gave him even greater authority in all he said, a voice that made you believe in him. His hair was now paper white and retirement was beckoning but Rick was reassured when he heard that rumble once again.

"Come in, Georgia. I hear you've been having a tough time. Well, we're going to help you out. This is Paul Lawrence, he's a community psychiatric nurse and he'll be helping you over the next few weeks."

"Hello, Georgia," the nurse said kindly.

"Hi."

"Are you happy for Rick to stay or would you rather speak to us yourself?"

"No it's fine, Rick can stay," she replied barely above a whisper while she gripped Rick's hand once again.

"OK. Tell us what's been happening to you."

She detailed her feelings since Emily's birth. She told them that Emily seemed like an alien to her and she had no idea how she could look after the little life that was now her responsibility. She said that she felt isolated and found it difficult to relate to anyone including Rick. She felt guilty that she couldn't be the mother she wanted to be but she couldn't bring herself to be with Emily.

"The good news, Georgia, is that what you're feeling is not that uncommon. We can help you. Now I'm not one of those doctors who believe that prescriptions will solve everything but I am going to give you something that will give you a bit of breathing space so that you can begin to get better. The pills will help with some of the chemical and hormonal imbalances that can result from childbirth but Paul will help you with the fears and concerns you have about parenthood. I think everyone suffers those feelings when they become a parent for the first time but for some women they become overwhelming. Paul will give you all the support you need. Does that sound like a plan?"

"Yes, thank you," she said quietly.

"We'll get you feeling better in no time," the nurse said.

While the doctor printed a prescription form he said, "Make an appointment to see Paul for Tuesday of next week and I'll see you in a couple of weeks."

He handed the prescription and the couple left the room hand in hand. Rick believed that things were finally going to start getting better and it was a weight he would be glad to discard so that their family life could become what he had always hoped it would be.

✝

There was a small gang of officers in the Station Bar, but Carrick had attached himself to Alex and Russell. The others kept a polite but friendly distance from their superiors. The bar was crammed with the Friday night office workers happy to escape for a weekend free of work. As well as the officers of Stewart Street station, the bar was popular with a host of different people including fire officers, railway workers, civil servants and even on occasion the musicians of the Royal Scottish National Orchestra.

Carrick had offered little in the way of conversation as he destroyed two bags of crisps with his pints and then when it was his round, he announced that he had an urgent appointment and left the bar.

"Miserable bastard," Russell muttered as the DC left. "Tighter than a duck's arse in a hurricane."

"Are you married, sir?" Alex asked after she had bought a Coke for herself and a pint of real ale for Russell. He had decided to leave the car at the station so he could enjoy some sort of relaxation after the week they had suffered.

"No, I used to be," he replied with a sigh.

"The job?"

"Naw, the wife. She was a one hundred per cent nutcase. She was jealous of any woman who came within a few hundred yards of me. Even accused me of shagging a lassie that I put away for killing a lad in a bar fight."

"That's tough."

"What can you do? It took me eight years to see what I was living with, at least you knew before he put another ring on your finger."

"I suppose so." It didn't seem like a lot of consolation to Alex at that point but she knew what he was trying to say.

"Sorry, that was insensitive. You must be devastated."

"I am but you're right, it's better that I know now rather than after the wedding."

"Ah don't understand guys like that. Why do they think that kind of behaviour is acceptable?"

"They probably think that they'll never get caught. Until I walked in on them I had no idea that he was like that or what he was up to, I thought he truly loved me."

"He probably did, in his own distorted way."

"Men, eh?"

Russell laughed. "We're not all cut from the same cloth."

"I hope not."

If she was honest she had only gone to the pub to delay the journey home but she knew she had to face it some time. She decided to leave and offered Russell a lift home but he said he was staying for one more and that he would get a taxi.

She drove home with a sick feeling in the pit of her stomach as she thought of her flat. When she opened the door it was just after nine o'clock. The absence of noise was the first thing she noticed and it was quickly followed by the memories of the previous day that came flooding back. Had it really only been a day and a bit since her home life had crashed down around her ears? There had been so much to think about at work that she had success- fully blotted out the images of that traumatic experience from her head. Rather than let it dominate her thoughts again, she decided to take some action.

After a quick shower she began the process of remov- ing Andrew from her life. She bundled the sex-stained bedding into a bag and dropped it into the external bin. Framed photographs of the couple in happier times were also consigned to the landfill.

She was working her way through them with little regret until she found the first photograph that was taken of the two of them as a couple. She had met him at the wedding of one of her friends from school. He was a pal of the groom and they had been placed at the same table during the meal. She was attracted to him instantly and after a night of drinking and dancing, he invited her out on a date. They had gone to Strathclyde Park and laughed like children as they rode rollercoasters and played arcade games. The photograph came from a photo booth and the two of them looked so naturally happy that she had treasured it and kept it.

Within a year of that first glorious day, he asked her to marry him and she was delighted to accept. Until the discovery of his betrayal, she had believed that they had a near-perfect relationship. He understood the demands of her job and was supportive when she brought some of her challenges home with her. His career as a surveyor was going from strength to strength and he had even talked of setting up his own company after they got married.

She wondered if she was in the correct career if she couldn't even detect that the man she thought was her soul mate was a cheating bastard with the morals of randy stray dog. The shock of what she had discovered had cut her deeply and she decided to take a little revenge for the humiliation she felt.

She found the most expensive of his clothes and ran a sharp knife over several of the seams. Trousers, shirts and jeans were reduced to pieces of cloth hanging together by a single row of stitches. She then folded everything neatly and placed it in a suitcase that she would send to her erstwhile fiancé. She knew it was petty but it proved to be very therapeutic.

The relief it gave her was fleeting and before long the melancholy swept in again. She got ready for bed but couldn't bring herself to sleep in the room where Andrew had betrayed her with that woman. She nestled inside a duvet on the living room couch and cried herself to sleep.

JOURNAL

Father Tierney was the worst. His sermons were packed with nothing but the wages of sin. Anyone disagreeing with his distorted view of the world was a sinner condemned to spend eternity in hell. One day a friend said to me that he thought even the Pope would be rejected at the heavenly gates if Father Tierney took Saint Peter's place.

My father had forced me to become an altar boy, all part of him projecting an image of solid, Christian dependability. I hated the whole dressing in gowns, waving incense and standing about with a goblet of wine but the one time I challenged my father he beat me and broke a rib. The hospital accepted his tale of my falling down a flight of stairs.

When I was about thirteen, one of the other lads brought a pornographic magazine in to a rehearsal for a big Easter service. Everyone was keen to see the pictures of the naked women and it was passed around eagerly. It arrived at me, and I was looking at the pictures when Father Tierney walked in. I remember the deathly silence of the other boys, they turned away from me and I was left facing the wrath of the priest on my own. He grabbed my arm and hauled me to his office. He screamed at me for being a pervert and a disgrace to the church. He hit me with the edge of a ruler and drew blood from my cheek. He then detailed all the tortures that my soul would face in the pits of hell. He told me I would be boiled in acid, my penis would have a hot poker inserted into it and the Devil would trample my soul with his cloven hooves.

I went home to my father, who had already been telephoned by Tierney. His self-righteous rage was the worst I ever suffered. The resulting broken cheekbone was explained away as a collision with a swinging door. That time the hospital staff were a little more cynical but nothing was reported. It was a domestic matter.

I suffered the worst nightmares in the wake of that incident. The images of the painful treatment I would suffer plagued me for months.

Now those images are back but this time it is

my poor, long-suffering mother who is the focus of the Devil's attentions. I am compelled to act to remove from my mind the doubt that she is among the angels; I must know that she is not being punished for my killing her before the last rites could be administered.

Unfortunately I am no closer to the answer I seek.

The heart of the woman I killed was not the source of her soul; there was no visible ascension from her chest that would indicate that she had begun her journey to glory; there was nothing when she passed over.

The police will be angry with me now; maybe I have to let them know what I am trying to do, try to make them understand. I have to let them see that I am simply removing these poor people from the sad and lonely lives they lead. I am giving them a better life with God and all his angels. There is no pain or stress or sadness in heaven, just the radiance of the glory of the Lord Jesus Christ. They will be better, won't they? I hope I am not mistaken.

I will need to release another one from her own personal hell so I can be assured that my mother is in the mansion that God promised. I need to see that soul float up to be convinced that the word of the Lord is the truth. Thomas needed to place his fingers in the holes in the hands of Jesus; I need my own concrete proof to support my own faith.

God's messenger has led me to another woman, one racked by the tragedy of a childless marriage; a woman who has tried to take her own life. Now I will complete her task and she will help me in mine. I have given a great deal of thought to where else the soul may reside. Everyone talks about the eyes as the window to the soul; maybe they are also the doorway, the secret of our humanity. The brain and the heart are but the mechanism to communicate what the soul is, but the eyes are the channels to our very being. They are the way the soul absorbs and processes the world.

I am sorry that it is necessary but I must know that what I did for my mother was worth it, that she has taken her place among the saints; that her soul left its living body for a better existence. If I cannot find it, how will I ever reconcile what I had to do?

I am the Soulseeker and I search for the essence of humanity; the soul of man. I will not cease my quest until I find the truth.

Soulseeker

CHAPTER 10

Russell regretted his choice to leave the car when he started Saturday morning by calling for a taxi and having to pay the exorbitant fare for the trip from his home to the station.

Alex and Carrick were already in the office when he arrived at nine o'clock.

"Good morning."

"Sir," Carrick said, barely looking up from his computer.

"Good morning. Good night?" Alex asked.

"Aye but I forgot how bloody expensive taxis were."

He asked the other two officers if they wanted a drink, and when they said no, he made himself his usual strong black tea.

He was about to settle down in front of the computer when his mobile phone rang.

"Major Incident Team, Detective Superintendent Russell speaking."

"Superintendent Russell, it's Charlie Walker."

"Hi Charlie, sorry but we've got nothing for you as yet. You know I can't speak to you about an on-going investigation. You'll be briefed with your cohorts later today."

"That's not why I'm calling. I think I've got something for you."

"Really?" Russell said, more alert and ready to listen.

"I received an e-mail at the paper this morning and we've been asked to pass it to you. It's got an audio file attached and I think it might be from the killer. He calls himself the Soulseeker."

Russell sighed. "Charlie, every day during an investigation we get hundreds of crackpots confessing to everything from stealing a plain loaf to being the reincarnation of Jack The Ripper."

"No, I think you have to hear this. It creeps me out and I think it might be genuine. My editor wants to print it but I said we should speak to you first."

"That was sensible. You're that sure it's real."

"There's details in it that I've not read in any paper. You'll know if they are true or not, I can't judge that, but they do seem too precise for just some nutcase trying to claim credit."

"Right Charlie, I need you to forward that mail to me and keep your editor on side until I've read it. Do you understand?'

"The editor's not going to like it but will you keep me in the loop?"

"Charlie, I promise that you'll get an inside track on the suspect when we have one, as long as my boss approves it." Russell was careful not to give him an abso-

lute guarantee, as he knew that no such approval would
be forthcoming.

The young reporter paused before saying, "That's fair.
I'll do what I can at this end but you know what the
newspaper industry is like, Mr Russell. We need to get
something exclusive and get it to press before our rivals
so we can sell more papers. A serial killer with a name, it
would be a gold mine."

"I know, but the last thing we need is to panic the
public. It's quid pro quo between you, your editor and my
boss and me; we all need to play ball."

"Cheers. I'll send it over."

"Thanks Charlie."

Russell hung up the phone and told the other two
detectives what had happened.

Within a couple of minutes the mail arrived in Russell's
in-box. Originally it had been sent from a Hotmail
account but the details would probably lead nowhere.
The forensic IT team would try to trace the IP address of
the sender but with all the care he had shown so far, there
was little chance that the killer had sent it from his own
computer or used his own details to create the account.

The mail contained a single typed line of text.

***Please pass to the officer in charge of the murder
enquiry.***

He invited the others to gather round before he pressed
play on the audio file.

A distorted electronic voice filled the room.

***"I am the Soulseeker and I seek proof of human
immortality. I am sorry that people have to die but***

I am on a quest and I must complete it. I must find the secret of the human soul; I must know it exists and that after death it journeys to a better place. The people I choose are those who have darkness, loneliness and pain in their lives; they will be assured of a better life with God. I respect the sacrifice that each of them is making and have given them full Christian rites by cremating their bodies and giving them a token of Christ's love. I will stop when my mission is complete. I know you will try to catch me but I must finish my quest before you do.

I am the Soulseeker and I search for the essence of humanity; the soul of man. I will not cease my quest until I find the truth."

A hush descended on the office for a moment before Carrick, wearing a stupid grin, said, "Well, we better go and arrest Stephen Hawking."

His attempt at humour was greeted with stony silence and a dark look from Russell and Alex.

She was chilled to the core of her being by the message and the way it had been delivered. The computerised voice made it seem almost robotic, with a lack of intonation or emotion. It was like something you would hear in a science fiction movie when a computer had gone rogue.

The message and the meaning behind it disturbed Russell in equal measure. Now it was definite they were dealing with a deeply disturbed individual who was likely to kill again and there was little they could do about it unless they got a significant break in the case.

"What's happening?" Rick Johnstone asked as he arrived.

"Get your coat off and listen to this."

The voice filled the room once more and Alex watched Rick's face as it flowed from shock to disgust to outrage. Stephanie Anderson walked in and caught the end of the playback.

"Good morning, what are you listening to?"

"We think that it might be a message from the killer," Alex replied.

"Can I hear it?"

Russell clicked play and they all listened intently once again.

When it was over DC Johnstone asked, "Do you think we'll be able to get a voice print from it?"

"No, that's a computer reading text," Anderson said confidently.

"How do you mean?" Russell asked.

"The killer has typed that into the computer. There is a program on the computer designed to help partially sighted people to interact with the machine. He has used a program like that to capture the words and then saved them as an audio file. He has recorded it to ensure there is no way we can obtain a voice trace or comparison." Anderson was completely sure of her analysis and her tone indicated that she would tolerate no disagreement.

"I think DS Anderson is correct, sir. It doesn't sound like a human voice that has been distorted, it's too mechanical," Alex added in support.

"Shite. So all we've got is a lunatic's message telling us

that he is going to kill again and no way of tracing who the hell he is."

"Another reason for digitising the voice may be to disguise the sex of the killer," Johnstone suggested.

"No, this must be a man. There's no way a woman could move the dead weight of a man."

Although Anderson was correct in what she said, Alex couldn't help but be irritated by her unswerving arrogance and the belief that she was accurate in everything she said. When they worked together in the Vice Squad, Anderson frequently dismissed ideas and opinions from other officers with contempt. Generally, she had good instincts as a detective but on a couple of occasions her dismissal of other people's input had cost the squad time on difficult investigations.

Russell was annoyed at the way Anderson had spoken to a colleague and offered a gentle rebuke to the DS. "As we have about three hundred thousand men in this city, knowing it's a man doesn't help. First of all, do we think this is genuine?"

"I believe so, sir, he mentions a token of Christ's love, that must be the cross we found with each of the victims. I doubt there is anyone other than the killer that could have that kind of knowledge, " Alex asserted, and her words were greeted with agreement by everyone.

"So we're dealing with a killer who is driven by a need to find the human soul. He has said he won't stop until he finds it or we catch him. As he's highly unlikely to find what he's looking for, we better stop him soon or there will be a lot of bodies piling up. What can we deduce about him?"

Alex offered, "What he thinks of as motive was probably created by something traumatic. The loss of a family member, or maybe he has a terminal illness and he wants to know there is something beyond this life."

"He seems almost reluctant to commit the murders but he feels compelled. There is a sense of guilt because he knows what he is doing is wrong," Johnstone contributed.

"He must have some medical background," Carrick said.

"He has access to a van and it might be the primary crime scene," Anderson added.

Russell seized upon her words. "Good. The van is key. His reasons for doing this are irrelevant in some ways but something physical should help us. If we can find the van, we find the killer. It's about the only concrete thing we know about this guy. This distortion of religious teaching is just the symptom of a disturbed mind and it doesn't give us a clue as to who he is. There are plenty of nutters who use religious excuses for what they do but it has nothing to do with God, it's about their own psychosis. We'll leave that to the psychiatrists to write papers about him once we catch the bastard, but we're police officers and we need to go on solid evidence to find the guy that did this, so let's get to it."

Alex could see a steely determination being revived in Russell. He had no time for the analysis of the killer that although valuable was unlikely to lead to an arrest; he preferred action that would bring them closer to their target.

He began to initiate those actions. "William, check those CCTV tapes with the van on and see what you can come up with. Stephanie, see if you can find out anything about the guy Theresa was supposed to meet. Rick, find out about her travel arrangements and then talk to anyone who might have seen her on the night she was murdered. Alex, when Tina Bartram arrives, can you work with her on the people who attended the meeting that both Theresa and Graeme were at? We need to know who they were and any other connections that they may have to the victims. I'll forward the e-mail to the IT bods but we'll get nothing from them at least until Monday. I'll keep myself busy with the medical records to see if there's anything that would indicate they were treated by the same doctor or at the same hospital. Everyone happy?" he asked.

There was general agreement from a group of officers now desperate to find a chink in the armour of the killer.

They dispersed to the desks and an air of busy concentration settled on the office. The next two hours were filled with the chatter of phone calls and the clicking of computer keyboards. There was little interaction between the detectives or the uniformed staff who had joined them; everyone was absorbed by their individual assignments.

The first to offer new information was Carrick. "We've got a white van turning into Bilsland Drive from Maryhill Road at 2:21a.m. on the morning of the second murder. It approached from a northerly direction, so it could have come from Milngavie. It's tough to make out the registration but I guess it'll be another dud if it's our guy."

"Get it to IT and ask them to tidy it up. They're going to be our biggest fans," Russell said sarcastically, knowing that the forensic IT team were often overloaded with work and this case was generating a huge amount of evidence to process.

"Will do. What else do you want me to look at?"

"Give Stephanie a hand tracing the mysterious boyfriend."

"I'd rather not, I prefer to work alone," she said before Carrick could move.

"What is it with this place and moody cows?" As usual, Carrick's mouth opened before his brain engaged and he quickly apologised before Russell could give him a bawling out.

"Sergeant, I expect a bit more in the way of teamwork from you, this is not the time for egos," Russell warned Anderson.

"I am happier when I have complete control of a situation. I am methodical and another person will disrupt my method." Anderson appeared to be immune to the ripples she was causing.

"I don't think it'll matter, sir," Johnstone interrupted. "I've been speaking to one of Theresa's workmates and she has remembered a bit more about him. His name is Doctor Brendan Harcourt and he works at Gartnavel."

"A doctor? Interesting. Doesn't Gartnavel have a specialist psychiatric unit?

"Yes, sir. It might tie with the forensics report from Graeme Mathieson's flat. They found anti-depressants, same as Theresa Asher."

"Very interesting. Let's pay Dr Harcourt a visit. Alex, you're with me. The rest of you follow your assignments and let me know how you get on. DS Anderson, aid DC

Carrick in widening the search for the van on CCTV, see if you can get that registration."

As she followed her boss out of the office, Alex smiled at the look of distaste on Anderson's face.

Gartnavel Hospital is in the north west of Glasgow. There is both a general hospital and a specialist unit dealing in mental health. Alex and Russell weren't directed to either of those buildings but instead towards the Beatson Cancer Centre, which is the primary medical treatment clinic for the disease in the west of Scotland.

The receptionist at the front of the building was reluctant to let the officers speak to the doctor as he insisted that Dr Harcourt was a very busy man. The mention of a murder enquiry was enough to persuade him that it would be appropriate to disrupt the doctor's day.

The two detectives were shown to an office and asked to wait. Harcourt appeared ten minutes later, breezing into the room with a confident stride. The officers introduced themselves and the doctor folded his six-foot-four-inch frame into an uncomfortable-looking old chair.

At first glance, Alex could see what would have attracted Theresa to him. She reckoned that he was in his late twenties or early thirties, a handsome face with good bone structure underpinning a tanned, even complexion. His green eyes and reddish-brown hair suggested Celtic ancestry but when he spoke it was with a North American accent.

"What can I do for you, officers?" he said with an affable smile.

"Doctor, I believe you know a Ms Theresa Asher," Russell said.

"Yeah, we're due to go on a date tonight, why?" Suspicion crept into his voice as he spoke.

"How long have you known her?"

"We met a couple of weeks ago. Is something wrong?"

"Where did you two meet?"

"At a friend's party. Now can you please tell me what this is about?" His suspicion had blossomed into a near panic.

"You haven't read the newspapers?"

"No, why?"

"Doctor, I'm sorry to have to tell you that Ms Asher was found dead on Thursday morning."

"What?" his shock seemed genuine but Alex knew enough about the behaviour of sociopaths to treat his reaction with a degree of scepticism.

"Now can you tell us a little more about how you two met?"

"You can't think I had anything to do with her death, I only met her once."

"Please answer the questions, Doctor."

"I was invited to a party by a friend, Leo Baines. We're in the same rowing club. Leo's wife invited Theresa; they went to the same gym, I think. I thought she was very attractive; we started talking and found we liked each other, so we arranged a date. Tonight was the first time that we were both free. That was all there was to it."

"Did you speak to her after the party?"

"We had a brief chat on the phone last Monday to confirm where we were going and the time."

"Are you a religious man, Doctor?"

"What? What's that got to do with anything?"

"Please answer the question, Doctor. Are you a religious man?"

"Detective, if you saw what I see every day in here, kids whose lives haven't really begun having to undergo therapies that are almost as bad as the disease, some of them dwindling away and dying despite all the training and facilities I have at my disposal, would you believe in a loving higher power?" The difficulties of treating a disease like cancer, where the illness is often the winner, were obvious on the junior doctor's face.

"Many people can find faith even in a place like this."

"Well, I envy them something that comforts them but losing the battle for a child is not something I can find any positives in."

Alex's gut told her that this was not the man they were looking for. She changed the tone of the questioning. "Did Ms Asher tell you about any fears she may have had about feeling threatened or being watched?"

"No, she seemed to be quite upbeat. She told me at the party that she had found it difficult to make friends in Scotland since she arrived. She worked long hours and was feeling quite lonely. I told her that I had felt the same when I first arrived from Calgary but that it would get better."

"Is there anything she said that might help us to find her killer?"

He made a show of trying to remember. "No, I don't think so. We were both looking forward to going out on the date; it was all I could think about. I didn't know her well enough to judge if there was something else worrying her, I'm sorry."

Russell was equally convinced that another possible route for the investigation had just closed. "OK, Doctor, thanks for your help. We'll let you get back to your patients. If anything occurs to you, give us a ring."

When the detectives were back in Russell's car, he banged the steering wheel in frustration.

"Fuck, this is crap. We can't catch a break."

"I know. But I do think there is something in the medical angle. The killer spoke about how he was putting people out of their darkness, loneliness and pain. Mathieson's break-up and Theresa's sense of isolation had caused them to feel depressed or anxious enough that they had to consult a doctor. Were they referred to a psychiatrist, did they go for a private consultation? It might be the connection we're looking for."

"You might be right but I'm hoping the bloody white van leads us somewhere."

As the car drove down Great Western Road, Russell's phone rang.

"Get that for me, would you, Alex?"

Alex picked up his mobile from the console between the their seats.

"Hello, Alex Menzies."

"Alex, it's Rick. Is the boss there?"

"He's driving. What's up?"

"It's the chief super. His wife called, he's in the Royal Infirmary with a suspected heart attack."

"Oh no. Is he OK?"

"She says he seems not too bad but they're giving him

tests at the moment."

"OK, thanks Rick. I'll let the boss know."

When she finished the call, Russell asked, "Let me know what?"

"Chief Superintendent Blair's in the hospital. They think he's had a heart attack."

"Oh, I knew I should have phoned for a doctor last night. I thought there was something wrong."

"It's not your fault, you couldn't have known."

"You didn't see him. He looked like death warmed up. He said it was the flu, stubborn old goat that he is."

"Do you want to go to the Royal?" Alex asked.

"No, there's no point just now."

"Have you known the chief super for a long time?"

"He was my DS when I first became a detective and we've worked together a lot. He helped me get a place on the MIT. He's a good copper, a good boss and a more than just a colleague."

"I understand."

Russell retreated into silence as he began to think about the implications of his friend's absence from the office. Alex realised that he didn't want to talk about it and they completed the journey with no further conversation.

Rick Johnstone had waded his way through many layers of bureaucracy before eventually finding the names of the train crew that had worked on the train that had taken Theresa Asher home. After some cajoling and informing the roster clerk that the crew weren't under any suspicion, he was given the mobile numbers of the driver and the ticket collector, who had the imposing title of 'Revenue Protection Assistant'.

As the driver would have little interaction with the passengers, Johnstone decided to give the RPA a call first.

"Hello, George MacIntosh speaking."

"Good afternoon, Mr MacIntosh. My name is Detective Constable Johnstone from Stewart Street CID."

"Whit kin ah dae fur ye, son?"

"You were working the Milngavie route on Wednesday night, I believe."

"That's right."

"Do you remember a young black woman on the 21:28 from Central?"

"Aye, she wis a stunner, ah couldnae help but notice her. That wis the lassie that wis killed, right?"

"That's correct. Do you remember if there was anyone else paying particular attention to her?"

"Wait a minute, noo. Ah've goat a special technique fur remembering things. I'll walk through the train in ma heid, gies a minute."

Rick smiled as he waited for the man, who by the sound of his voice was well into middle age. He could hear slight mumbling as Mr MacIntosh did his virtual walkthrough.

"The train wis quiet that night. There wis wan other passenger in the same carriage. A boy aboot eighteen ah reckon. He wis plugged in tae wan o' they music players."

"Did he appear to be interested in Ms Asher?"

"Well if he hud eyes and a pair o' baws he probably wid've noticed her but he didnae seem to be that bothered."

"What about at the station, was there someone waiting for her?"

"Wait a minute. Intae ma heid again."

Rick would normally have been frustrated at the man's antics but as he it seemed to work for him, he thought that he might as well let him continue.

"There wisnae anybody at the station but there wis a moator sittin' ootside it. Ah wis walkin' up the ootside o' the train tae go and talk tae Alice, the driver. When the black lassie walked up the road, ah noticed the car pulled alang side her."

The detective sat up and grabbed a pen. "What can you tell me about the car?"

"Ah'm no great wi models, son but it wis quite a wee moator. Maybe a Fiesta or Corsa, somethin' like that. It was hard tae be sure in the light but ah think it wis light blue."

"I don't suppose you saw the registration plate?"

"Naw son, ma eyes urnae that good."

"Did you see what happened next?"

"Ah'm afraid no, son. Ah jist thought she'd bumped intae somebody she knew. Didnae think anythin' o' it, till you asked me."

Johnstone was a little disappointed but the ticket collector had proved to be an excellent eyewitness and he may have given them their first real break. "Thanks a lot, Mr MacIntosh."

"Yir welcome, son. Ah hope ye get the bastard."

When the call finished, Johnstone told the other officers what he had discovered.

Stephanie Anderson took control. "I'll contact the Transport Police and ask them to check the CCTV from the station."

"Shouldn't we let the boss know?" Johnstone asked.

"Let the boss know what?" Russell said as he walked through the door.

Anderson replied before Johnstone could open his mouth, "We've got a lead on a car that stopped outside Milngavie railway station and the driver seemed to speak to Ms Asher. I was about to contact the BTP for access to their CCTV coverage of the station environs."

"I like your initiative, sergeant, but I also expect to be kept informed of any significant development."

"Yes, sir." The reply was loaded with her anger at the shot across her bows from the superintendent.

"Anybody else got anything they want to tell me?" Russell's mood was still coloured by the news regarding the chief superintendent and not even a significant lead seemed to have lifted it.

PC Bartram stood up. "Sir, I've checked out the people who attended the meeting. Apart from the police officers there were seven others. None have a record or a medical background."

"Good work, constable. Thanks."

"We've had no luck with the CCTV either. The rain made it difficult to read the registration plates. The best we got was a partial and according to the DVLA records none of the possible matches were a white Luton van."

"OK, it's as we expected, he's using false plates and is probably clever enough to change them for every kill. We need to find that fuckin' van somehow. Suggestions?"

No one responded and Russell slammed his desk in frustration. "This bastard is playing us. Come on, people, help me out here."

Alex could see that there was more to his reaction than the lack of progress in the case. Things were in danger of unravelling in the squad if they didn't get a breakthrough soon.

"We'll need a warrant for the victims' medical records, William, can you get that prepared tomorrow for Monday?" Alex requested.

"Will do."

"I think we should call it a day. Try and get some decent rest and we'll see what we can do tomorrow." Russell needed some space.

The officers drifted away, leaving Russell alone, exhausted and contemplative.

Aileen Fletcher finished towel drying her striking red hair and pulled a hairband over it. She looked in the mirror at the face she had seen for thirty-six years. Little sketches of lines were beginning to appear at the corners of her eyes and the edge of her mouth. Even she could see the sorrow in those emerald green orbs; she looked into them, into her very soul, and it definitely showed the depth of the agony she had felt, but maybe there was a little bit of light there too.

Ten years of trying to have a baby had taken their toll on her both mentally and physically. After the doctor had informed her that the latest fertility treatment had failed and there was little chance that she would ever be pregnant, her spirit had crashed like a fallen tree; she collapsed in on herself, wondering what the point of life was if you could not have a child. Three months of anti-depressants had helped stop the slide but hadn't improved her life as much as she had hoped. The community psychiatric nurse had encouraged her to try regular exercise as a way of lifting her mood. She joined the gym and for the last two weeks had worked on the various machines four nights a week. A Saturday night was a good time to come as it was always quiet and she felt more comfortable with fewer people to judge her performance. She was beginning to feel the benefit as she felt the angst begin to lift. The future no longer looked so bleak and she had even suggested to Gary, her husband, that they should consider adoption after years of rejecting the idea.

She packed her bag, put on her coat and plugged in her earphones. The gym was a fifteen-minute walk from her home and although the rain was still falling as it had all summer, she liked the cool touch of it on her skin after a hard workout. She stepped out into the mild air and felt the raindrops begin to patter down on her hood. She turned her face to allow the water to hit her skin and for the first time in a while it felt good to be alive.

She started walking through the deserted streets. A dog walker and the lights of the occasional passing car were the only signs that she wasn't the only person on the whole planet. Five minutes from home she thought nothing of the light blue Corsa that stopped at her side of the pavement. The driver had pulled over so that his door was close to the kerb. As Aileen stepped closer the door swung open, blocking the narrow pavement.

"Sorry," the man said as he smiled. He motioned as if to close the door and she moved to step around him. When she was level with him, she felt a sharp pain. She turned towards him to see him putting a hypodermic syringe into his jacket pocket.

"Hey, what are you..." The world seemed to waltz around her and she felt her legs fold like they were made of cardboard. Her sports bag fell and he stepped forward to catch her before she could follow it. A cold fear passed through her as she sunk into unconsciousness. He opened the back door of the car and levered her into the seat, then picked up her bag and threw it casually on to the passenger seat. He closed the door and, with a quick look around to ensure that nobody had seen him, got into the driver's seat and pulled away.

CHAPTER 11

Alex felt a cold hand of dread grab her when she awoke to the sound of her phone ringing once again. The clock told her that it was three-twenty and somehow she knew that the Soulseeker had struck again.

"Hello," she mumbled into the handset.

"Alex, we've got another one," Russell uttered the words she had feared.

"Where?"

"Balgrayhill, in an abandoned pub."

"Same MO, I take it."

"Looks like it. A woman called the fire in about thirty minutes ago, the brigade at Springburn responded and found the body. It hadn't been burning long and the Springburn CID report that it's another woman."

"I'll be there in about half an hour."

"Right, see you there. I'll give Rick a ring."

When the call was complete Alex was on the move. She dressed in a casual blouse and jeans, pinned up her hair and set off for the scene.

✝

The old pub had once been the focal point of the community but it had slid into neglect and finally disuse. It stood above a small row of shops that offered the necessities of life to the residents in one of Glasgow's poorest areas; fast food shops and a bookmaker.

When Alex arrived, the normally deserted shell of the bar was a hive of industry. A hard hat was required on the site and she collected a white one marked with the Strathclyde Police badge along with her protective suit from the SOCO's van.

A feeling of déjà vu overtook her as she approached yet another scene lit by floodlights where a gathering of people was posed around the burnt remnants of a human being. There was water pouring in from a variety of holes in what was left of the roof. Large droplets splashed over the equipment and the people below. Rick Johnstone was standing with Russell and a small man that Alex didn't recognise.

"Alex," Rick acknowledged her she approached.

Russell turned to her and said with resignation, "Looks like he wasn't kidding about his need to continue killing people."

"Hello, I'm Terence Owens. I'm the assistant fiscal, I'm covering for Fiscal Kerr," the little man said as he offered a formal handshake. He looked distinctly ill at ease and Alex felt some sympathy for him. She wouldn't have been surprised if this was the first time he had been involved with a murder investigation and he looked like he might scamper for cover at the first loud noise.

"Pleased to meet you," she replied with a smile she hoped might reassure him a little.

She nodded at Noel Hawthorn who was recording the scene with his usual detachment. He returned her greeting but was back at work immediately. Doctor MacNeil had once again been the unlucky on-call pathologist and she was making notes about the body.

Alex could see that the fire had not had time to wreak the same amount of damage on the victim that was evident in the first two cases. Her face was still intact and at first Alex thought the killer had left her eyes open. It was only when she leaned closer to the body that the full horror was exposed.

"Has he removed her eyelids?" she asked the pathologist.

"I'm afraid so. Both upper and lower lids have been removed with a very sharp knife. Considering the medical connections with his previous victims, I would guess it was probably done with a scalpel."

Before he could throw up all over the body, Mr Owens ran from the scene and deposited the contents of his stomach into a dark corner.

"Bloody hell," was Rick Johnstone's response. His belief that the killer was nothing more than an evil bastard had just been reinforced and no amount of psychological analysis would change that view.

"Why?" Russell asked rhetorically but Alex answered him with her first thought.

"The eyes are a window to the soul," she whispered, chilled by the thought she may just have made a connection with the disturbed thought processes of a deeply disturbed individual.

Russell could only sigh in response. This whole case

was proving to be impossible for him to comprehend. Greed, passion, revenge; all of them were motives he could understand, but this kept taking them into an undiscovered landscape of psychosis. How could he catch a killer whose thought processes were so alien?

"As you can see the woman has been undressed and then covered in a simple shroud."

The shapeless cloth had been wound around the victim like the very loose bindings of a mummy.

"Have you checked her hands yet, doctor?" Russell asked.

"Not yet."

"May I?"

The doctor reached into her kit and gave the detective an evidence bag. Russell bent close to the woman's right hand. The smell of carbonised flesh filled his lungs but he dismissed it from his thoughts. The poor woman's hand had suffered some damage from the flames but he was able to carefully prise open her fingers. In her palm was the familiar gold cross; he tried to remove it but the heat of the blaze had branded the shape into the woman's palm. When he felt resistance, he gave up trying to pull it away.

"I'll leave it for you at the PM," he told the doctor.

She gave a grim nod. Even with all that she had seen during her training and in her professional career, this case was affecting her in the same way as the members of the police team.

"Rick, you know the drill," Russell turned to the detective constable.

"Yes, sir. I'll organise an escort."

"Sean," Russell called to the senior scene of crime officer who was supervising the search of the building.

"Hello."

Russell and Alex walked to where he was standing.

"Tell me you've got an ID on both the victim and the killer and that we can mop this up by midday."

"Oi wish oi could. This shoite is gettin' on my tits.' Sean's Dublin accent was thicker than Alex had ever heard it.

"It's loike chasin' a feckin' ghost."

"I had an awful feeling that was going to be your answer."

"Oi'm sorry, Tom but there's feck all here that amounts to evidence."

"OK, pal, keep looking."

"I'm looking for Superintendent Russell," a shout rose from just outside the building.

"That's me."

The crime scene manager approached the detectives and said, "Detective Sergeant Morris, sir. I've got the woman who called in the fire, I thought you might like a word."

"Thanks sergeant, I'll be with you in a minute."

Alex joined the superintendent and they dumped the protective clothing in the box at the technicians' van.

They hurried through another depressingly heavy downpour to where the sergeant was standing sheltering in a doorway with the female witness. She was in her early fifties and was wrapped in a thick, quilted jacket. A cigarette released smoke into the air around her right hand. Her hair was dyed black but the grey of her roots showed through and she reminded Alex of a badger. Her skin had aged like dried-out old parchment as a result of her smoking habit but it had been decorated liberally with hastily applied make-up. As the two police officers approached she allowed the jacket to fall open to give them a view of her plunging neckline and her considerable breasts, which were spilling out in all directions from a bra that was too small for the task of supporting them.

DS Morris introduced her. "This is Mrs Fenlon, sir."

"Hello Mrs Fenlon, I'm Detective Superintendent Russell, this is my colleague Detective Inspector Menzies."

"Pleased to meet ye," she replied as she offered her hand like she was a Hollywood starlet waiting for Russell to kiss it.

He twisted his hand into an awkward position to allow him to shake hers and Alex did likewise, although Mrs Fenlon offered her hand at a normal height rather than for a kiss.

"I believe you were the one who reported the fire."

"Aye, ah wis."

"Could you tell us what you saw?"

"Ah wis up huvin' a coffee; ah find it hard tae sleep when there's no' a man beside me tae keep me warm, if ye get ma meanin." She fluttered her eyelids and drew in a breath that encouraged more of her breasts to make an attempt to break from their constraints.

"Yes, I think we understand," Russell replied, but to Alex he seemed a little flustered.

Mrs Fenlon brought the cigarette to her lips with a

slow gesture heavy with what she obviously believed were sexual undertones. She blew the smoke out seductively and then continued her story. "Ah wis jist staunin' wi' ma fag and ma coffee when ah saw this guy comin' doon the sterrs fae the auld pub. At first ah thought he wis a junkie, know? They're aye goin' in there tae get high when it's rainin'. Daft bastards, that auld wreck could faw oan tap o' them at any time. Anyway, he gets in this white van, quite a big wan wi' a kinna boxy back. He was jist away when ah saw the flames then ah rang 999 and goat the fire brigade oot."

"That's great Mrs Fenlon…"

"Please, caw me anytime." She laughed before continuing, "Ah mean Roberta."

Over Russell's shoulder Alex could see DS Morris close to laughter as he studied the face of her extremely uncomfortable boss.

"Roberta, did you happen to see the man?"

"No' his face, naw. He wis wearing a black hoody, in fact he wis dressed aw in black. Looked like the guy fae the auld Milk Tray adverts, so he did."

"OK, thanks for your time. If there's anything that comes to mind, give me a ring," Russell said as he handed her a card.

"Anything?"

"Anything at all." He walked into an obvious trap.

"Well, ah'll be sure to ring ye and ye come up an' ye take doon ma particulars." She cracked a lascivious grin that only increased the number of wrinkles on her already craggy countenance.

Russell turned away, "Detective Inspector, I believe we

will have to get going."

"Nice meeting you, Roberta," Alex said before rushing to catch up with her quickly retreating boss.

"Are you alright, sir?"

"Fuck, as if I've not got enough on my plate without a sex-starved pensioner chasing me."

"I think you should take it as a complement, sir," Alex suggested with a smile.

Russell stopped. "Alex, we've not known each other very long and up until this point I thought I liked you, but now I'm not so sure." His face was set like granite but Alex thought he was kidding; at least she hoped he was.

As they were making their way back towards the crime scene, Russell's phone rang.

"Superintendent Russell."

"Sir, it's DS Quinlan. I've got a gentleman here that I think you should speak to. The guys from Bishopbriggs have brought him in. His wife went missing late last night and he's very anxious about her."

"Have the hospitals been checked?"

"Yes, sir. They've done all the standard checks."

"Right, try and settle him down and we'll be there as soon as we can."

When the call was complete, Russell turned to Alex and told her what had transpired.

"At least there's a chance we'll be able to identify the victim quite quickly this time. I hope it's not the gentleman's wife but it certainly sounds a possibility."

"I know. It's a shitty conversation to have with anyone."

Another brief exchange with those involved in the investigation of the locus confirmed that the killer was careful to minimise the forensic evidence he left behind. Sean O'Reilly's language had slipped further into fierce Irish curses as his anger increased at his team's inability to make a breakthrough.

Arrangements were made to transport the remains of the woman to the mortuary and the two detectives prepared for their meeting with the anxious husband. As they walked to their cars, the first of the press corps had arrived and shouted questions about the death, but they were ignored. Russell was glad that there would be no lurid headlines that day as the Sunday papers would already be printed and there were no evening papers later that day.

Alex drove on autopilot back to Stewart Street while she tried to think how to break this case, how to find the connection that would point them to the deluded killer, but the lack of obvious connections was making it impossible. She felt guilty for thinking it but the only good thing about another victim was the possibility of a more obvious thread appearing. It was little compensation for her as she and her colleagues had failed to prevent the woman's death by catching the killer. She hoped that today would bring some good news.

CHAPTER 12

Russell had beaten Alex back to the station and he was standing in the reception when she walked in. Detective Sergeant Quinlan pointed them to a waiting room where a red-eyed, crumpled man sat with a female PC. The officers had given the man a coffee and a sandwich but they lay untouched on the small table in front of him.

As the two detectives entered, the man stood up. "Have you found her? Is that why they brought me here? Is she OK?" he asked in hurried apprehension.

The constable introduced the man, "Sir, Ma'am, this is Mr Fletcher."

"Thanks constable, we'll take it from here," Russell said.

"Yes sir," the uniformed officer acknowledged the detectives with a nod as she left the room.

Russell introduced himself and his colleague. Alex took the lead by indicating the seat and then sitting beside the distraught husband as he flopped back into the chair. He was in his late thirties with a receding hairline. He wore dark-rimmed glasses that sat in front of bright blue eyes on a face that was filled with all the signs of distress both detectives had seen often. "Mr Fletcher, it might help if you tell us what happened and also a little about your wife."

"I've already told the other officers."

"We understand that but it is better if we hear it directly from you, sir." Alex kept her voice calm in an effort to still his restless concern, it was important that he detail the facts without too much emotion getting in the way.

He understood what she was trying to do and gulped in a large breath. "My wife Aileen goes to the gym regularly; it's part of the therapy her psychiatric nurse suggested to help her recovery from depression." At the mention of the nurse, Russell glanced at Alex.

"What was the source of her depression, Mr Fletcher?" Russell asked.

"We were told six months ago that we would never have kids. We had been trying for ten years and had three sets of IVF treatment but they were unsuccessful. The doctors told us that there was a congenital problem with her womb and that the chance of her becoming pregnant and carrying a baby full-term was virtually non-existent. When we received the news she became very distant and for a while I was worried that she might harm herself. I got some help from our GP and he referred her to the community psychiatric nurse. She's been going to the gym for a month and it has definitely helped her."

"So what happened last night?"

"She went to the gym as normal about nine; she preferred to go late in the day because it's quieter. She's very self-conscious about her shape and she doesn't like it when there are too many people around. She normally stays until the gym closes about ten-thirty. Last night I was waiting for her to come home but I fell asleep. I awoke about ten to one and I thought she'd gone straight to bed but when I got upstairs there was no sign of her. When I realised she wasn't there I called the police immediately." His voice began to crack and the emotional strain began to creep back in to his body language as he rubbed his arms as if hugging himself.

"How does she travel to the gym, does she use a car?" Alex said gently.

"No, it's just fifteen minutes' walk from our house."

"Do you have a picture of her?"

He reached into his jacket and took out his phone. He tapped a few instructions on the screen before turning it to let Alex see the photograph. An attractive woman smiled out from the picture; her face was beaming with an undisguised joy. Alex felt the pain of recognition as she realised that it was almost certainly the same woman they had found in the abandoned pub.

Fletcher read her expression. "Have you found her?"

Alex carefully took the phone from his hand and showed the photograph to her boss.

Russell felt the same feeling of foreboding at what he saw but the unfortunate man had to know the truth. "Mr Fletcher, the body of a woman matching the description of your wife was found in the early hours of this morning."

"Oh no, oh no, oh no…" He repeated the phrase like a litany while Alex tried to calm him. There were no tears as he seemed to stare off into the distance, his mind tried to disassociate him from the reality of the situation and his mouth worked automatically, repeating the same two words relentlessly.

It took ten minutes before he was calm enough for Alex to ask him, "Is there someone we can call?"

"Eh… my brother. My brother."

"What's his name?" Russell was still holding the phone and was ready to use it to call the man's relative.

"Paul, it's Paul."

Russell scanned the contact list on the phone and when he found what he believed to be the right number, showed it to Mr Fletcher. "Is this him?"

"Yes."

Russell stepped out of the room and dialled the number.

"Derek, what the hell are you doing phoning at this time on a Sunday morning?" was the grumpy and tired response from Paul Fletcher.

"Mr Fletcher, my name is Detective Superintendent Russell."

"Oh hell, what's happened?" The shock was all too noticeable in the man's voice; a hundred different thoughts racing through his head and none of them good.

Russell informed the man of all that had occurred and the belief he had that his sister-in-law may have been murdered. He asked him to come to the station while they arranged a viewing for formal identification of the woman at the mortuary. Paul Fletcher agreed and promised that he would be there as soon as he possibly could.

Alex sat with Derek Fletcher, listening to him speak of his wife and comforting him when the tears did eventually flow as he slowly emerged from the stasis of the initial shock. Paul Fletcher arrived after about twenty minutes. He looked older than his brother in both features and manner of dress. A tweed jacket and Farah trousers aged him beyond his forty-odd years. He moved to console his brother when he arrived and Alex left the two men to talk, her own emotions already drained by a husband's grief.

She climbed the stairs to their office where Russell was sitting at his desk resting his feet on his desk. He looked as stressed as she felt. He told her that he had spoken to the staff at the mortuary and arranged a viewing for nine o'clock.

"Any doubts?" he asked

"No, you?"

"Unfortunately not. There are days when I hate this fuckin' job."

"I know exactly what you mean."

Alex sat and typed up some notes while they waited for the time to come when they had to take Derek Fletcher on a journey that would haunt him for the rest of his days.

The two detectives and the two brothers sat quietly in Russell's car as they made their way through the tranquil Sunday morning streets to the mortuary building. The pain that the two men felt was like an enormous weight on the detectives, making the vehicle feel particularly claustrophobic. The dark skies and drizzling rain only added to the feeling of despair.

When they arrived, Russell led the two brothers through the public entrance where a tastefully decorated reception was a more welcoming site than the entrance the police normally used.

A member of the mortuary staff was waiting for them and guided them to a waiting room. As they were about to enter the room, there was a sudden commotion from behind the door that led to the viewing room. There was a lot of swearing and the sound of violence.

"If you take a seat, gentlemen, we'll be with you in a moment. Can you stay with them until we sort this mess out?" Russell asked the woman from the mortuary.

"Certainly," she replied, only too glad to be out of the firing line as she had a good idea what was happening on the other side of the door.

The two detectives burst through the connecting door to find four uniformed officers trying to separate two groups of people who were trying to throw punches at one another.

"What the fuck is going on?" Russell shouted, which caused a brief pause in the proceedings. An obscenely obese woman turned towards him with fist clenched. She tried to connect with a punch but Russell caught her arm and whipped it behind her back.

She screamed in pain. "Yir breaking' ma fuckin' erm!"

"No' yet, but ah will if ye don't fuckin' calm doon."

Meanwhile, Alex had grabbed another antagonist and bound his arms with a cable tie. He was a man in his early twenties with the emaciated appearance of a habitual drug user. The other officers had used the interruption to restrain the rest of the combatants, who all looked like they were no strangers to entanglement with the police.

"Noo, will somebody tell me, whit the hell is goin' oan here?" The rage that had been building up in Russell as the case had progressed seemed to have burst through and he looked as if he would flatten the first person that moved in an aggressive manner.

"Her bastard son killt ma boy!" a middle-aged man screamed in the direction of the fat woman who was still being restrained by Russell.

"His bastard killed mine, so he did," the fat woman screamed back.

There followed a number of further accusations being shouted back and forth between the two groups and the level of tension rose again.

"Shut the fuck up, the lot o' ye!" Russell's voice had an instant effect.

"Constable, can you please tell me what's going on?"

"Sorry sir. There was a gang fight last night. There were knives involved and it ended up with two fatalities. The two families were supposed to be here at eight and eight-thirty respectively but they arrived within ten minutes of each other. This lot came through towards the viewing room before they were told and the other lot were still here. That's when the barney erupted." The young cop looked flustered by what had transpired.

"Fuck me. Ah've goat a family next door who have had a real tragedy, an innocent wummin murdered and this fuckin' scum cannae even behave themselves in a mortuary. Arrest the lot o' them, throw away the fuckin' key. If ye need backup, call it in."

There were shouts from both sides but all were rounded up and placed in two separate police cars to be taken to Govan station where they would be charged.

When the area was cleared, Alex noticed that there was blood on the floor from the nose of one of the younger men. She went back to the waiting room and asked the mortuary attendant to come outside. She discreetly asked that someone clean up the mess before the two brothers were taken through to see the body.

Alex went back into the waiting room while her superintendent took a brief walk outside the building as he tried to calm himself.

"I can only apologise for the wait and the disturbance, I know it's the last thing you need right now," Alex said to the shocked pair.

"How can they behave like that in a place like this?" Paul Fletcher asked sadly.

"They're incapable of any emotion other than anger, it's the way they live their lives. They'll blame each other, they'll blame us, but they won't take responsibility for the fact that two men went out carrying knives, looking for trouble and that they are dead because of it."

"They sicken me," Paul replied with resignation.

"Most people would agree."

Russell returned, the flush of anger still visible on his face. "They're ready for us now, Mr Fletcher."

Paul had to help his brother stand and aided him to walk through to the now quiet viewing room. The younger man's hands were trembling and his legs seemed to be too weak to keep him upright.

There was a line of chairs against one wall and Russell invited the two men to sit.

"The curtain will open and you will be able to see the deceased through this window. I know how difficult this will be. There has been some damage done to the face that will disturb you, so if you don't feel up to it or you would prefer your brother to do it on your behalf, please tell us now."

Paul turned to his brother, "It's OK Derek if you don't feel up to it."

"No, I need to do this for Aileen's sake."

They stood up and Russell gently knocked on the door between the viewing room and the room where the body was laid out.

The curtain was drawn and the woman's body was revealed. The lighting had been arranged to highlight her face, protecting the viewer from some of the horror of what had been done to her body.

Derek Fletcher stepped forward and said very quietly, "It's her. It's Aileen. Why are her eyes open?"

Before either of the detectives could respond he suddenly said, "Oh God, her eyes. Someone's cut her eyes, her beautiful eyes." It was too much for him. The power went completely from his legs and his brother had to catch him before he fell.

"Oh Paul, they cut her eyes." His brother held him tightly as he wept copiously. Alex stood and let her own tears trickle down her face as she watched the wretched man's anguish pour into the arms of his brother.

She looked at her boss who also seemed to have been

diminished, a strong man reduced to a shell by the worst that he had ever encountered or would ever encounter. He nodded to the mortuary attendant, who closed the curtains.

After ten minutes, Paul Fletcher managed to get his brother to his feet and they walked back through to the waiting room. Alex spoke to the mortuary attendant who organised some sweet tea for the two men.

Derek Fletcher was persuaded to sip it and slowly he began to regain some composure.

"Why did he do that to her eyes?"

"We don't know yet," Alex replied.

"Is it the same killer, the one that's been in the newspapers?"

"It's a distinct possibility."

"Did he do that to the other victims?"

"I'm sorry, Mr Fletcher but we can't reveal those kind of details."

"I understand. What happens now?"

"We will conduct a post-mortem on your wife to establish the cause of death."

"Then will I be able to organise the funeral."

"I'm afraid not. We are obliged to allow any defence team the opportunity to conduct their own post-mortem, so we will have to retain her body for a period of time."

"Oh. I didn't realise that. There's a lot of pain in this process for the victims, isn't there?" he observed.

Alex had to agree, "Yes, I'm very sorry there is.'

He fell silent again, retreating into himself once more. When they had finished the tea, the two detectives drove the men to Derek and Aileen Fletcher's home; a home that would never be the same for anyone who entered. Alex told them that a liaison officer would be in touch and Paul promised to look after his brother. The police officers left the family to begin the grieving process in earnest.

"How are we going to catch this bastard, Alex?"

"Good police work, sir. It's all we've got."

"Do you think we need help?"

"Maybe. But who do you think could help?"

"A profiler, maybe?"

"You know they are only able to give a generic profile of a suspect, it isn't going to lead us right to his door." Alex felt she had to play devil's advocate, as she was convinced that Russell didn't want anyone else involved but was vocalising his own doubts in the hope she would dismiss them.

"Aye, I know. It's just that he's a slippery bastard, clever. Give me the dumb fucks anytime." his faced formed into a slight smile.

At that moment, Russell's phone rang. Alex didn't need to be prompted, she picked it up from the centre console of the car and said, "Superintendent Russell's phone, DI Menzies speaking."

"Shite. Eh… it's Paddy Niven. Tell Mr Russell, number one in the 2:15 at Kempton."

Alex was about to reply when the call ended abruptly.

"Who was that?"

"Paddy Niven. He said something about number one in the 2:15 at Kempton?"

"Good. That means he's got something definite for me and I've to meet him in the bookies in Dundas Lane at quarter past two."

"How do you know it's something definite?"

"Number one is a definite lead, number two is some basic information or a rumour. Kempton is the code for the bookies in Dundas Lane and the time is obvious."

"It's certainly elaborate."

"I told you, he's paranoid. I think he's watched too many spy films."

"Maybe it's the break we're looking for."

"I hope so, Alex. I certainly hope so."

CHAPTER 13

By the time the pair arrived back at the station, the office was a hive of fevered activity. The uniformed officers were all on the phone, as was Stephanie Anderson. Carrick and Johnstone were like eager puppies when the two senior detectives walked into the room.

"Sir, we think we've got something on the van," Johnstone said. His words ran together due to his almost childish excitement.

The older DC looked a little peeved that Johnstone had beaten him to the punch. "We think we know the origin of the van," he added.

"How?" Russell and Alex were both suddenly lifted from the gloom that had descended on them over the course of the morning and had asked the question simultaneously.

"We did some work on the images we got from the CCTV on the computer. I noticed the there was something close to the back of the van, a section where the paint looked different. See?" Carrick showed them an image of the van, an isometric view that showed both the front and the side of the van from a camera somewhere above it.

Alex could see that the reflection of the streetlights looked different at a small patch of the van; there was an area where the reflection was more distinct.

"We used the image software and changed the angle."

Another picture appeared on the screen, a close-up of the section that had been skewed to show the side as if the camera was facing it.

"We enhanced the contrast and this is what we got," Carrick was like a proud child showing off to his parents.

The superintendent had glazed over as the process was described but he perked up when they showed him the final picture.

The next photograph revealed the same image but the settings had been adjusted to increase the difference between light and shade. It showed the faint outline of the old logo for the NHS, it was the area that had been covered by a decal, preserving the paintwork underneath from the vagaries of the working life that the rest of the paintwork on the van had suffered. The two constables had indeed found the origin of the van.

"Well done, lads. Brilliant." Russell's praise was genuine and heartfelt.

"Another medical connection," Alex observed.

"Let's see if we can find out how many of these vans have been sold in the last year and who to," Russell instructed.

"I have already started that search but there aren't too many administrative staff on duty on a Sunday, so it is proving difficult," Stephanie Anderson said as she finished her phone call.

"Keep at it, we might find somebody." Not even the lack of any respect from Anderson was going to affect the burst of positive energy Russell now felt. The news from Paddy Niven and the discovery in the pictures was enough to make him believe that they were finally on the road to finding the killer and getting some justice for the victims and the bereaved.

His mood was so positive that he arranged to buy everyone a brunch from a local café that opened on a Sunday. Various rolls with sausage, egg, bacon, potato scone and one tuna salad - for Stephanie Anderson, who refused to consider fried food - were delivered to the station. A large pot of strong tea and cups of coffee were made and Russell got the team to take a break from their various tasks. He encouraged them to enjoy their food; Carrick took him literally and helped himself to three of the crisp, Scottish morning rolls with their unhealthy but very tasty contents. Anderson sat away from the main group. Russell was glad that he would be rid of her when the case came to an end.

Alex finished her bacon roll, and then she moved to the side as she called the Royal Infirmary to check up on their boss.

She called the ward and nurse with a bubbly voice answered.

"Hi, I was wondering if you could tell me how Mr Blair is?"

"I'm sorry, Mr Blair is gone."

"What?" Alex asked, her voice laced with shock.

"He was discharged this morning."

"Oh, thank goodness, I thought for a minute you meant something else. Is he OK?"

"False alarm, thankfully. His heart is fine and the doctors think he may have caught some form of virus."

"That's fantastic, thank you." She completed the call and turned to her colleagues. "More good news, the boss is fine. Docs think it was just a virus."

There was a small cheer from nearly everyone, even Anderson. Carrick made a half-hearted attempt to look pleased but he knew that the chief super wasn't his biggest fan. Russell on the other hand looked almost exultant; the terrible morning had improved little by little.

Russell's mobile rang. The others watched as he nodded agreement and muttered positive responses.

"That was Doc MacNeil. The PM is scheduled for one o'clock. I've got to meet my pal Niven, Alex, can you and Rick attend please?"

"Yes, sir," they both replied.

A look at her watch told Alex that they would have to get going within the hour.

Russell called the team together to run over the details of the third victim of the Soulseeker. The photographs were equally bleak as the team realised how little they told them about the killer and how much extra work still needed to be done to catch him and prevent him adding to his grisly tally.

The majority of the team spent the remainder of the hour talking to some of the people who had attended the same meeting as Graeme Mathieson and Theresa Asher. Every call proved fruitless, as the witnesses had failed to see anything that would indicate anyone had taken a special interest in either victim. The checks had produced nothing more serious than speeding fines on any of the attendees and in the wake of the third murder, the calls were made more out of procedure than with any belief that they would produce concrete results. Russell told them to begin looking into the movements of Aileen Fletcher.

The time came for Alex and Rick to go back to the mortuary and as they walked out the door, Russell asked to be informed immediately of anything significant. They confirmed that they would ring him and set off.

The trip and the procedure were already familiar to Alex. It was obvious to her that this was a process that would become increasingly common over the next few weeks and months. There would be stabbings, strangulations, murder by blunt instrument, road traffic injuries and occasionally gunshot wounds but the day the chase for a killer became routine and something to dismiss as just another part of the job, she vowed to herself, would be the day she quit.

The two detectives were guided to the same room as Alex had been in for the previous post-mortem. Doctor MacNeil was there once again, looking exhausted from a week of early starts and seemingly endless bodies to be investigated. A sour-faced Aberdonian called Matthew Hogan had joined Eilidh MacNeil in the room; he grunted a surly greeting at the two detectives. Hogan's reputation as a thoroughly sombre and unlikeable character had reached Alex's ears long before this first encounter. The joke among most of the CID squads across the city was that Hogan had been made to become a pathologist to prevent his living patients from dying of depression.

Alex watched the same formal routine play out with professional detachment as the pathologists and technician performed their tasks. As the senior officer, she took the lead and asked the odd question but much of what was discovered was similar to the previous victims. There was no obvious sign of a cause of death and chemical analysis would be the key to revealing the murderer's method. The pathologist repeated her belief that Aileen Fletcher's eyelids had been carefully removed with a scalpel or a similarly sharp instrument. She stated that due to the haemorrhaging, she believed that Aileen Fletcher was alive when her eyelids had been sliced off.

Alex and Rick Johnstone both shuddered when they heard the doctor's analysis.

The doctor worked carefully to ease the decorated cross from the heat-contracted palm of the victim. She showed it to the two detectives before registering it as evidence.

There was little else of note until Doctor MacNeil focused on the womb of the victim. She removed it and Alex could see her measuring something within. There was a moment's silence before the pathologist uttered the awful phrase. "The victim's uterus shows signs of an embryo consistent with a child of approximately ten weeks' gestation."

"She was pregnant," Alex said with a sigh that was filled with dismayed disbelief.

"Yes, I take it you didn't know that." The doctor's

professional detachment was put on hold as she absorbed the tragic truth.

"Neither she nor her husband knew. Their doctors had told them she was incapable of having children," Alex said just above a whisper. She turned away from the screen for a moment's quiet reflection as the procedure paused. She could see Rick Johnstone's doleful face, as his thoughts drifted to home and his own family.

Doctor MacNeil continued the PM. Her bearing told its own story of the cost that events like this could take, even on a medical professional that would see the worst that fate and violence could throw at human beings in the course of her career.

When the PM was complete, the evidence was collated before being dispatched for further analysis or storage for the criminal proceedings.

Before they began the drive back to the city centre, Alex called Russell.

"Fuck, fuck, fuck," was the angry response when she told him about the baby.

"Alex, I know it's shit but could you go and tell Mr Fletcher? I don't want this left to family liaison."

"Yes, of course."

"I'm sorry to do this to you, Alex but we need to let him know."

"I know."

"I'll see you later."

"Bye."

Russell received some strange looks from the shoppers

in Buchanan Street as he walked towards the bookmakers in Dundas Lane. His expletives had filled the air of the relatively quiet street and he could see some people diverting away from the idiot screaming swear words into his phone. He couldn't blame them.

He arrived at the brightly lit betting shop, a very different experience to the bookies of his youth. When he was a rookie cop, he would be a frequent visitor to his local betting shop to have a punt on a horse or to do his football coupon on a Saturday. Back then, the shops were dingy, almost seedy, with little natural light and always filled with a heavy pall of cigarette smoke. They would be rank with the smell of working men; sweat, cheap aftershave, tobacco and alcohol. Now they are hospitable sanctuaries with coffee machines, comfortable seating and 'puggies' that allow you to lose money with even less effort on your part. The other big difference is the range of bets you can make and Russell was glad he had put his fondness for a flutter behind him; he may well have been an addict if he was still a regular patron in the church of random chance.

He could see Paddy Niven standing against a wall, studying the horse-racing pages of a newspaper that were pinned to a board above him. The meetings were always the same; Niven would ignore the detective completely and Russell was not allowed to acknowledge his informant. Niven wrote down a bet and then left another little scrap of paper when he moved away to make his bet. Niven believed that anyone watching him would think he was leaving a horseracing tip rather than information that might lead to the apprehension of a criminal. Russell on the other hand thought his informant was a little mad but played along as he was a good source of what was happening among Glasgow's criminal classes.

He allowed Niven to complete the pantomime and leave the shop clutching his hopes for the afternoon's betting in his hand.

Russell didn't look at the little sliver of paper that might have a vital clue until he completed the final part of the routine that Niven insisted upon. He had a quick look at the race card, where he spotted a horse called 'An Inspector Calls'. He regarded it as decent omen and bet £5 each way on the 6-1 shot.

Outside the bookies he retrieved the paper from his pocket. Scrawled in an untidy, almost childish hand was an address and a brief message.

Perkins Motir Accessories, Osborne Street. Lisens plates.

Osborne Street was in area that Russell was all too familiar with. Close to the High Court, it was filled with small businesses that somehow survived against the odds, each with a niche that was big enough to sustain them. Some may have been money-laundering operations but that was of little concern to a detective on the trail of a serial killer. The only exceptions to the struggles of modern business were the defence lawyers, whose premises were dotted around the court. Somehow they always seemed to have the odds on their side; at least that was how it appeared from Russell's perspective.

"William, can I speak to DS Anderson, please?" Russell said into his mobile as he walked back up Buchanan

Street.

There was a brief pause before Anderson's superior tone could be heard, "Sir?"

"Meet me in the car park in ten minutes, we're going on a trip."

Anderson agreed with little enthusiasm; she didn't even ask where they were going.

"Snooty cow," Russell muttered when the call was complete. She was a pain in the arse and someone who didn't seem to understand the need for teamwork. He hoped that he wouldn't come across her too often in the future.

He strode back up to the station with a renewed sense of purpose; things were beginning to move.

CHAPTER 14

The trip to the car accessories shop was conducted in stern silence. Anderson didn't seem capable of small talk and Russell couldn't be bothered trying to engage the DS in conversation; he doubted she would have anything interesting to say anyway.

The shop was an expansive space that was absolutely packed with anything that anyone could possibly need to customise his or her car. There were huge exhaust pipes to make a Fiesta roar like a Ferrari; body parts to add muscle to a Micra and shiny chrome wheels to add some razzle dazzle to a Reliant Robin. There were even some furry dice to hang from a rear view mirror. Russell thought of proposing a sticker for his windscreen that would read 'Tom and Steph' but he decided against it; his temporary colleague was unlikely to see the funny side.

"Cin ah help yous?" a hirsute man asked from behind the counter. He had long thick black hair that merged into an equally thick beard, neither of which looked very clean. His bare arms were covered in elaborate tattoos and ended in brawny hands that looked stained by engine oil. Around his neck he wore a series of thick gold chains.

Russell flashed his warrant card. "Detective Superintendent Russell and this is Detective Sergeant Anderson."

"Aw fuck, whit've we done wrang noo?"

"We need your help. We don't care what interesting dodges you might get up to. We're from CID and this is about trying to catch a killer."

"A killer? What the fuck?" He was a man who was used to dealing with the police but obviously never in connection with a murder. The colour drained from his face, washing out his features and leaving a vivid contrast between his pallor and coal-black hair, all of which combined to make him look like the subject of a Victorian photograph.

"We believe you sold a series of licence plates recently."

"Ah sell hunners o' plates aw the time."

Anderson suddenly interrupted, "I think you know which plates the detective superintendent is referring to. Don't be obtuse."

"Ob… whit?" He looked even more flustered.

"What the detective sergeant is trying to say is that we believe you had a customer who bought a large number of different plates, probably within the last month or so."

The shop owner gave a brief show of trying to remember before he said, "Aye, there wis a guy bought ten different sets a few weeks back but ah get dealers needing new plates aw the time, ah didnae know he wis a fuckin' murderer, honest," he said, unnerved.

"We're not saying you did but if you can give us a description or tell us what plates he bought it would be a big help."

"He wis like an ordinary bloke. He wore a baseball cap wi' a Scotland flag oan it. It wis pulled doon quite low o'er his face but fae whit ah could see he wis about late-thirties maybe early-forties, brown eyes ah think. It's hard, man, it wis a while ago."

"That's great, Mr…"

"McCulloch. Jimmy McCulloch."

"Do you remember the plates he ordered, Mr McCull-och?"

"Ah'll hiv it in ma book. Gie's a minute."

The police officers waited patiently while McCulloch retrieved a large ledger from below the counter. He flicked the pages and scanned each column of information. He found what he was looking for and exclaimed, "Got it."

He wrote the details on to a sticky note and handed it to Russell.

"Did he leave a name?"

"Jist, Mr Smith. He ordered them wan day and came back the next tae pick them up. Paid by cash as well."

"That's fine, Mr McCulloch, thanks for your help."

"Ah didnae know anythin' aboot him bein' a killer. Ah widnae have helped him if ah realised, honest."

"We know, thanks again."

They were a few steps from the door of the shop when Russell turned to Anderson and said, "Did you learn fuck all about building rapport with a witness when you were at Tulliallan?"

"I'm sorry?"

"What the fuck was that? Obtuse? Jesus Christ."

"He knew exactly what you were asking him but chose

to pretend ignorance."

"We had just told him that we were investigating a murder; a guy whose worst crime will be helping to ring a car. Co-operation doesn't come easy to these guys anyway but the thought of murder is bound to put the shiters up a petty criminal like him. We're lucky he didn't clam up and tell us nothing."

"I don't see that there is any cause to swear," she bristled into a defensive posture.

"D'ye know what really scares me? It's that emotionally deficient fuckwits like you will be running the force within ten years. Clutching your investigation manual in one hand and a calculator in the other. God help us all." He walked in silence back to the car making no attempt to hide his disgust.

Anderson for her part was unperturbed as she didn't even understand why Russell was so upset. He's just a Luddite, she thought, a dinosaur that thinks policing is about gut instinct rather than proper procedure.

When she arrived home, Alex kicked off her shoes and dumped her bag in the hall. The day had been one of the worst she had ever experienced on the job and after the trauma of the crime scene, the identification of the body and the PM, the visit to Derek Fletcher had capped it in the worst way possible.

Rick Johnstone had accompanied her on her miserable mission and she was glad of his support. Paul Fletcher had shown them into a bright, modern living room where his brother was waiting. There was a brief moment of hope that the killer had been found when he saw the visitors but Alex sat him down and took a wrecking ball to those hopes. She felt that every word she uttered was destroying another piece of the already brittle man sitting beside her. The news that he had lost not only his wife but their child seemed to be too much for the shattered man to take. The four people sat in that room and it seemed to close in on them, turning it into the deepest subterranean cavern where not a beam of light could reach. They sat in silence for around half an hour before the detectives left the family members, who were now gathering to comfort the distraught husband.

They had returned to Stewart Street and the last hour of the day was filled with paperwork but the atmosphere in the office had once again begun to flag as the news of the pregnancy had permeated their thoughts.

Russell and Anderson arrived back with the details of the ten registration plates they had received from the car shop. It was a rare piece of concrete evidence that might help but it couldn't alleviate the simmering anger and devastating despair that had descended on the team.

The working day had ended with the details of the plates being disseminated across the Strathclyde force with orders to report any sighting. Anyone spotting the van was to monitor it but under no circumstances were officers to challenge the driver until they had back-up.

Alex was glad to leave the job behind for a few hours and although the flat still seemed quiet without Andrew, her problems had been sharply brought into focus by the events of the day. Andrew had left a pleading - and by the sound of it drunken - message on her home voicemail. She listened to it but the only feeling it aroused was contempt. The sense of betrayal was too deep and there was no reconciliation possible with him after what he had done. She deleted it.

She cooked herself a quick meal with little real interest in what she was eating; after the day she had endured everything tasted a little sour.

A long soak in a bath seemed like a good way to ease some of the tightness that had built up due to the job and the change in her situation. The water was noisily gushing into the tub when she heard her mobile ring. For a moment she considered ignoring it but in the end professionalism won out and she turned off the water, walked to the living room and found the phone. The display told her it was Craig Campbell, her erstwhile lover who remained a good friend. The temptation to ignore it was strong but she tapped the answer button.

"Hi Craig," she said wearily.

"Hi Alex, you sound knackered."

"I am and if you're looking for any favours, I'm afraid it will need to wait."

"No, not at all, I was just wondering how the new job is going."

"Pretty crappy to be honest. I've got three murders within a week and we think they have all been committed by the one person."

"The fires?"

"Yip. So I've definitely had better weeks."

"That's tough. How's Andrew?"

"That's the other part of my week which hasn't gone too well."

She proceeded to tell him all that had happened. She tried to hold on to the anger but by the end of it the emotional weight became too much.

"I'm sorry, Alex. I thought the two of you were good together," he sympathised.

"So did I." The statement was enough for the tears to fall once more. She took a moment to compose herself before telling him how she had dealt with Andrew in the immediate aftermath of the discovery.

"You twisted his gonads?" Craig laughed.

"It was the least I could do," she responded as the memory brought a smile to her face. It was one she would have to hold on to, that simple and painful act of revenge.

"Look, if there's anything I or Carol can do, let us know."

"Thanks, Craig but I'll work through it myself, eventually. However, there is one thing you might be able to help with. It's work related."

"Anything, I owe you plenty."

"We've got a set of registration numbers we believe were purchased by the killer. I'll send you the list and if you see a white Luton van with any of these numbers can you give me a bell right away?"

"Of course. Is there anywhere in particular to look?"

"The north of the city seems to be his territory but you don't need to go out of your way."

"Alex, it's the least I can do, particularly if it helps you catch this guy."

"Cheers, Craig."

"And if you need to talk to someone, you know where we are."

They exchanged farewells and Alex thanked her friend

once again.

She luxuriated in the welcoming warmth of the bath; the scent of the herbal bubbles helped to ease her fatigue and to quiet her mind.

She went to bed hoping that there would be no early morning call to say that the killer had struck again. Tomorrow had to be a better day, surely.

CHAPTER 15

When she arrived at the Stewart Street incident room the following morning, Russell was once again in situ at his desk. She wondered if he ever went home. It took a single look to know that he was in a furious mood and hopes of a better day began to dissipate quickly.

"Have you seen this?" he said, brandishing a morning newspaper.

'SOULSEEKER CLAIMS THIRD VICTIM,' the headline screamed. Alex took the paper and scanned the story. It was full of dramatic prose about the serial killer and his motivation but little in the way of concrete facts.

"Damn, how did they find out?" she asked as she handed it back.

"Apparently, when his little message to Walker didn't provoke the desired response he sent the fucking thing to every paper in the country. We're going to have every arse wipe in the world phoning us to claim that they're the killer and we're going to be wading in shite for days." He slammed the paper on to the desk.

"Why would he do this?"

"Maybe he wants his fifteen minutes, maybe his mother didn't fucking breast feed him, how the fuck should I know?"

"We need to try and rationalise this, sir."

"We'll talk when the rest get in. Sorry Alex, but this guy is getting on my fucking wick."

Alex wondered if Tom Russell was the next one who would be rushed to hospital with a suspected heart attack if this case continued much longer.

The team assembled over the next half hour, each ready to start the new day with the hope that they would be closer to catching the 'Soulseeker' and ending the fear that would now be gripping the city.

Russell assembled the team in front of the incident board that now featured an additional collection of macabre photographs to add to those of the first two victims. He was about to start the briefing when the office door swung open and a large, middle-aged man in full police uniform walked in carrying a briefcase. The braid on his hat and the line of medal ribbons told them that it was a senior officer, one who obviously rejoiced in his superiority.

"Chief Superintendent Logan. You must be Superintendent Russell," he said as he thrust a well-manicured hand at his subordinate.

"Yes, sir. How can we help you?"

"I'll be looking after you until Chief Superintendent Blair is on his feet. You were about to address the troops, don't let me stop you." His attitude seemed to indicate that he thought he was an army general rather than a copper who had brown-nosed his way to a position of middle management.

Russell ran through the latest information on the third victim - Marsha Collins was visibly upset when he repeated the fact that Mrs Fletcher had been pregnant. He detailed the news of the licence plates and the hope that it may give them their first big break.

He was about to continue with the allocation of the work for the day when Logan interrupted him. "How many resources do we have committed to this operation?"

"Not enough," was Russell's succinct reply.

"Well, we have to be careful. We can't afford too many people all running off in different directions. Too many cooks… etcetera."

"Bollocks!"

Everyone turned to see the formidable figure of Chief Superintendent Blair walk in to the office with the stride of a man who was re-staking his claim to his territory.

"Sir, what are you doing here?" Russell uttered the question on behalf of the shocked team.

"I'm fine, Tom. Just some wee virus and it'll take more than that to stop me catching this bastard - sorry Marsha. Now, as I was saying, you're talking bollocks, Jack. We need as many resources as we can get, it's a fucking serial killer - sorry Marsha - not somebody dipping the till at the local supermarket. Now you can go back to HQ and play with your spreadsheets and leave us to do the real police work. Go pick what colour of Jag you fancy in the reorganisation and then make another 100 real coppers redundant. It's what you live for, isn't it?"

"Well, there's no need for that attitude, Fraser."

"Jack, fuck off - sorry Marsha - and gie's peace, please," the final word was delivered with a sarcastic smile.

"I'll be reporting this. That's a disgraceful way to speak to a colleague." Logan stormed out and a universal grin spread around the team.

"Tosser, thinks a uniform and a few medals makes him a polis."

"Are you sure you're OK, sir?"

"Never better now that I'm back here. I've got a lot of livin' to do and you can't do that from a sick bed." The Elvis reference brought further broad smiles; the boss was back. Marsha Collins was so pleased that she stepped forward and gave him an all-enveloping hug.

"Enough of that now Marsha, a man in my condition can only take so much excitement. Tell me where we are with the case, Tom," he said as his focus turned to business.

For the second time that morning Russell ran through the progress that had been made and the new problems they faced.

"I'll leave it to you to allocate the tasks for the day but folks, we need to bring this one to an end soon. Work hard and bring this bastard in - sorry Marsha - before he inflicts any more pain. Meanwhile, I'm sure to get an entertaining call from the ACC when Logan tells him what a bad boy I am." It was obvious that he wasn't too worried about what he might have to face when his superior called. He headed to his own office as Russell resumed the discussion.

"Alex, you had some thoughts about the publicity?"

"I think it's worth considering; this sudden desire for coverage in the media, I mean. He has gone out of his way to be careful in terms of the forensics, the false licence plates and the handling of the bodies. Why would he suddenly want to go public about what he's doing and why he's doing it?"

Stephanie Anderson spoke before any of the others could react. "At some point serial killers want their crimes to be acknowledged, they thrive on the notoriety. By announcing himself to the world he begins to be famous."

"I'm not sure. If you listen to that message, he doesn't sound like a man who is enjoying the crime. He only sees it as a means to an end. There's a pain there that is driving him on and he wants someone to put an end to it. Is he reaching out to the public in the hope that someone will supply the answer? Is he hoping that some religious leader or spiritualist will give him the proof he needs?"

"Christ, Menzies, you sound sorry for him. He's a prick that gets his kicks out of killing innocent folk and now he wants everyone to know what an arsehole he really is. Soulseeker, fanny," Carrick sneered as the cracks in the team were emphasised by the professional frustration that they were all feeling.

"Rick?" Russell was keeping his thoughts to himself but was keen to know what everyone else felt.

"I can see what Alex is saying. In the message there is a feeling that he wants it to stop but that he can't until he sees his idea of a soul ascending. But I do think that on some level he feels that he has to be recognised for his crimes."

"Does anybody think it really matters? We need to

catch him and his need for publicity is an irrelevance," Russell said.

"If we can understand something about his motivation maybe it helps us narrow down the kind of person he is." Alex was defending her corner but she knew that profiling would only help up to a point.

"What kind of person is he, based on what we know?"

"He's an organised killer, methodical. He's probably a professional person from a medical background or with medical training. He has had some kind of trauma that has flicked a switch in his head and now this pursuit of the soul has become an all-encompassing, overwhelming obsession. He has probably lost a child, a parent, a partner or a sibling and that's what has changed his behaviour. He was probably raised in a religious environment where heaven and hell were a part of his daily life and that's what is driving him now."

"It doesn't narrow it down much does it?"

"No, but we're learning more all the time."

"How does any of that crap justify what he's done?" Carrick was both dismissive and angry at the opinions Alex held.

"It doesn't justify it to any reasonable-thinking person but he's not a reasonable-thinking person. He's deeply disturbed and has a distorted view of the world that, at the moment we can't understand that view."

"I know what you're saying, Alex, but we need to use the physical evidence we have and try to piece it together from that." Russell held on to the kind of policing he had conducted his whole career; the rationale of a serial killer had never been something he had ever needed to consider and he didn't want to start now.

"Yes, sir." She fell silent, knowing that her boss was right. Solid police work was only effective when they had concrete leads to pursue; anything else was only slightly better than a guess.

Russell ran through the various assignments for the morning. He took a twisted pleasure in assigning Carrick and Anderson to go to the gym that Aileen Fletcher attended to see if anyone noticed anything or if the security cameras had captured the killer. The two detectives deserved each other. The uniformed team and Rick Johnstone were assigned the task of tracing the medical connections for the victims. There was a strong feeling that there had to be a link, particularly as all three victims had been treated for depression.

Russell wanted Alex to help him study the geography of the murders to see if they could pinpoint somewhere that might be used as the killing zone. They had just rolled out the map of the city when Russell's phone rang.

"CID, Superintendent Russell speaking."

"Mr Russell, it's Charlie Walker."

"Charlie, I'm not saying anything about that bloody tape."

"That's not why I'm calling. He sent me another one, a different one."

"What?"

"It arrived in my inbox this morning."

"Can you send it to me?"

"I will but I've got to go to print with this. The editor's doing his nut because we missed an exclusive with the previous one. I've got no option." He sounded genuinely apologetic.

"I understand, Charlie, the genie's out of the bottle. But you know that every word you print makes our job more difficult."

"I know, but you don't pay my wages."

"Fine, but your paper will be briefed at the same time as everyone else when we eventually bring this guy in." Russell knew that Charlie had a job to do but it was still exasperating that something as important as the capture of this menacing killer was secondary to circulation figures. He felt there was little he could do as the Leveson inquiry had highlighted relationships between the press and the police that were corrupt and it had left a stain on the character of the force. He couldn't apply pressure to the editor of Walker's paper without the possibility of further damaging the reputation of the police. Every member of the newspaper industry would pounce upon claims of censorship and they would use it to help prevent the reforms that very industry needed.

"I'll send it over."

"OK. Thanks."

When the call was over, Russell briefed the team on what Walker had told him. They waited patiently until the file appeared in Russell's computer.

The same metallic voice filled the silent room.

"I'm sorry. My quest must continue, as I still do not have my answer. There are people in this city whose lives are too horrible for them to tolerate; those are the people that I will help. They are the distraught and displaced, the forgotten and forlorn

and by helping them I will help to discover the truth I seek. When it is over, no one else needs fear, for I will end it and accept gladly the punishment that the Lord has reserved for me.

I am the Soulseeker and I search for the essence of humanity; the soul of man. I will not cease my quest until I find the truth."

"What the fuck does that mean?" Carrick asked through a mouthful of a bacon roll that he was demolishing with his usual greedy enthusiasm.

"He's going to commit suicide when he gets his answer," the matter-of-fact reply came from DS Anderson.

"And good riddance to him."

"What good is that if another fifteen people are going to die before he's ready to kill himself?" Alex asked with annoyance.

"Right, let's think about this," Russell interrupted before the simmering resentments could boil over.

"He's resigned himself to committing suicide," said Anderson. "There is nothing to hold him back now; the level of atrocity may increase and he may even change tactic to force the issue." She was once again detached from the emotion that should have accompanied her statement. Alex thought that the DS was as robotic as the killer's substitute voice.

"Do we need help?" Russell asked with resignation.

"What kind of help?" Rick Johnstone asked.

"A profiler or at least an officer from another force

who is experienced in dealing with this kind of crime."

"You're not giving up, sir?" the young DC asked cautiously.

"Am I fuck - sorry Marsha. I'm just beginning to think that we don't have the skills to find this kind of killer."

Despite his denial, Russell looked defeated. Every turn the case took, it seemed to go further away from what he understood, a little more foreign to what his training and experience had prepared him for.

Alex was disturbed at Russell's tone; most senior investigating officers hated to have 'experts' thrust upon them but Russell was advocating just that. She was about to argue her case when a shout came up from PC Bartram. "Sir, a van with one of the plates has been spotted by a patrol car."

It was like someone had applied a defibrillator to Russell as he jumped from his seat. "Where?"

"It's heading east on Great Western Road coming from Knightswood."

"Tell them to follow it but under no circumstance have they to approach."

"Yes, sir."

"Rick, call the armed response team and put them on standby. We need them to be ready to move at a moment's notice. Anderson, let the chief super know what is happening and co-ordinate the operation from this end. Alex, you're with me."

He grabbed his coat and they both rushed towards the front desk.

"Terry, have we got a spare radio car?"

"Yes, sir."

"Can I have the keys? We might have a lead on that killer and I need to connect with control."

"There's a grey Focus available," he said as he retrieved the keys, which were hanging in a box close to the desk.

"Cheers. Let my lot know I've got the radio."

The sergeant nodded as he watched Alex and Russell run to the car park.

The car was marked discreetly with Strathclyde Police decals over the gunmetal-coloured paintwork. As Russell started the engine, Alex was on the radio.

"Control, this is DI Alex Menzies, I'm travelling with Detective Superintendent Russell. I need to be patched through to the patrol car following a white Luton van on Great Western Road, over."

There was a brief pause before the female controller said, "This is control, ma'am. Car Alpha Papa Six is monitoring that vehicle, over."

"Understood, thanks. Alpha Papa Six, this is DI Menzies, over."

"This is Alpha Papa Six, PC Neil Murphy speaking."

"What's the current status, PC Murphy?"

"We're still following the van on Great Western Road. We've just passed Gartnavel hospital."

"Understood, we're on our way. Keep us updated."

Russell drove as fast as he could, occasionally giving a blast of the horn to slow moving cars. He had decided against switching on the lights and the siren as he did not want the suspect to realise they were in pursuit.

"DI Menzies, this is PC Murphy. The suspect has turned into Queen Margaret Drive."

"Understood." The two detectives were crossing the

River Kelvin on Great Western Road as the message arrived. They were now not far from the Queen Margaret Drive junction.

"Suspect has turned into Kelvin Drive and has stopped. We have driven past and parked about fifty yards away."

"Understood." Alex then relayed the information to both her colleague and the controller, whom she asked to dispatch the armed response unit to the scene.

Russell waited impatiently to turn into Queen Margaret Drive and when the traffic allowed he swung the car sharply to the right. He drove speedily, crossing the Kelvin again before turning left into the street where the white van was parked. He drove past it and the marked car, which was sitting a little further up the street.

The two detectives walked back to where one of the constables was standing outside the car.

"Where is he?" Russell asked without preamble.

"He's gone into the house, sir," the young PC was eager to impress.

"Do you think he noticed you?"

"No, sir. He didn't seem suspicious when he exited the vehicle. He seemed intent on getting into the building as quickly as he could."

"Thank you, constable. You can go now, the ARU are on their way."

The young man's face fell. "We could wait until they arrive, sir. Just in case you need us," he said hopefully.

"No, thanks for your help and diligence. I'll be sending a letter to your commanding officer."

"Thank you, sir." The officer took the hint and left with his partner.

The armed response unit were based in Baird Street station and within ten minutes their van had arrived. The well-drilled team of officers were quickly and quietly assembled outside the building, ready to move when the command was given. Tom Russell and Alex Menzies joined them and the team leader approached them.

"What have we got?" she asked in an unnecessary whisper.

"A single suspect, we've no idea how many others in the room. He is unlikely to be armed with a gun but you never know," Russell replied.

"Do you know which flat?"

"No, I'm afraid not."

"OK, we'll work it out."

She moved back to her squad and began giving commands. The team of armed officers moved towards the door of the building that the driver of the van had entered. There were four flats in the Georgian terraced house. One of the team pressed the button for the bottom right flat.

"Hello," a sleepy voice said.

"Post," the officer said.

The buzzer sounded and the team entered the door. They were about to check the flat they had buzzed when a woman's scream was heard from the flat on the opposite side of the hall. A battering ram was brought up rapidly and the force of the officers' swing brushed the door aside as if it was made of balsa wood. The team swarmed through the doorway and shouts of 'clear' were heard from a variety of rooms until there was a shout from one of the bedrooms.

"On the floor, hands behind your heads."

Alex and her superintendent joined the small throng of armed officers in the room. For the second time in a week, Alex found herself in a room with two naked people. A man in his early thirties was lying on the floor. On the opposite side of the bed a middle-aged woman was struggling to preserve her dignity while obeying the commands that were being shouted at her.

"Fuck, if this is aboot the VAT, I was gonnae pay it, honest," the man shouted through frightened tears.

The woman was screaming almost incomprehensibly about her husband and how she didn't want to die. Alex stepped forward. "I think the lady can get up now, don't you?" she asked the officer who was standing over the prostrate figure.

She gently lifted the terrified woman from the floor, covering her with a sheet as she stood.

"Are you hurt?" she asked kindly.

The woman looked at Alex as if she was crazy. "Why would I be hurt?"

"We heard you scream."

"Oh, that was something else," she replied as a flush of red raced up her face.

Alex felt almost as embarrassed for the poor woman as she was for everyone in the team.

"Get him back to the station," Russell said as he indicated the man who was now lying shivering with cold and fear.

Alex spent some time speaking to the woman but it was obvious that she knew little of the man's life other than their affair. She called for a liaison officer to come to speak to the woman and arrange for the replacement of her front door.

Russell had been pacing outside the living room while Alex consoled and interviewed the woman. When she was finished he said, "Come on, let's get back to the station and find out what this bastard knows."

Back at Stewart Street there had been many members of the team who wanted to get a look at the suspected killer. A small stream of people had wandered past the interview room or stuck their head in on some pretence but no one spoke to him until Superintendent Russell arrived.

When he arrived he strode into the interview room with Alex close on his heels. The man in the chair was a wreck, tears were still snaking down his face and he sniffed constantly as he tried to control the drips from his nose while his whole body shook violently.

"Name?" Russell asked.

"Frankie McCutcheon."

"So Mr McCutcheon, where did you get your van?"

"Ma van?"

"Aye, the van."

"Ah bought it aff Gumtree last year."

"Why did you buy it?"

"Removals, ah run ma ain removals business."

"So that's what you were doing today, removals?"

"Denise, ye mean? Look it's jist a bit o' harmless fun, know? Ah met her last month when ah moved her stuff fur her when she left her husband. She was up fur it, so ah thought better no look a gift horse in the mouth, even if the horse is a bit of an auld nag that's ran its best race, know whit ah mean?" He smiled faintly thorough the snot and tears. Alex made her disgust obvious.

"Where were you last Monday night?' Russell asked, his voice hard with determination.

"Monday. In the hoose probably."

"What about Wednesday?"

"Same probably. When ah'm finished, ah'm normally pretty knackered. Whit is it ah've supposed tae huv done?"

"We'll ask the fuckin' questions," Russell shouted and McCutcheon cowered back in his chair.

"How many times have you changed the registration plates on the van?"

"Whit? The van's no' nicked. Ah bought it fair 'n' square. Ah paid fur it."

"And you have the documentation to prove that?'

"Of course. It's in the office."

"Sir, can I have a quick word?" Alex said.

Russell walked out of the room without saying anything else to the puzzled and scared suspect.

"It's not him, is it?" Russell's question was rhetorical; he already knew the answer. The man they were holding just didn't feel right, he didn't fit the profile of a professional person or someone with the intelligence to carry out such well-planned crimes, not unless he was the greatest actor since Brando.

"What about the van?" Russell asked.

"Have we checked those registrations?"

"You think the murderer has used some that are real

vehicles?"

"A good chance."

"We'll go upstairs and get someone to check with the DVLA." Russell seemed enervated by the latest setback and the energy was draining away from him once again. Alex realised that he was a man whose emotions were always close to the surface; she would never have to work very hard to know what he was thinking.

It took just fifteen minutes to establish that Frankie McCutcheon's van was one of five genuine registration plates that the killer had ordered from the accessories store.

"Why didn't some bastard check this? Do you need to be told every fuckin' thing?" Russell roared his annoyance at a staff that quietly accepted the rebuke, too intimidated to offer any resistance. He stormed out, heading in the direction of the chief superintendent's office.

When he returned he ordered Alex to complete the formalities of letting the unfortunate McCutcheon go. An apology and some smoothing was needed, the senior officer didn't feel up to it. Alex did as she was ordered and McCutcheon seemed too relieved to think about suing for wrongful arrest but given time, it was something that may well creep into his head.

When she got back to the office, Carrick and Anderson arrived close behind, each looking as if they were ready to kill the other. The trip to the gym had been as unproductive as almost every other interview the team had conducted and once again the killer's care in all that he did was proving to be complete; he had constructed his crimes so carefully that they were the perfect barrier to the police making any progress.

Alex had no idea what it was going to take to get this case resolved.

JOURNAL

I remember my mother lying on that bed. She was still and apart from the lack of movement, she could have been sleeping. As time has passed, I doubt my recollection. Maybe she wasn't as peaceful as I remembered and there were signs that she had not crossed peacefully.

I told God's messenger what I had done. He understood that it was necessary, that to leave the poor woman to suffer any longer would have been truly cruel.

Now I am driven by only one thought; is she really at peace? There is only one way to prove it.

The philosophers lied. The eyes are not the windows to the soul. That woman died but gave me nothing. Even with her eyelids gone, there was no trace of the change I desired, the indication that the soul is real and bound for Heaven.

Where is the answer if not in the brain, the heart or the eyes? Maybe I am approaching this from the wrong direction. Could it be how you die that is the key to the visible soul? I think that if you die like one of the great martyrs, your soul will ascend like theirs did and you will sit at God's right hand. The great martyrs all had painful deaths and this pain might be the key. Up to this point I have protected them from the pain but it is time to try something different, something more dramatic. Then it will be obvious that there is more to life than flesh and blood; tangible proof that there is something beyond this mortal world.

Of all the great saints, the one I admire most is Joan Of Arc. She was truly chosen by God, a woman of unshakeable faith who died with great courage. God will have reached down to lift her soul from the flames and guided her to her rightful place by his side. That is the method I must use to free the next pained soul brought to me by the servant of the Lord. Her sacrifice will be worth it and she will join Jesus and the angels in heaven.

I am the Soulseeker and I search for the essence of humanity; the soul of man. I will not cease my quest until I find the truth.

Soulseeker

CHAPTER 16

Russell took the team into a conference room and encouraged them to review everything they had garnered so far; it was an effort to find that important detail that they had overlooked. They pored over the crime scene photographs, the tens of interviews that had been collected from witnesses, CCTV footage and the audio files that had been sent from the killer.

Late in the day as the individual detectives felt their energy levels were dipping, Tina Bartram appeared clutching a piece of paper.

"Sir, these are the three people we've found who may have some connection to all three victims. We've just listed the males, but there are also four women if you need them, sir."

Russell almost snatched the paper from her hand, as he muttered, "No, this'll be fine Thank you, constable. Great work."

Bartram took it as a dismissal and retreated.

The sheet of A4 paper had three names with a brief

description of their possible link to the victims.

Dr Mohammad Ahmed - Locum GP who has covered for the regular doctors at the health clinics attended by the three victims. No criminal record.

Marcus Scott - Representative of a drugs company who has been conducting trials of a new anti-depressant with three GPs at the various clinics. Arrested but not charged for his part in a bar fight.

Paul Lawrence - Community psychiatric nurse who serves all three clinics. Arrested in 1995 for assault. Given 300 days community service and a 1 year suspended jail term.

The list was passed around the detectives who each took time to absorb the information before it made its way back to Russell.

He initiated the discussion. "Thoughts?"

Stephanie Anderson was the first to respond, "I think we can rule out the GP."

"Why, because he's a doctor?" Carrick scoffed.

"No, because - judging by his name - he's a Muslim," Anderson replied.

Carrick looked a little sheepish and his antipathy to his colleague deepened. Alex almost felt sorry for Carrick who had once again reacted long before any thought process had started. Maybe there is no process where he's concerned, she thought.

"Either of the other two could have access to the

patient's records or even contact with them. Rick, what's wrong?" Alex asked as she noticed that the junior officer had suddenly gone very pale.

"I know the last guy. He was assigned to help Georgia with her post-natal depression."

Russell pounced on his comment. "What did you think of him?"

"I...I don't know. He didn't say much."

"Does he know you're a cop?"

"Not unless the doctor told him."

"We need to bring them both in for a conversation, I think. We'll play it a bit cooler than this morning's debacle. Alex, you and Rick, go get Mr Scott, Stephanie, you're with me. Mr Carrick, you can get a full background on our two main suspects."

In the main incident room, the addresses were retrieved for the two men and the detectives set out to begin what they hoped would be the final stage of the investigation.

Marcus Scott lived alone in a flat in Finnieston. Alex and Rick were walking up the stairs to his door just fifteen minutes after leaving the station. The journey had been spent with Alex reassuring Rick that she was sure Georgia was in no danger.

Scott opened the door wearing expensive casual clothes and a confident smile. He was in his early thirties with well-trimmed hair, trendy spectacles and skin that glowed more than was natural for any man. He looked every inch the successful, image-aware young professional.

His smile weakened slightly when Alex flashed her

warrant card and asked if she and her colleague could come in.

"Eh... sure, what's this about?"

"We would like you to accompany us to the station to answer a few questions."

"Can't you just ask them here?" he asked when they walked into the living room. It was a very masculine space dominated by a huge flat-screen TV that was surround by games consoles, media drives, a Sky TV box and a surround-sound system. To one side of the room there were shelves decorated with a number of action figures of characters from science fiction movies.

Scott saw Alex looking and said, "It's my inner geek."

She said nothing in reply but thought that it was his outer child that was responsible for the purchases.

His anxiety was plain to see as he asked, "Do I need a lawyer?"

"I don't think that will be necessary, it's just a few questions to help us with our enquiries."

"OK, give me a minute or two to get ready." He looked uncomfortable with the attention from the police officers as he walked back through into the hall.

"Keep an eye on him," Alex told Johnstone. Both officers walked into the hall and while Johnstone stood by Scott's bedroom door, Alex stuck her head into the other two rooms. There was a kitchen and a second bedroom, neither of which looked likely to be the primary crime scene.

Scott reappeared wearing a soft leather jacket and a pair of designer trainers. "Are you looking for something in particular?"

"No, just being nosy. It comes with the job," she replied calmly.

She noticed his hand shaking slightly as he locked his front door. Her instincts were telling her that Mr Scott wasn't all he appeared to be.

Paul Lawrence lived in Drumchapel, the sprawling estate of social housing that was built in the fifties as an escape from the crowded inner streets of Glasgow's slums. The lack of amenities soon turned it into an isolated ghetto where social problems spread like a particularly virulent cancer.

Lawrence's home was a semi-detached house in a respectable street that had been built as a part of the latest attempt at regeneration.

There was a young child's pink bicycle in the small well-maintained garden at the front. As Russell rang the bell, the shouts of excited children could be heard from somewhere in the house.

A plump woman who looked to be in her late twenties opened the door.

Both detectives had their warrant cards ready. "I'm Detective Superintendent Russell and this is Detective Sergeant Anderson. We'd like to speak to Paul Lawrence."

"Fuck, cin you lot no; gie him a breck?" She moved the door until it was almost closed and the two officers heard her bawl back into the house, "Paul, it's the fuckin' pigs."

"Delightful lady," Russell said quietly to Anderson.

They were left standing in the rain and a leaky gutter

meant that the DS had to take a step back to ensure she didn't have the water running down her back.

Lawrence appeared a few moments later and opened the door warily. He was in his mid-thirties but looked older due to a wispy attempt at a moustache that occupied his top lip. His hair was cut in a side parting, probably the style he had favoured since he was a small boy. He wore a blue checked shirt and dark blue jeans. His dark blue eyes were wary as he studied the police officers.

"Mr Lawrence?"

"Yes."

"We'd like you to come to the station to answer a few questions."

"What is it I'm supposed to have done?" his reply was filled with jaded resignation.

"We'd just like to ask you a few questions."

"Your lot are forever just wanting to ask a few questions. Drugs go missing, ask Lawrence a few questions, he's got previous. Fight in the local, ask Lawrence a few questions, he's got previous. What horrendous crime is it that I'm supposed to have committed this time?"

"We'd rather not discuss that here," was Russell's simple response.

"I've done nothing wrong," he protested weakly.

"As I say, a few questions and you can be on your way."

"Christ, I suppose so. Ella, phone the lawyer, tell him to meet me at…" He turned to Russell.

"Stewart Street."

"At Stewart Street station."

"Do you want your wife to come with you?"

"She's not my wife, she's my sister," he replied with

contempt at the idea he could be married to such a woman.

He stepped back inside briefly before he returned wearing a large anorak.

Russell's car steamed up as the air from the warm bodies condensed on the cool windows. He blasted the air through the vents and when the glass was clear, he pulled away to begin the journey back into the city. Lawrence sat with a grim look and said nothing, but there was no sign of any anxiety. Alex imagined that he had been questioned so often that the process was not in itself stressful for him.

When they arrived at the station he was put in an interview room across the corridor from where Marcus Scott had been placed on his arrival. A uniformed officer was assigned to keep an eye on him and the detectives went to the office to see what the background checks had revealed.

Carrick had been working diligently on his task and had compiled a report for each of the suspects.

Russell decided to give the DC a chance to shine and asked him to brief the team on what had been found. As Carrick stood in front of the incident board, he brushed away the detritus of his dinner from his shirt.

"Marcus Scott was born in Edinburgh in nineteen seventy-nine. He studied pharmacology at Edinburgh University for two years before he was thrown out after an incident in the Students' Union bar. The Lothian and Borders force interviewed him but charges were never brought due to a lack of evidence. He spent some time as a car salesman with one of the big outfits in Edinburgh before he moved to Glasgow to start his current job two years ago. He's never been married and lives alone.

"Paul Lawrence comes from Drumchapel. By all accounts he was a magnet for trouble in his youth. He was in front of the children's panel when he was thirteen for persistent vandalism and his early criminal career culminated in him brawling with another seventeen-year-old in a bar fight. He did three hundred days' community service but avoided further trouble and as a result has never seen the inside of a jail. During the community service he was helping some youngsters with learning difficulties and got interested in the brain and then psychology. He studied through college to get some school level qualifications before studying to be a nurse. He's worked as a community psychiatric nurse for just over a year. He was married but it didn't take and has been living with his sister for about six months."

"Well done, Constable. A good job in such a short time." Russell's praise was well received by the detective.

"What do you think?" Russell opened the debate to his colleagues.

"Any mention of any connection to organised religion?" Alex asked.

Carrick glanced at his notes. "Lawrence has done some fund-raising for his local church but that was all I could find. Nothing on Scott at all."

Anderson, as usual, was the first to offer an opinion. "Both have some medical knowledge, both have had police trouble in the past, both seem to be reformed characters and both will have access to the sedatives that have been used in the murders. If I had to choose one it would be Scott. He's a loner and that is what would make me think he was more likely."

"I'm not sure. There's something we're missing but I can't put my finger on it," Alex said thoughtfully.

"I just hope that it's not Lawrence," Rick Johnstone said. His thoughts were purely for his wife and the hope that she had not come into contact with a dangerous individual.

"We'll only know when we get some questions answered. So Alex and I will take Lawrence, Stephanie and Rick will deal with Mr Scott. Sergeant, I want you to take the lead but if you think you're getting somewhere, I want you to come and get me. Do you understand?"

"Sir," was all she said. Alex wondered if the chance to grab some personal glory might prove to be too much temptation for the ambitious woman to resist. She said nothing to Russell, she didn't feel it was her place and she didn't want to undermine the authority of her boss.

"William, keep up the good work and check what vehicles they own."

"OK." The effect of the praise had worn off when he realised that he wouldn't be involved in the questioning of the suspects.

"Right, let's bring this one home," Russell said forcefully. It was now seven in the evening and everyone looked tired. Russell hoped that he could get a bit more out of them before the day ended.

Soulseeker

Anderson and Johnstone were the first to leave, followed closely by the other two detectives. All four were hoping that they were on their way to ending the week of nightmares.

CHAPTER 17

Superintendent Russell and DI Menzies received a shock when they opened the interview room to find Mark Pirelli sitting in the chair beside their suspect. He was dressed in another suit that was immaculately tailored from fine cloth; a white silk shirt and red silk tie completed the image of the successful, well-paid lawyer that he was.

"Mr Pirelli, twice in the one week. We are honoured." Russell did well to cover his surprise with a healthy dose of scorn.

"Detective Superintendent, a pleasure as always," The lawyer replied with an equal measure of distaste in every word.

"The NHS must be paying better than we think, eh Alex?"

"Mr Lawrence was a friend of my late brother and is a friend of the family. I have been taking care of his affairs for some time now."

"Lucky boy. We'll start with a simple question, shall

we? Do you own a pale blue or light-coloured Corsa?"

Lawrence immediately looked to Pirelli and Alex noticed something in the exchange but wasn't sure what. Pirelli nodded.

"No."

"Do you have access to such a vehicle?"

"No."

Over in the other interview room, the response was different.

"Yes, an SRi as a matter of fact. Has it been stolen?" Scott asked anxiously.

"No, sir. We are simply trying to establish some facts. Tell us about your car," Anderson suggested. She remained incredibly still and spoke very quietly. Her behaviour seemed to be having an unsettling effect on the worried man.

"I get a Mondeo from work but the private mileage was costing me a fortune. I got the Corsa as a weekend runabout."

"Where is the car?"

"I keep it in a small lock-up not far from my flat."

Anderson held her poker faced expression but there was an internal leap of excitement at the possibility of finding the primary crime scene.

"What about a commercial vehicles?"

Scott looked puzzled. "Commercial vehicles? What, like a van?"

"Exactly like a van."

"No, why would I need a van?"

"I occasionally use a van if there are no cars available when I'm visiting agoraphobic or housebound patients," Lawrence answered the question after once again consulting with his lawyer.

"Where were you a week past Monday, around eleven o'clock?"

"You don't need to answer that," Pirelli interceded.

"I'm asking a simple question. If your client has nothing to hide why would he refuse to answer?"

"My client's private life is simply that, private. He has no need to answer a question like that unless you are accusing him of something in particular."

Alex had come across some smugly arrogant defence lawyers during her career but Pirelli was in the premier league of arseholes. Russell's fiery stare at the advocate indicated that he found him equally irritating.

-

Scott was more forthcoming when he was asked about his whereabouts.

"I was at home."

"Can anyone verify that?" Rick Johnstone asked and received an annoyed glance from the Detective Sergeant.

"No, I was alone." The forlorn way he said made it sound like solitude was quite a common situation for him.

"What about last Wednesday evening into Thursday morning?"

"Eh… At home again, no witnesses again, I'm afraid."

After the initial pause the words came rolling out too quickly for either officer to believe he was telling the truth.

Anderson sensed the lie and fired her next question, "Are you sure about that, Mr Scott?"

Scott looked petrified and Anderson pressed home her advantage, "Maybe the reason you are lying, Mr Scott, is because you were out killing a woman, then you set her on fire and left her to burn to ash." Her tone was suddenly louder and more aggressive in a way that even shocked Johnstone.

"No, no that wasn't it. Oh God, I'm sorry." He looked down into his lap where a damp patch was slowly spreading from his groin.

"What about Wednesday into Thursday, or is that too private as well?" It was Russell's turn to be acerbic.

"The same rules apply, Paul," Pirelli advised.

"No, it's fine, Mark. I had to work late when I needed to get some social work help for one of my patients. I finished around nine-thirty and got home late, about eleven-thirty. My sister will verify that."

"I'm sure she will," Russell replied.

"And what about Saturday night around ten-thirty?"

"I was at a twenty-first birthday party in town."

"Whose birthday party?"

"A colleague from work. Yes, Mr Russell, there were plenty of witnesses." His countenance was now the mirror of his lawyer's self-satisfied confidence.

Rick Johnstone stepped out and brought back a set of forensic coveralls that allowed Scott the opportunity to get out of his wet trousers. Anderson left the two men while Scott changed and Johnstone put his wet attire into a large plastic evidence bag. He summoned Anderson back in to the interview, where Scott was now sitting in abject embarrassment.

"I'm sorry."

"We've seen worse." Anderson couldn't quite bring herself to add sympathy to the sentence.

"Now, would you like to explain what you were doing that night?"

"You won't cause any problems for this person if I tell you?" he pleaded.

"That will depend on what you say."

"Please, I don't want to get her into any trouble."

"Just tell us!" Another sudden change to her voice nearly brought another unfortunate accident.

"OK. OK. I was with a prostitute in a hotel."

"This woman's name?"

"I only know her as Melissa. I found her on the Internet. She's pretty expensive but very classy."

Anderson recognised the name from previous encounters during her spell in vice. "I'm aware of this individual. We'll need the name of the hotel."

Scott was now eager to help and gave the officers all the particulars of the encounter, with rather more detail than they really required, as if confessing his sins was a cathartic exercise for him.

"As my client has supplied you with alibis for two of the days you were interested in, I believe we're finished here." Pirelli stood and gestured to his Lawrence to do the same.

"Don't go far, Mr Lawrence. I'm sure we'll have some more questions for you." Russell was obviously enraged by the conclusion of the interview. His gut told him there was more to this suspect than they had been able to reveal.

"Thank you for your hospitality, Detective Superintendent, Detective Inspector," Pirelli said with a little bow and a grin as he left the room.

"Fuck, fuck, fuck," Russell screamed.

"Shit," Alex added supportively.

"There's something about that bullshit that's not right."

"I agree, sir."

"That bastard is lying about something. Those alibis are all a little too convenient and why wouldn't he tell us where he was on the Monday night?"

Alex could offer him little in the way of suggestions but a sixth sense was telling her that her boss was spot on.

They trudged back to the office where Anderson and Johnstone were sitting with a hot drink.

"Well?" Tom Russell asked.

"Not him, sir. He's a pretty sad loner but he's a mouse," Johnstone replied.

"What happened?"

Anderson took over and detailed all that had occurred during the interview. She was convinced that Melissa and probably the hotel staff would confirm the details. The suspect's lack of urinary control was the subject of a little light relief for a beleaguered and exhausted group of people.

Russell asked Alex to tell the others about Lawrence. Their suspicion that Lawrence was hiding something did nothing to allay the fears of Rick Johnstone and he resolved to prevent Georgia from attending the meeting with the psychiatric nurse the following day.

"I want more on Lawrence and what the story is with him and that prick Pirelli. We'll get on it in the morning. Go home, get some rest."

They drifted away gradually, leaving Detective Superintendent Russell to contemplate where the case was going. The intensity of the work of the past week was taking its toll physically but he knew that there was still much to do.

When Rick Johnstone arrived home his wife was sitting under a blanket watching some programme about property on the TV. He bent to kiss her and she didn't turn away, which he hoped was another positive sign that her climb out of the depths was beginning.

They had a brief conversation about how her day had been. Although she was still having problems relating to Emily, Georgia was at least making an effort to be out of bed and to look after her appearance.

"I don't want you to go to the nurse tomorrow," he said tenderly.

"What? Why?"

"I can't say why but I want you to leave it tomorrow."

"You've been going on about this for ages and now I've got an appointment, you don't want me to go?"

"I'm not saying you should never go. I just want you to postpone it tomorrow."

"I don't understand this. It's been really difficult for me to admit something is wrong. If I don't go tomorrow, I might never get the courage to go again."

"Please Georgia, just for tomorrow. I'll explain later, I just want you to promise me that you'll phone and cancel," he pleaded with her.

She looked at him with a steady gaze. He seemed to be serious and in truth she was worried about going to the clinic.

"OK, if you think I shouldn't go, I won't."

"Thank you." His relief was obvious.

"There's a pie in the oven."

"Cheers, I'm starving."

He went through to the kitchen leaving his wife to wonder at the change in his attitude.

JOURNAL

I must act now. The police were too close to discovering my secret and I cannot fail now when I know I am so close. I can't let them stop me.

God's messenger has found the next soul that I can rescue. She is a woman with darkness in her heart, a darkness that prevents her from loving her child. She must be brought to the light and begin the final voyage to God's palace.

Tomorrow it will end, I am positive.

I am the Soulseeker and I search for the essence of humanity; the soul of man. I will not cease my quest until I find the truth.

CHAPTER 18

Early the following morning, Alex and Stephanie Anderson were detailed to interview the woman known as Melissa. Her real name was Helen Plant and she lived in a beautiful penthouse flat in the old Sheriff Court building in the Merchant City.

When she opened the door, she cracked a grin at her visitors. "Ladies, come in." She was used to regular visits from officers of the law and appeared relaxed and unfazed by this early morning call.

The two detectives followed her into a spacious and airy living room. Luxurious fittings and furniture were complemented by original art on the walls and sculptures on the sideboard.

"Can I get you a tea or a coffee before you arrest me?"

"No, thanks. We're not here to arrest you, Miss Plant," Alex replied. On the journey to the flat, she had warned Stephanie Anderson that she would take the lead and she expected the DS to stay in the background and take notes.

"Oh, that makes a pleasant change. What can I do for you?" She sat in a plush armchair with languid ease. She was a stunningly gorgeous woman and Alex imagined that she would command a huge fee from the men who visited her.

"We need some information about a client of yours."

"Detective Inspector…"

"Menzies," Alex told her.

"Detective Inspector Menzies, as you know mine is one of the oldest professions in the world and with it comes a certain code of conduct. The gentlemen that come to see me expect a degree of discretion that I would be foolish to ignore if I want to stay in business." Her voice was refined and Alex thought that it might well have been the result of a private education.

"The man in question requires you to be an alibi for him. We have already spoken to him with regards to a very serious matter."

"Oh, what's his name?"

"Marcus Scott."

"I don't have a Marcus Scott on my list but then they are reluctant to tell me their real names. Particularly the policemen, lawyers and politicians." She leered as if sharing a great secret with the two other women.

"He told us you might know him as Peter Parker."

"Ha, yes I know him very well." She laughed with bubbling humour.

"The night in question is last Wednesday through to Thursday morning."

She took a moment to think before saying, "Yes, that would be right. He's as regular as clockwork. Wednesday night, once every four weeks."

"Did he stay all night?"

"Yes, he always pays for the full night. He likes to spend the night beside me in the bed after I've played whatever character he desires for that session."

"What kind of characters?' Alex asked as she probed for a hint at his psychology.

"On Wednesday, it was, let me think. Oh yes, I was Wonder Woman. He's got a thing about superheroes."

"Has he ever been violent towards you?"

"No, he's a pussycat. Very gentle and loving. He treats me like I'm a real girlfriend, he even brings flowers and chocolates."

"You're sure he couldn't have left in the middle of the night?" Anderson asked.

"I'm positive. Believe me detective, I kept him occupied well into the early hours, and he's always very tired by the time we're finished," she replied proudly.

"Thanks for you help, Miss Plant," Alex said. She shook the young woman's hand and the two detectives left the flat.

The visit to the hotel proved to be a bit more difficult as the manager vehemently denied that her establishment could be used for such purposes. Eventually she gave in and checked her records. Miss Plant had indeed taken a room for an evening with a gentleman guest.

Scott's alibi had held up and from all they had heard the

two officers doubted that he was capable of the callous killing of three people. By mid-day they were heading back to the office.

☩

Rick Johnstone had left his wife that morning convinced that he had persuaded her to delay her appointment and was feeling relieved.

When he arrived at the station, Russell asked him to accompany him as he checked the alibis of Paul Lawrence.

The social worker Geraldine O'Rourke had confirmed the emergency call and that Lawrence had left the client around nine-thirty. It still left a sliver of doubt in Russell's mind as the next part of the story Lawrence had told still had a huge time gap. There was little point in interviewing his sister as she would say whatever she thought would protect her brother. There was certainly a possibility that he had time to get to Milngavie in time to meet Theresa Asher at the station and from there take her to her death.

Their second port of call was one of the health clinics that Lawrence served in his role as a community nurse. They were there to meet the woman whose birthday was celebrated on Saturday night.

"I'd like to speak to Clare Middleton, please," Russell said as he produced his warrant card.

"She's on her break. Is it urgent?" the receptionist asked.

"Yes," he replied impatiently.

"I'll take you through." She came from behind the desk and showed the two detectives to a small room that contained a square kitchen table, a microwave, a kettle and all that was needed to make a tea or coffee. Clare Middleton was sitting at the table with a plate of pasta and a mug of tea. She looked younger than her twenty-one years despite the orange glow of a fake tan, huge false eyelashes and heavy make-up. Her hair was dyed a deep ebony black and hung in gentle curls around her face.

"Clare, these policemen want to talk to you," the truculent receptionist told her.

"Oh, right," she tried to smile but there was a trace of concern in her face.

"Miss Middleton, we'd like to talk to you about your party on Saturday."

"I'm not related, in case you're wondering," she said.

Russell misunderstood. "To Paul Lawrence?"

"No, silly. To Kate and Pippa. People are always asking."

"To be honest, miss, I couldn't give a damn either way. I'm here to talk to you about your birthday night out last Saturday."

"OK, no need to be cranky," she said with a childish glower.

"I believe that Paul Lawrence was invited."

"Yes. He's a nice bloke but there was a whole big gang of us."

"What time did he arrive?"

She searched her memory. "He was there at the start of the night, around nine o'clock."

"Did he stay until the end?"

"I was a bit drunk but I think so. He got a taxi, I think. No… wait, he wasn't drinking because he had his car."

"What time did he leave?"

"I'm not sure but it was late."

"Did he leave the pub at any point?"

"I honestly couldn't say for sure but I don't think so. He didn't sing in the Karaoke, I remember that. That was a laugh, Colleen was pissed and was trying to sing 'Somebody To Love' and kept getting the words wrong."

"So you can't be sure that Lawrence was there with you?"

"No, not sure."

"Can you give me the names of some of the other people that were at the celebration?"

She listed four names and supplied some telephone numbers.

"What's he done?"

"Probably nothing. Thanks for your help." Russell indicated to Johnstone that they should go. The younger policeman said goodbye to Miss Middleton, who wasn't related to royalty.

One of the people who had attended her party worked in the same clinic but once again he couldn't state categorically that Lawrence had been there for the length of the party.

Russell and Johnstone visited two more partygoers and telephoned the remaining female member of staff who wasn't on duty when they visited the clinic. They all said the same thing; they knew that Lawrence had been there at the beginning and the end of the evening but no one could say that they had seen him around the time of the Karaoke.

When they had left the last witness, Russell said, "We'll

check the CCTV outside the pub. If he left, we might be able to spot him. I'm convinced there's something shady about our Mr Lawrence. Let's get back to the station."

It was three o'clock when the team was once again assembled in the main office. Alex reported that Scott was in the clear while Russell raised his suspicions that the alibis Lawrence had given weren't watertight. DC Carrick was still compiling information regarding the relationship between Lawrence and his legal representative, so the CCTV analysis was left to Alex and Rick Johnstone. Rather than wait for the data to be sent from the control room, they made their way to the city's CCTV monitoring site in Blochairn Road.

George Robson, a former detective who worked at the centre, met them at the door.

George was an effusive character who would generally enjoy talking to the detectives that came to visit but when Alex told him the purpose of the visit he became serious and focused on his task.

He took them to a room away from the banks of monitors that showed pictures from the cameras that covered a large part of the city centre.

"Right, where aboots is the pub?" George asked.

Alex told him and gave him the date and time they were interested in.

The former policeman typed on a computer keyboard with a single finger and Alex found that she was desperate to push him aside and take over the typing to speed things up. After a short time the files he needed were available.

He was more skilled with the video cueing controls than with the computer. He scrolled through the video, varying the speed as Alex or Rick asked him to concentrate on a specific person. The clock on the screen showed nine fifty-five when Alex said, "Wait, go back a bit."

George complied and at nine fifty-three and fifty seconds a man that looked like Lawrence could be seen leaving the pub.

"Can you zoom in?" she asked enthusiastically.

Once again he manipulated the controls and managed to get a close-up of the man they were interested in.

"Is it him?" the retired detective asked.

"It certainly could be," Rick replied.

"It's him, I'm certain. Let it run and see where he goes."

The video played in slow motion and they watched the man turn left and out of shot.

"Are there cameras in that street he turned into?" Rick was feeling the same excitement.

"Aye, ah'll call it up." George couldn't help but feel the infectious exhilaration that was now permeating the room.

There was another hiatus as the files were retrieved from the server. George's skill with the cueing software meant that he synchronised the two sequences on the screen. At the moment he disappeared from one picture, the man could be seen on the other. He let the video run at half-speed as the man approached the second camera and once again magnified the face. This time both detectives said simultaneously, "It's him."

"Follow him," Alex said.

The camera had been tracking as Lawrence walked

past and they watched as he got into a small car with a Vauxhall badge. The camera hadn't been upgraded to a colour unit, so all they could tell was that the car was a light colour that could be blue.

"He lied about the car," Rick observed as he took note of the registration.

"And that's not all," Alex replied. "Let's see when he got back to the pub."

The original video was cued again and George sped through it a six times normal speed. Around eleven fifty-five on the video clock, Rick said, "Wait, that was him."

The operator rewound the sequence and they watched as Lawrence greeted the bouncer before re-entering the pub.

"Got him, bastard," Rick shouted.

Alex was not quite so sure. "If it's him, he left the pub, abducted Mrs Fletcher and then went back again before going back to kill her in the early hours of the morning?"

"Could be that he wis tryin' tae make sure he hud an alibi," George suggested.

"That must be it," said Rick. "It all fits. He had access to the records of all three victims; he has medical knowledge and access to the drugs. He's been a sly bastard, making sure he's covered from every angle."

"You're probably right," Alex said. There was a part of her screaming that there was a huge gap in the logic of Lawrence as the killer, but she couldn't put her finger on it.

'Can you send some stills from the video to Superintendent Russell?"

"Aye, nae problem."

"Thanks for you help, George."

"Yir welcome, pet. Any time."

She ignored his use of the patronising term and instead was on the phone to Russell as she and Johnstone hurried back to the car.

"Good, I knew there was something about him," Russell said when she told him what they had found.

She gave him the registration details of the car and he said he would get someone to check them with the DVLA.

"Get yourself back here, then we'll go and pick him up."

CHAPTER 19

Alex drove the dark grey marked Focus back to the station and there was a palpable air of excitement and determination between the two officers. Neither had eaten since breakfast and they decided they needed a quick stop at a chip shop to get some food. As they stood in the queue, Johnstone's phone rang; the screen showed that it was his mother.

"Hi Mum, what's up?"

"Rick, has Georgia called you?"

"No, why?"

"I've not heard from her since she went to see the psychiatric nurse. I tried calling her but there was no reply."

Panic nearly swamped Johnstone but he managed to stay calm as he said, "She's probably gone for a bit of shopping and she's always forgetting to charge that bloody phone."

"Aye, you're probably right. I'll see you later."

"How's Emily?"

"She's fine, lying here playing with her baby gym thing."

"OK, I'll speak to you later."

The call ended and Johnstone turned, grabbed Alex and rushed out of the shop. "We need to go."

"What's up?" She could sense the level of alarm that her colleague was feeling.

"It's Georgia, I think Lawrence has her."

"What?"

"She went to see him today despite me saying that she shouldn't. She's not arrived home and Mum can't reach her on her phone."

"Look, what you said to your mother may well be true. Take a breath and give Georgia a ring."

They had arrived back at the car and Johnstone rested against the bonnet as he made the call. When the phone went immediately to voicemail, his mind drifted back to the crime scenes and the people at the centre of them.

"Voicemail," he told Alex.

"Right, let's get to the clinic and see if she's still there. Maybe he was running late with another patient or the session has been overly long."

"All right."

"I'll drive again and you can ring the boss and tell him where we're going."

He moved like an automaton as he opened the car door and settled into the seat.

Alex understood the importance of keeping the DC as calm as possible but she too was fighting the visions of what Lawrence was capable of. She drove quickly when she could through the rush hour traffic. She was tempted to put on the lights and siren but that would only increase the feeling of consternation in Johnstone.

When Johnstone called Russell, the superintendent was measured and cool as he told the young officer to contact him when he knew more.

They eventually pulled into the car park at the health clinic half an hour later. There were a couple of patients sitting in the waiting room, which was directly in front of the reception. Alex had told Rick that she would take control of the situation but before she could ask the receptionist a question, he blurted out, "Where's Lawrence?"

"I'm sorry?" the middle-aged woman replied.

"Where's the psychiatric nurse?"

"I'm afraid that's none of your business."

Before Johnstone could let his anger spill over, Alex flashed her warrant card and addressed the woman. "Is Mr Lawrence available?"

"No, he left when he had finished with his last patient. What's this all about?" The confused look on the woman's face told its own story.

"Who was that patient?"

"I'm sorry, but that's confidential," she stated.

"Was it Mrs Georgia Johnstone?" Rick asked loudly, which caused the two people in the waiting area to look at him with a measure of trepidation.

"I'm sorry, sir. I can't give you that kind of information."

Alex couldn't prevent Rick's anger exploding. "I'm her fucking husband and if you don't help us she could be dead. Now do you understand?" he screamed at her, causing the woman's eyes to fill with tears of terror.

"Yes. It was Mrs Johnstone."

"When did he leave?"

"About quarter to four, I think."

"Did Mrs Johnstone leave before him?"

"No, they actually left together. Paul said he had an appointment with his bank about something, so he left a little earlier than usual."

"Oh shit." Johnstone's anger had morphed into anguish.

"Thanks for your help," Alex said. "My apologies for my colleague's language but he is very worried about his wife."

"I understand," the receptionist said as she reached for a tissue.

Alex took Johnstone back to the car and then she called Russell.

"Alex, what's happening?"

"Lawrence left with Rick's wife nearly two hours ago."

"Fuck. Is he up to dealing with this?"

"No, I don't think so, but somehow I doubt we'd be able to stop him."

"We'll meet you at Lawrence's house but don't go in if we're not there."

"Understood."

This time she had no hesitation about switching on both the blue strobe lights and the siren as she sped along Great Western Road and out towards Drumchapel. She switched them off as she approached the street that Lawrence lived in and parked away from the house but in a position where she could still see the front door.

"Right, let's go," Johnstone said, his hand on the door

handle.

"No, we have to wait until the others arrive."

"It's my fuckin' wife he's got."

"Rick, I know how you're feeling but anger is not going to help us deal with this professionally. You don't want that bastard walking on some technicality because you couldn't control your temper." She spoke firmly in the hope that she could get through the mantle of rage that was controlling him.

"I know you're right but I just want to see her again, Alex. To know that she's safe."

"I understand that, Rick, believe me, but we have to be professional about it."

They waited five minutes before Russell's car accompanied by three marked cars arrived in the road.

The officers were on the move almost before the vehicles stopped. Russell signalled to three uniformed constables to go around to the back of the house while he and three others stood at the front.

He hammered on the door just as Alex and Johnstone joined him. "Open up, police."

He was about to give permission to break the door when it opened and Lawrence's sister stood blocking their way.

"Whit the fuck dae yous lot want noo?"

"Where's your brother?"

"How the fuck should ah know? Ah'm no his ma."

"You won't mind us coming in to have a look around."

"Fuck off, ye need a warrant fur that."

"Not if we believe that there is someone in danger. We think your brother has abducted a woman and killed three other people. We have a right to search your premises for that woman. Now you can let us in the easy way or I'll have the lads here take you in for perverting the course of justice and then we'll give the social workers a call to take your weans into care." Russell broke into a caustic smile.

"Fuck you, the whole fuckin' lot o' yous. He's no' fuckin' here and he's no killt naebody but come in an' waste yir time if ye want."

Russell turned to Rick Johnstone, "You stay here."

"But sir…"

"That's an order, constable," Russell said with a tone that left little room for argument.

"Sir," Johnstone said unhappily.

The woman stood aside and allowed the team of officers to begin searching the premises. As they found their way into every room it quickly became obvious that Lawrence was not at home. Alex was searching the bedroom of the youngest child when she came into the room. She was about seven years of age and looked angelic in her pigtails, a pink shirt and blue jeans.

"Ur you fae the fuckin' polis?"

Alex looked down at her, "You shouldn't use language like that."

"Whit fuckin' language? Ur ye a polis?"

"Yes."

"Ah didnae know wimmin could be pigs," she said, and walked out of the room.

Alex thought that the girl would probably see a few 'polis' in the years to come and probably the inside of a few prison cells.

As the team drifted out of the house one by one, Lawrence's sister stood at the door. "Ur ye fuckin' satisfied? Look at the fuckin' mess o' ma hoose, ya dirty bastards."

"Shut the fuck up. Now where is your brother? If you fuckin' know and you don't tell us, I'll have you up on charges of accessory to murder, believe me." Russell was standing toe to toe with her.

"Ah don't fuckin' know but he's no capable o' killin' anybody."

Russell looked to Alex who gave him a brief shake of the head to indicate she didn't think the woman knew what her brother had been up to.

"If he turns up, ring us right away." He gave her his card and she slammed the door closed.

"Constable," Russell shouted to one of the uniformed officers who were standing at the garden gate.

"Sir?"

"You and your neighbour stay here until we can get an unmarked car to keep an eye on the place."

"Yes, sir."

"Try to stay out of sight if you can."

"Will do."

The rest of the police presence was ordered away. Russell walked with Alex and Johnstone back to their car. "Get on the blower to control and tell them we need extra vigilance when looking for those van plates. We'll go back to the station and see if Carrick or Anderson have discovered anything that might help find this prick."

On the drive back, Johnstone broke down and wept.

Alex said nothing but her thoughts were growing equally dark.

It was a sombre group that assembled in the main office including DCS Blair and a host of extra detectives who wanted to help when they heard that the wife of a colleague had probably been abducted.

The DVLA confirmed that the car belonged to Lenny Thompson, who had an address two streets away from where Lawrence lived with his sister. Mr Thompson was currently suspended from driving and the detectives surmised that he had given Lawrence use of his car.

Russell briefed all present on what had happened in the past few hours and the urgency of finding Lawrence. Russell deferred to Blair when it came to the allocation of resources. A team of people were assigned to find out all they could about Lawrence's acquaintances and places he would regularly go. The meeting was breaking up when Russell's mobile rang.

"Sir, it's Constable McDermott at Lawrence's place. He's arrived at the house but there's no sign of the woman."

"He's there?"

"Yes, sir. He walked in bold as brass just a minute ago."

"Right, keep an eye on the house, I'll get Drumchapel CID to come and pick him up."

A buzz of conversation ran through the ranks of officers in the room, as they understood what the conversation meant. Russell smiled broadly when he put the phone down; surely they had him this time.

There was a nervous wait until the phone rang again.

"Superintendent Russell."

"Sir, it's DS Cochrane from Drumchapel. We've got him and we're on our way."

"Did he give you any trouble?"

"No, sir. Came as quiet as a lamb."

"Thanks Sergeant, we'll see you shortly. Bring him in through the back, I don't want the press swarming."

"Yes, sir."

A loud cheer rang round the room when Russell reported that Lawrence was in police custody but he tempered the mood of optimism when he said Georgia Johnstone was unaccounted for.

DC Johnstone said, "Let me at him when he comes in, sir."

"I don't think that would be a great idea. Believe me Rick, he'll tell me what he knows whether he likes it or not." He rested a hand on Johnstone's shoulder in a supportive gesture that he hoped would calm the dangerous current of anger the younger man was feeling.

"Sir…" Johnstone's protest died in a sigh. He knew that no matter what he said, Russell would not relent.

Blair announced to the rest of the team, "Listen, we still need to find Georgia. Get those checks on people and places that are connected to Lawrence."

Everyone broke away, some retreating to other offices with the urgency of people intent on saving a life.

✠

Georgia Johnstone opened her eyes and quickly closed them again as a bright light shone directly into them. She tried to lift her arm to shade them from the glare but there was a strong resistance and she had little energy to fight against it. She couldn't think what was wrong with her arm and she was unsure if she was completely conscious; it felt like she was somewhere between wakefulness and sleep. Her mind was foggy and she found it difficult to bring her thought processes to bear. She began blinking in an effort to allow her eyes the chance to adjust to the light. Finally, she was comfortable enough with the brightness to keep her eyelids open and she could see that the lights over her reminded her of being in a dentist's chair. It was so intense that she wanted to turn away from it but then she discovered that her head was as restricted as her limbs and she could not move it to either left or right.

Slowly her mind began to replay the events that had led to her staring into the glaring illumination. She had boarded the bus for the short journey from her house to meet the community psychiatric nurse. He was a lovely man and they had a great chat about Emily and how she was feeling. He had suggested some techniques that would help her to feel better and begin the process of making a maternal connection with her child. When the session was over he had asked her if she needed a lift home as he was going past her house on his way home. She was delighted to accept, as she didn't fancy waiting in the deluge of rain that was once again tumbling down on the city.

She had walked with him to his light blue Corsa and she had admired its metallic paintwork. She had sat in the comfortable seat and begun chatting about something on the television when she felt a tiny pinprick of pain.

She looked down to see the nurse complete the depression of the plunger on a hypodermic needle. All she could remember was that a black cloud had swirled in and then nothing.

Until that point she had been relatively calm but when she comprehended the danger she was in she began to scream.

CHAPTER 20

Paul Lawrence was sitting with his hands clasped on the table when Tom Russell and Alex Menzies walked into the interview room.

"All on your own?" Russell asked. He knew the answer already as DS Cochrane had briefed the investigative team when he brought the suspect in. Lawrence had not asked for Pirelli to be present and even signed a declaration to that effect. The team spent some time brooding over his decision; what was different about this time?

"I'm fine, thank you."

"Mr Pirelli unavailable?"

Alex noticed the muscles twitch on Lawrence's face as if they were about to form a grin but he controlled the impulse. It gave him a slightly manic air.

"He's busy."

"So Paul, it looks like you've got some explaining to do."

"And why would that be?" he responded, his face a picture of detached innocence. It was like his thoughts had taken somewhere else, far from the confines of the interview room.

"We have a missing woman and you were the last one to see her from what we've heard," Russell said.

"And who would that be?"

"Don't play fuckin' games wi' me, you know damn well who I'm talking about."

Alex added quietly, "It would be better for you if you didn't provoke my boss, he's on kind of a short fuse at the moment."

"I'm not playing games. I meet lots of women."

Russell jumped his feet, leaned over the table and screamed into Lawrence's face, "Stop your fuckin' lies, you pathetic little twat. Now where is Georgia Johnstone?"

"I have no idea where Mrs Johnstone is at the moment," Lawrence replied carefully.

"Maybe you're some kind of idiot but you don't seem to realise that a fourth murder charge is only going to make things worse for you. If there is any chance she is still alive then you have to help us find her."

"I don't have to do anything but as it turns out I don't know where she is and I have not murdered anyone." There was little doubt that Lawrence believed that what he was saying was true.

"You're not going to come out with all that bullshit you sent in the message about releasing them from their pain are you?"

"No, Mr Russell, I mean that I haven't killed anyone. I haven't murdered, executed or released anyone. Do you understand?"

"Sir," Alex laid a gentle on her the arm of boss before

he could do something that he would later regret.

Russell sat back in his chair. "Lawrence, here's a wee tip for you, when you give the polis an alibi, we are going to check it. We don't say, 'Oh well, it couldn't have been him.' Now where is Georgia Johnstone?"

"I will say this for the last time, I don't know where she is."

"Look you little shit, maybe you don't know but Georgia Johnstone is the wife of one of my officers. You hurt one of us and you hurt us all. There are plenty of large men and women who will happily arrange an unfortunate accident for you if you don't want to co-operate."

At the mention of Georgia's relationship the first flicker of fear could be seen in Lawrence's face and manner.

"I don't have her, I don't know where she is."

Alex had been monitoring his answers and noticed how careful Lawrence had been with the language he had used. An idea struck her. "You don't have her but you know who does?"

The question she had asked obviously pinpointed what Lawrence was trying so hard to conceal as he reacted by squirming in his seat. There was a moment of silence as the detectives waited for the now uncomfortable suspect to respond but his mouth stayed firmly closed.

"Answer DI Menzies. Do you know who has Mrs Johnstone?"

Lawrence stared straight ahead as if in a trance and said nothing. Alex's phone vibrated in her pocket, it sounded like a pneumatic drill in the silence of the interview room. She took it out and noticed that the call was coming from Craig Campbell. She ignored it and put the phone back in her pocket.

"Sorry," she said to Russell, who was now ready to launch everything he had at the recalcitrant suspect.

"Who the fuck else is involved in this? There's a woman's life at stake." He suddenly threw back his chair and grabbed Lawrence by the collar with enough force to lift him from his seat.

"Give me the fucking name!" he screamed as he shook Lawrence like he was beating the dust from an old rug.

"I can't," Lawrence shouted back.

"Sir! Maybe we should take a break," Alex shouted.

Russell let Lawrence collapse back on to his chair.

"I can't," Lawrence whispered.

Alex firmly guided her boss out of the room. When they were in the corridor Russell apologised to her as he leaned against the wall.

Alex could feel her phone vibrating again against her leg and she pulled it from her pocket it with annoyance. It was a text from Craig and this time her annoyance turned to shocked excitement.

"Alex, pls ring. I think I've fnd the van u were looking 4."

Georgia Johnstone dreamt of being on a boat in the middle of a loch. Overhead, grey clouds had begun to form, growing bigger and more ominous with every second. She was with Rick and Emily but there was no one else on the loch. She could see

all the other boats tied up at the jetty on the shore but they were drifting further and further away. The light disappeared until all she could see was her husband and daughter through the rain that was now hammering down on the little wooden craft.

"We need to go back, Rick,' she screamed into the deluge, but he didn't seem to hear her.

Suddenly the boat began to rock as the wind buffeted it and waves crashed over the sides. The rocking increased and then a huge wave swept a screaming Emily out of the boat.

Georgia shrieked loudly and with a terrified intensity, "Rick!"

Her husband turned to her; he looked forlorn as he dived into the black waters of the loch, leaving his wife screaming his name over and over. She knew she would never see either of them again.

She awoke with a start, tears still streaming down her face and a feeling of rawness in her throat. She was still very groggy and could feel that whatever she was lying on was moving in much the same way as the boat had pitched and rolled in her dream. It was nearly completely black but when her eyes adjusted to what little light there was, she could see that she was in a small room. It can't be a room, she thought, I wouldn't be moving unless the bed is vibrating in some way. Slowly her mind put it together and she grasped that she was in some kind of vehicle. An attempt to move her arms and legs established that she was still strapped to the bed, although the restraint on her head seemed to have been removed. The crook of her right arm had something pressed into it, which reminded her of when she was in the hospital for Emily's birth. There was a faintly mechanical noise and she felt tired again. She tried to fight it but sleep engulfed her and she was back at the centre of the loch, desolate and alone.

"Craig," Alex said into her mobile without explanation to her boss as to why she had decided to call her friend in the middle of an interview.

"Alex, thank God you called back." She could hear the drone of traffic in the background and it was obvious that Craig was using his phone in speaker mode.

"Where are you?"

"I'm in the car on Royston Road. I was on the way home after dropping off one of Carol's pals when I spotted the van. It's a Luton van and it's got one of the registration numbers that were on the list." He told her the registration of the vehicle he was pursuing.

"Which direction are you going?"

"We're going east and he's about five cars ahead of me. What do you want me to do?"

"Stay with him, we'll get cars there to support you as soon as we can. When I'm in the car I'll ring you. Craig, for once in your life try not to put yourself in harm's way, stay away from this guy."

"Yes, Detective Inspector Menzies. Message received and understood."

He hung up and Alex sighed. Previous experience had told her that her friend was not a man who was good at following orders and she was worried that this would be no different.

"What is it?" Russell asked.

Alex told him what had happened and before she could finish the whole story he was racing away and up the stairs to the office.

When she caught up with him he had already started to fire orders at the detectives who were all on their feet and ready to move. When he was finished, he shouted to Alex to join him as he led an exodus of bodies from the office.

Once they were in the car, Alex asked the control room to contact any car in the vicinity of Royston Road to try to pick up the van before she redialled Craig's number.

"Craig where are you?'

"Still heading east. I can see the Red Road flats now."

"OK, got you." Alex became the relay of the information she was getting from the private detective to other cars that were involved in the search for the van.

"Wait, he's signalling, turning left into..." There was momentary pause as Craig looked for a road sign. "Broomfield Road."

"Got it. All cars, he's going north on Broomfield Road."

The police cars were driving as fast as was safely possible but they were a long way from the target.

"He's turning right at a roundabout on to... Ryehill Road."

Alex once again repeated the message but they were

suddenly brought to a halt by a queue of traffic. A huge puddle had formed in the middle of the road and the cars were going through it very slowly, trying to prevent their engines from being flooded. Russell turned the air blue with a string of expletives.

The man who called himself the Soulseeker indicated and then steered the van to the right and into the final street of both his physical journey and the quest that had haunted him for so many years.

His destination was an abandoned church; the holy ground where he believed he would finally achieve his goal. In his distorted mind, the consecrated ground would be the perfect place for him to sacrifice someone in the manner of a true martyr. These things combined were guaranteed to bring the view of the ethereal ascension he so desired.

The main door of the old kirk faced the street but he wanted privacy and drove the van around to the right of the building where there was a small car park. He reversed the van into position beside a small door that led into a deserted vestry and from there into the main altar at the front of the church.

He quickly pulled a ramp from the back of the van and leaned it against the opening of the cargo area of the van. He was moments from his goal and he could hardly contain the excitement he was feeling but he had to continue to be careful. He focused on the task of wheeling the woman - the one who would be his saint - into the church from where her journey to glory would complete his hunt for the truth.

CHAPTER 21

Craig Campbell watched the van turn to the right but he couldn't see the name of the street and informed Alex of roughly where he was. She explained the problems they had met on the road and that they were still ten minutes away from joining him.

"I'll see if I can delay him."

"Craig, wait. No heroics," she warned.

"OK. I promise I'll delay him, nothing else."

He followed the van along the street and noticed that its destination lay at the dead end of the narrow road. He turned the car to the left at the last junction before the church and found a parking space.

"He's at an old church."

"OK, understood, we'll find you. Be careful."

He stepped out into another cloudburst of summer rain but the sky in the distance was bright, the silver hue of a herring's scales. It was a faint promise of better weather to come.

He walked cautiously towards the blackened stone of

the Victorian building; the cloak of soot and dust that covered it stood as a reminder that Glasgow was once both a devout and an industrial city.

He reached the corner and edged his head out to see what was happening in the car park. He watched the man set up the ramp and then roll a hospital bed with a woman strapped to it straight through the door at the side of the structure.

He made a snap decision on how he could delay the killer to allow the police a chance to intervene. He ruffled his hair, made his clothes look unkempt and stepped into the view of the man who was now back to put the ramp in the van.

"Haw, ur you the priest?" he shouted as if he was just another Glaswegian drunk.

"No, I'm sorry. Please go away."

"A minister, then. Ah want tae confess ma sins. Ah've no' been a good person. Drank too much, look at me, ah'm pished again. Ma wife left me cos ah hit her but ah didnae mean it, it wis jist the bevvy, know whit ah mean?"

"I'm sorry for your troubles but I can't help you."

"Whit, d'ye think yir too fuckin' good fur the likes o' me? You fuckin' religious bastards ur aw the same. Holy fuckin' willies, as the Bard said ye wur. Aw full o' yir ain self-importance. That's no' whit Jesus wis like, He wis a workin' man, jist like masel'."

"Look, I'm extremely busy, please go away!" The killer took an aggressive step towards him.

"Hey, look, jist cool yir jets. Gie's a fiver an' ah'll get oot yir herr."

The man was not in the mood to negotiate and placed

his hands on the drunk and pushed hard. Craig decided that he needed to go down so it would look as if was as inebriated as he appeared. Before he could react the man had retreated back inside the church and closed the door. The sound of a key turning in the lock ended any chance of the private detective taking any further action.

In the distance, he could hear the sirens of the police cars and he hoped that he had done enough to give them time to catch the killer.

Alex took another call from Craig just the police cars turned into Ryehill Road.

"How far up the road did you turn right?" she asked.

"Second, I think. Alex, please hurry, he's in the church and he's locked the door."

"OK, we're nearly there."

Within a minute a fleet of flashing blue lights were zooming to where Craig was standing opposite the church.

Alex was the first out of the lead car and she ran towards him.

"Where is he?" she shouted.

"There's a door on the right," Craig replied.

"Stay there," she warned before disappearing with her colleagues around the side of the building.

Inside the dark nave, the killer had been shaken by the confrontation with the drunk. His perfect plans were nearly ruined by another sinner; maybe he should invite him in. It would give him another chance to complete his task if the woman failed him.

He had wheeled the old porter's bed into the main body of the church, now stripped of pews and strangely empty except for the ghostly noises of echoes, creaks and drips from the incomplete roof. Earlier in the day, in front of the altar, he had made a pyre of wood that he had collected from a builder's merchant. He wheeled the old hospital bed beside it, unstrapped Georgia Johnstone, lifted her and then laid her gently on to the pile with a reverent bow of his head. He reached into his pocket and lifted a tiny gold cross that glimmered in the light from the torch he carried. He raised Georgia's right hand, laid the cross in her palm and tenderly folded her fingers around it. He then folded her arms over her chest, carefully to ensure he didn't dislodge the cross.

He began to pray. "Dear Lord, accept into your tender care the soul of this poor distressed woman. Give her peace and grant her a place among your saints. Allow me to complete what I started and give me the knowledge I require. Amen."

Suddenly he heard police sirens penetrating the eerie sounds of the haunting old building. His heart began to thump in his chest and a dreadful terror of failing his mission gripped him. He swung the torch round to where he had left the bottle of lighter fuel that he needed to begin the final stage of his plan. He reached for it and opened it. The smell of the fuel escaped into the musty air. He could hear that the police cars were getting ever closer and he hastily began to pour the liquid on to the wood. He was now close to panic; surely he couldn't come so close to all that he had worked for only to fail at the moment of his triumph.

His hands were shaking as he lifted the matches from his jacket. The trembling prevented him from striking the match properly a couple of times before it finally flared and with a silent plea to God, he dropped the match onto the bonfire.

When the police reached the door they confirmed that it was locked and Russell tried kicking it open but the old oak and substantial lock and bolts held firm. Alex rushed back and called for the battering ram.

Two detectives sprinted to a car and fetched the equipment. They battered the door and although it moved the lock still held.

His exasperation obvious, Russell shouted, "Put your back into it for fuck sake." Alex understood exactly what he was feeling but the door was made from thick wood and the lock was substantial.

It took another two swings of the ram to finally burst both the bolts and the lock.

Russell was first through the door with Alex close behind. They raced through the vestry and across a short corridor and burst into the nave of the church where a grotesque scene greeted them. A ring of bright yellow flame encircled the still body of Georgia Johnstone. Off to one side a man was spinning like a dervish as flames began to engulf him.

Alex felt a rush of engrained terror as his screams of pain reached into her deepest fears and hauled them to the surface. She stopped in her tracks but Russell's voice broke the spell.

"Alex, we have to get Georgia."

He was kicking the burning timber to try to create a gap. Alex, still fearful, joined him. Her breath was laboured, her heart was racing but the sight of Georgia Johnstone's prostrate form at the heart of the blaze was enough to drive her on. They created enough space to allow them to reach over and grab an arm each. They hauled at the unconscious woman and pulled her through the ring of flames. Some of the shroud that she had been dressed in was alight but the two detectives stamped on the flames and quickly put them out.

"Please, tell me she's alive," Rick Johnstone shouted as he bent down beside his wife and cradled her in his arms.

"I'm so sorry, darling," he said into her hair.

Something in Alex made her consider that their suspect was about to escape justice if she didn't do something. She took off her coat and ran over to the still screaming man. She wrapped the damp coat around him and threw him to the floor, rolling him until she had managed to extinguish the raging flames. She rolled him onto his back and unwrapped the coat from his body. She looked down at the face of the Soulseeker. She could not have been any more surprised.

Russell and Johnstone had confirmed that Georgia was still alive and Russell told another detective to call an ambulance.

"Better make that two," Alex said to her colleague.

Russell left Georgia Johnstone in the loving care of her husband and walked towards Alex.

"Who is this fuckin' loony?" he said contemptuously.

When he looked down on to the face of the man he had been chasing, he declared his surprise.

"Pirelli?"

"Now I'll never know. I'll never know if she was saved," Pirelli croaked before he lapsed into unconsciousness.

CHAPTER 22

It was nine o'clock before Alex Menzies and Tom Russell arrived back at Stewart Street station. The press had obviously got wind of what had happened and were out in force. The two detectives walked through the noisy scrum of reporters without even an acknowledgement of their existence.

They climbed the stairs and went straight to DCS Blair's office to brief him about what had happened.

"What I don't get is why the hell would someone help someone to do this?" Blair asked.

"I agree sir, and with your permission I would like to interview Lawrence again." Russell was equally keen to remove that particular burning question from his mind.

"Of course. If you both feel up to it, I'll listen in on the video link."

Despite her fatigue and shredded nerves, Alex agreed to join Russell in the interview room.

Lawrence cut a despondent figure as he sat alone at the small table.

"Mr Lawrence, we have some important questions for you and we need you to be honest with us, for your own sake. You are implicated in the deaths of three people and the attempted murder of a fourth. It will go better for you if you tell us the truth now." Russell's opening statement was formal and said with quiet authority.

"At this juncture Mark Pirelli is in hospital in our custody. We know that he is the killer but we need you to tell us all you can about his activities."

Lawrence looked up for the first time since the two police officers had walked into the room. "You're lying," he said, but there were traces of doubt in his response.

"Take a deep breath, you'll be able to smell the smoke from the fire that Pirelli set under Georgia Johnstone. She was still alive when he lit the blaze under her and he was willing to burn her to death. The fire he started caught on the accelerant he had accidentally spilled over himself and it nearly killed him."

Lawrence leaned forward and sniffed.

The truth of what they were telling him was something that he was reluctant to accept but something in their expressions told him that this was no strategy. The aroma of smoke from a fire erased his remaining doubts.

"Tell us about your history with him."

Lawrence sighed and said soberly, "I killed his brother."

"What?"

"I killed his brother Joseph in a pub fight. Another man was arrested for it but it was me. I was with a few mates in this pub; we'd been there most of the day. I was very drunk when this guy bumped into me and spilled his drink all over my brand new tracksuit. I was a very angry person back then, I reacted and I took out a knife and stabbed him. In the chaos that followed my mates and me got out of the bar before the police arrived. I was doing community service at the time and there was no way I could get caught. They would have thrown the key away." He fell silent.

"Then what happened?" Alex prompted.

"One of my mates was identified as the killer by a couple of eyewitnesses and was arrested. He committed suicide in the remand prison before he was brought to trial and the case was closed. I felt guilty about what had happened and I was going to go to the police but the rest of the guys told me that it would mean wee Gary would have died for nothing and told me to keep quiet." Guilt and shame were evident in Lawrence's body language and voice.

"So how did you link up with Pirelli?"

"I went to Joseph's funeral and pretended to be one of his friends. I stayed in touch with him and his mother, and tried to help where I could. Mark gave up his medical studies to look after his mother when she was diagnosed with dementia. He was convinced that it was his brother's death that had sent her loopy. She treated him like dirt as her illness got worse and then he helped her to die."

"You mean he killed her?" Russell asked.

"He never thought of it like that. He always talked about it being a mercy killing, like putting down a sick dog was how he put it. He just left the gas on in her bedroom, the police thought it was an accident due to her illness."

"When did this happen?"

"She died ten years ago. After she was gone, Mark got on with his life, decided he wanted to be a lawyer rather than get involved in medicine. He thought that all doctors were arseholes because they couldn't see that it was grief that was killing his mother. Anyway, I've stayed friends with him ever since."

"He started to feel guilty about what happened about five years ago, that was one thing we had in common. As the tenth anniversary of his mother's death approached he began to change. He began to obsess about whether his mother's soul had gone to heaven; whether him helping her to die had sent her to hell. He talked about the immortal soul every time I saw him and then about a month ago he came up with this plan. He wanted to confirm that the soul exists and decided that releasing people from the agonies of their lives was the only way to achieve it."

"Why did you help him?"

"At first I tried to dissuade him but then he started to quiz me about my relationship with his brother. He had worked out a long time ago that I was the one who had killed Joseph and said he would get the police to re-open the case if I didn't help. He was blackmailing me, basically. He told me that I could be God's messenger like the angel Gabriel. In truth I felt so guilty about what had happened to his whole family as a result of what I had done that I decided to help him. He promised that no one would suffer."

"What did he ask you to do?"

"I had to find patients that were suffering from depression or anxiety. I hadn't consulted with any of them until the last woman. I would go through the records of patients that had been referred to the CPN service and find possible targets. The last one, Georgia, I only picked her because he was getting more desperate with every passing death. He demanded I bring him another one quickly and as she was my last patient of the day, it was easy."

Russell sounded weary as he said, "You must have known that what he was doing was never going to bring the results he wanted."

"I hoped that he would see something that he thought was the soul ascending. He was going to kill himself as soon as he was sure that he had found what he was looking for. Then it would be all over and I would be in the clear."

Russell stood up and walked out of the room, his abhorrence too deep for him to want to be in the same room as the pathetic creature that was Paul Lawrence.

Alex told Lawrence that he would have to give a full statement in the morning and then called for the custody officer to place him back in the holding cell.

The news from the hospital was that both Georgia Johnstone and Mark Pirelli would be fine. Georgia had suffered a couple of minor burns and from smoke inhalation. Pirelli's injuries were more extensive and he would require skin grafts on his legs where the fuel had caused the fire to burn more intensely.

DCS Blair had offered his thanks to the remaining detectives and ordered them to go home. There would still be work to be done the following day to help present the evidence to the fiscal's office, but it could wait.

Alex and Tom Russell were the last to leave.

"Pirelli will probably be sent to Carstairs rather than prison," Russell said.

"Probably, and it's maybe where he should be. He's definitely not of sound mind."

"He wasn't that nuts that he couldn't plan meticulously and execute that plan in a way that left us with nothing. If it wasn't for your pal spotting that van, we might never have caught him. By the way, I'm not sure I'm too happy at you letting a civilian in on confidential information."

"I'm sorry, sir, but Craig's got good instincts and I thought another pair of eyes might not go amiss."

"You were proved right, inspector, but still. Anyway, you should get home, now."

"You too, sir."

"I will, I will, just not yet."

When Alex reached her crappy old Golf, the shock of what she had been through suddenly crept up on her. She decided that an empty house was the last place she wanted to be after a day like the one she had just survived. She took out her mobile phone and dialled the number of her parents' home.

"Hello," her dad answered.

"Any chance I could come and stay with you tonight?"

"Of course, darling. What's up?"

"I'll tell you when I get there. Thanks, Dad."

Soulseeker

She got into the car, put a music station on the radio and drove to where she could forget about the Soulseeker, death and flames.

THE END

About The Author

Sinclair Macleod was born and raised in Glasgow. He worked in the railway industry for 23 years, the majority of which were in IT.

A lifelong love of mystery novels, including the classic American detectives of Hammett, Chandler and Ross Macdonald, inspired him to write his first novel, 'The Reluctant Detective' featuring Craig Campbell. There are two further Reluctant Detective novels, 'The Good Girl and 'The Killer Performer.

Sinclair lives in Bishopbriggs, just outside his native city with his wife, Kim and daughter, Kirsten.

For more information go to
www.reluctantdetective.com
twitter: @sinclairmacleod

The first Reluctant Detective mystery

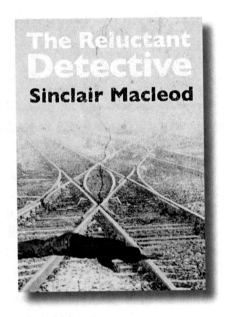

"I want you to find who killed my son."

Craig Campbell's quiet life as an insurance investigator is turned upside down when Ann Kilpatrick hires him to find her son's killer. He reluctantly agrees but doesn't believe he can really help.

Before long he is plunged into a world of corruption, deceit and greed. His journey takes him from the underbelly of Glaswegian society to the rural idyll of a millionaire's mansion.

Along the way, a death close to home ensures that he has a personal reason to face the dangers and bring the murderer to justice.

Available in paperback and for the iPad and Kindle

The Reluctant Detective returns

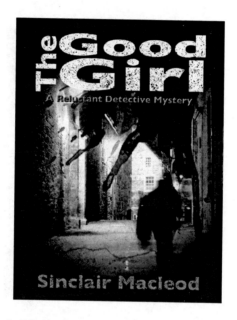

Craig Campbell leaves his native city to investigate the disappearance of a young woman from St Andrews. Initially, it appears to be a simple case of a girl escaping to start a new life but it soon becomes apparent that there are ominous undertones.

When a woman's body is found on a nearby beach the case takes an even darker turn. Craig focuses his attention on the seedy world of escorts and their clients. A pimp with a violent history and a number of witnesses with their own secrets to protect block his investigation.

He finally breaks through the wall of lies and discovers a gruesome truth that leads to a dramatic and explosive climax.

Available in paperback and for the iPad and Kindle

Death, Drugs and Rock 'n' Roll

It should have been Craig Campbell's dream job, working for a rock star who was his boyhood hero. But when the target of his investigation is murdered, Craig is the prime suspect.

Despite the police suspicions, The Reluctant Detective is released and begins his own pursuit of the killer.

His investigations bring him to the attention of a Glaswegian drug lord with a vested interest in the case. Craig's own safety is threatened and he is ready to walk away but as the body count mounts he feels compelled to continue the hunt.

Rival drug gangs, jealous musicians, a disturbed rival and a crazed voice from the past are all possible suspects. Craig must find the killer before the finale of their murderous performance brings the curtain down on another life.

Available in paperback and for the iPad and Kindle